I0620749

THE VENUS BELT

L. NEIL SMITH

PHOENIX PICK

an imprint of

ARC
MANOR
Rockville, Maryland

The Venus Belt copyright © **1980, 2009 L. Neil Smith.** All rights reserved. This book may not be copied or reproduced, in whole or in part, by any means, electronic, mechanical or otherwise without written permission from the publisher except by a reviewer who may quote brief passages in a review. Cover copyright © 2009 Arc Manor, LLC. Manufactured in the United States of America. Originally published by Balantine Books (Del Rey), 1980.

Tarikian, TARK Classic Fiction, Arc Manor, Arc Manor Classic Reprints, Phoenix Pick, Phoenix Rider, Manor Thrift and logos associated with those imprints are trademarks or registered trademarks of Arc Manor Publishers, Rockville, Maryland. All other trademarks and trademarked names are properties of their respective owners.

This book is presented as is, without any warranties (implied or otherwise) as to the accuracy of the production, text or translation.

ISBN: 978-1-60450-442-2

www.PhoenixPick.com
Great Science Fiction at Great Prices

Visit the Author's Website at:
http://www.lneilsmith.org

Visit the Author's Page at Phoenix Pick:
http://www.ElNeil.com

Published by Phoenix Pick
an imprint of Arc Manor
P. O. Box 10339
Rockville, MD 20849-0339
www.ArcManor.com

Printed in the United States of America / United Kingdom

To my parents, Les and Marie Smith, and to treasured memories of the lives and works of H. Beam Piper and Karl Bray.

CONTENTS

Let no one hail this occasion as binding together our myriad interests and separate wills. Those represented here, the, respectively, United States of America and Mexico, the former Dominions of Newfoundland and Canada, the Republics of Quebec, Alaska, California, Texas, and Cuba—all enjoy unique histories and traditions which must be neither lost nor rendered inconsequential.

Rather, let us say that the barriers between us have been cast down, so that those histories and traditions might live and mingle freely as they will, toward a new synthesis, greater than the parts combined to create this, our own new North American Confederacy.

> President Benjamin R. Tucker
> In Continental Congress
> July 2nd, 117 A.L.

1: ESPIONAGE CONFEDERATE STYLE

Tuesday, February 23, 223 A.L.

Denver's overzealous District Attorney wouldn't be raiding any more mom-and-pop porno stands. Not after last night's covert photo session in his basement—that extra room nobody's supposed to know about.

I'd chosen a wintry evening when he was out addressing Concerned Prudes Against Literacy, or whatever they call it. Breaking in was a cinch—I've had plenty of practice. So were the pictures—my light-amplifier's bigger than the camera it attaches to, the size of a .38 slug.

And what a collection! Whips, chains, video cassettes. I haven't seen so many rubber suits since they took "Sea Hunt" off the air. Next morning I sent a swell assortment of eight-by-ten glossies to the *News-Post* and *Rocky Mountain Liberty*, following up with an anonymous call, but I didn't linger on the phone.

It wasn't that I feared a trace, or SecPol's voice-analysis procedures. In the first place, the call was routed over a line that isn't even supposed to exist, courtesy of the Colorado Propertarian Party. And anyway, I used a Confederate-model vocal synthesizer, the kind chimpanzees and gorillas use to communicate with other folks. Took me six months to learn how to work the bloody thing.

In the second place, I'm totally above suspicion, with the pluperfect alibi: I've been dead for twelve years.

Mainly, I was in a hurry. I had an appointment in a broom closet, and was late for a game of golf. You might *call* it golf. I do.

My death? A reasonable, but fortunately unwarranted conclusion on the part of my former employer, the City and County of Denver, circa 1987. Though another several billion people—including critters I didn't even know about then—had called it 211 A.L. That's *Anno Liberatis*, and if you've got enough fingers to count up to 1776, you can figure out why for yourself. Now they're calling it 223 A.L., and in the good old U.S.A., it's 1999.

I put the phone away. The *News-Post* wanted the story, all right, and I wasn't much worried about the city's second largest paper, because, at that moment, Jenny Noble, *Rocky Mountain Liberty's* editor in chief—and national Propertarian chairperson—was handing me a grilled cheese sandwich. I moved my soggy topcoat so she'd have a place to sit—her desk, after all—and slung my shoulder holster over the back of my chair. The battle-worn Smith & Wesson .41 clunked a couple of times before it stopped swinging. The edition in Jenny's wastebasket was yesterday's, but I was two months out of touch with my native land, so it evened out. Jenny interrupted my perusal of the front page before it got started:

"You and your cute little camera have a busy night? I understand they're really going to run the pictures."

Slender and freckled, Jenny's a pleasure to be in the same room with, only partially because she's pretty. She communicates enthusiasm, and her horde of gentle revolutionaries seemed to get the work out just to please her. Somewhere in her early forties, I believe, but it wouldn't matter, even if she *weren't* getting antigeriosis in the Confederacy.

"You bet your sweet by-line they are," I answered through fried bread and melted plastic cheese. "Is it just me, or is there a new appreciation for the Bill of Rights over there? Lady on the city desk said they've been trying to get the goods on the D.A. for a long time."

She grinned, which I enjoyed, and shut her door against the clamor from the crowded office beyond. Printers clattered through the glass; people tossed jokes and good-natured insults across the room. An occasional paper SST dipped and soared among the light fixtures. "There wasn't always a *lady* on the city desk. Her predecessor got permanently blue-penciled by some lunatic from the Right to Life Action Squad—didn't change their editorial position on abortion, thank goodness, but it sparked a timely re-evaluation of the *News-Post*'s stance on gun control!"

I laughed. She reached past me for a sheaf of print-outs from the in-basket, leafing through to check the status of a hundred subversive little exercises like mine last night. Somebody entered from the din-filled boiler room and dumped off another two-inch stack of hard copies. She looked up with a little frown. "You really have to go home right away, Win?"

I nodded. Win is me: Edward William Bear, late of Denver's finest—even later for my golf game—former homicide dick, now P.I. and part-time spy for the North American Confederacy. If that's too melodramatic, how about loving husband and soon-to-be-father, at the astonishing (at least to me) age of damned near sixty?

I swallowed another bite. "I could lie and add 'regretfully,' but I'm getting pretty old for these uncivilized Colorado winters." I glugged down half the mug of Campbell's soup she offered, watching snow fall heavily outside the second-story corner windows. My feet were icy, soaked clear through, but it wasn't just the weather; it was a dozen years of growing accustomed to clean air, instant hassle-free transport, and virtually nonexistent crime. I glanced at the day-old headline again and shuddered:

87 MISSING IN LATEST KIDNAP ROUND

"Don't be ridiculous. You look ten years younger just since you smuggled that load of coke and silver over last December." She gazed out at the noisy, bustling office, remembering. "Now *that* was a merry Xmas!"

I couldn't help agreeing, on both counts—though ten years might be stretching it. Rejuvenation's a gradual thing, especially for a guy who lived his first fifty eating, drinking, and breathing all the wrong stuff. "Clarissa gets the credit—Win Bear's Practical Health Tip *Numero Uno*: marry up with a Healer, a beautiful one, if possible."

Another smug survey of the semifrozen brown slush in the street, and I finished my sandwich, set the mug firmly on Jenny's desk—it would most likely be buried in computer-droppings before anybody got a chance to rinse it out—and "Time to abscond. Tell your fellow-conspirators so long for me. Any time you need my talents as a burglar again..."

"You can't get off *that* easily, Officer!" She rose with me to deliver a crushing hug and a peck on the cheek. "Love to Clarissa, and I'd better hear the *instant* your daughter arrives, understand?"

"*Oof!* You'll be the first to know—in *this* universe, anyway." I gathered up my coat and gun, folded the newspaper under my arm, and threaded through the maze of desks in the outer office. Against one wall on a yellow flag, a stylized rattler warned DON'T TREAD ON ME!, while a hand-lettered sign read THANK YOU FOR POT SMOKING.

Half a hundred defiantly colorful posters advertised the recently launched Fraser campaign. D. Nolan Fraser had created the Party back in 1971, unaware that the Confederacy existed. Two decades later, as Denver's first Propertarian mayor, he'd pulled the city out of its share of a nationwide depression, and now, with a little imported help, the polls gave him an even shot at dragging the whole country, kicking and screaming, toward "civil liberties and economic freedom" via four years' residence at 1600 Pennsylvania Avenue. Hail to the Chief.

Hail, yes.

At the last desk, a girl had a dispenser of pop-ups printed to resemble federal neobucks; she blew her nose and threw the tissue in a wastebasket. The guy next to her repeated the gesture with genuine government-issue, and they both giggled at the green ink it left on the end of his proboscis. He grinned up at me and pointed to the placard taped to the wall above him: IN GOLD WE TRUST.

I shook my head and stepped into the reading-room, looking forward to some quiet. Halfway to the broom closet, I swiveled, surprised by the chattering of a printer even in this sanctuary. At a library table, typing furiously, sat—another Jenny.

"Last time I heard, you were doing business out on Ceres." I hefted my snow-soaked topcoat to a more comfortable position over my arm. "Very hush-hush. Got a chip from Lucy and Ed about it. How've you been, Prez?"

President of the Confederacy, that is.

"Ex-prez, *por favor*." She handed copy to an assistant, who hurried it off to god-knows-where. "I understand Olongo's thinking about a third term, poor masochistic old ape. Say, what's all this about his getting held up?"

That had been the day I left; I didn't know enough about it yet to tell her, but spread the paper out to show its chilling headline. "Crime marches on—everywhere, it seems lately. Why do you suppose they're only taking women?"

"Probably because they're *men*. This makes over a hundred fifty thousand, doesn't it?" She shook her head grimly.

"In the Americas and Western Europe, anyway. I haven't really been keeping score." I glanced down at another column. "Says here there's another dozen IRS men missing, too."

"Yes, and sales of canvas and quicklime are up in seven western states and rural New Jersey—old joke. But *nobody* supposes that's got anything to do with the kidnapped woman—it's just another *healthy* sign." She patted the protruding handle of a hefty automatic tucked into a holster underneath her jacket. "Anyway, thank goodness it hasn't spread to the Confederacy—and while I'm over here, it's not going to happen to me, either!"

Jenny Smythe is just as decoratively energetic as Jenny Noble, and for an excellent reason; while the latter was being conceived in the United States, her charming "twin" began existence in the Confederacy at precisely the same instant. Yet physiologically she's four years younger, due to some advanced paratronic skulduggery called stasis delay: her mama wanted her, right enough, but not just at the moment, thank you.

Complicated, isn't it? In the history I grew up with, Alexander Hamilton decreed a tax on whiskey, almost touching off a second revolution. President Washington mobilized fifteen thousand federal troops to quiet it down, abetted by a professor-type named Albert Gallatin who didn't want to see his fellow Pennsylvanians slaughtered.

End of Whiskey Rebellion.

In the Confederacy, Gallatin's counterpart organized the irate booze-farmers, conned the bluecoats into taking his side, and marched on Philadelphia. Old George went to the wall; Hamilton beat it Prussiaward, inaugurating a minor quasi-fascist movement that caused trouble for a couple centuries afterward.

End of Federal Government, however.

While Jenny Noble's riding herd over an unruly crowd of anarchists whom Gallatin might've kissed on all four cheeks in sheer Discordian delight, Jenny Smythe makes frequent visits stateside to lend a seditious hand. I'm not sure whether all this qualifies as "synchronicity"; it's just one of a million semi-coincidences that need better explaining, at least to this retreaded old flatfoot.

"Well," she said finally, "there's good news, too. Fraser's begun clicking with the media, almost a year before the Demagogues and Republicrats even nominate *their* mealy-mouthed barrel scrapings." She indicated the books lying open on the table, works that Gallatin had never gotten around to writing in this here branch of probability.

"So you figured Fraser might crib a stirring speech or two from *Rule of Reason* or *Principles of Liberty*?" I sneaked a peek at my watch, an annihilation-powered goodie from the Confederacy's fifty-year-old Lunar colonies.

"Hmmph! I've been known to give a stirring speech or two, myself."

"Yeah. The last one *started* this whole expensive, complicated, and probably unethical undertaking. Well, write on, sister! Dinner's a-cookin', and probably so's the little woman by now, late as I am."

Jenny's flunky stood waiting impatiently for the next batch of profundity. She let him fidget. "If Clarissa hears that 'little woman' crap, it'll be *you* doing the cooking, right up to your prominent ears in the soup!"

"No thanks"—I curtsied—"just had some—tomato bisque, I believe. And now, dear former Chief Executive, *au 'voir*. My closet awaits without."

"Pass," Jenny answered, turning down a terrific straight line, "I'll be back in Laporte by the time your daughter's due." She made a show of looking me over. "Guess I'm sort of morbidly curious how she'll turn out."

I replied with a raspberry cheer, turning again to the closet, the only Propertarian institution that hasn't changed in twelve years. Originally a tiny, insignificant splinter group valiantly determined to shove America back in the direction Tom Paine had pointed it, the Party had occupied a lonely disinfected cubicle here at Colfax and York amidst an otherwise pee-stained conglomeration of leftists, eco-freaks, and latter-day Luddites. Now Jenny's yahoos owned the building, printing presses, hundreds of telephones, even a lively public bar downstairs. *And* numerous less well advertised facilities that SecPol—the Federal Security Police—even in its presently chastened condition, would doubtless frown upon severely.

One of those was this closet. I forced the creaking door aside and squeezed in. Peace at last. Here were the old familiar dingy sink with a little brown spider homesteading it as always, a couple of rusted buckets, a plastic garbage pail, and a damp, moldering smell that titillated my gag reflex. There was also a dry rotted two-by-four on the wall with nails sticking out from which depended a ratty battery of mops and brooms. Pulling at the frayed cord dangling in my face, I squinted in the fifteen-watt illumination, counting nails on the rack, and pushed up *hard* on the third, fifth, third again, and seventh from the left.

A hole in the universe—the P'wheet/Thorens Probability Broach—irised open before me. When the aperture was large enough, I stepped through gingerly, unwilling to test its matter-annihilating properties with a coattail or the heel of my shoe. Behind me, the Broach dwindled like the little dot you used to get when you switched off a TV set, then vanished with a *pop!* and a tiny, star-bright flash of blue.

I'd made it safely once again, to the other side of reality.

2: VOICES FROM THE STARS

Eyes watering in the sudden glare of Laporte's Inter-world Terminal, I stepped through a glassed-in security booth onto the concourse. Commercial gunmen circulated, alert for the occasional unfriendly immigrant. The Confederacy welcomes strangers, but likes to look them over first. The only import we reject is hostile intentions.

Like many another "breakthrough," the Probability Broach got invented by mistake. A dolphin—*Tursiops truncatus*—name of Ooloorie Eckickeck P'wheet had been aiming for the stars. Her human partner, Professor Deejay Thorens—who might've looked more natural, *without* her labcoat, somewhere among the pages of *Penthouse*—had cobbled the prototype together, and I'd been their first unwitting sample, accidentally collected.

Laporte's a hop, skip, and a universe—call it sixty miles—from Denver. Each has its counterpart in the other's continuum, the former as a minuscule Fort Collins suburb, the latter as the sleepy village called Saint Charles-Auraria. Each was once a candidate for capital of Colorado, Denver for its railroad. But Confederate *stagecoaches* ran on steam, so Laporte, an Overland Trail depot, became a population center of two million.

Far across the stadium-size terminal, a giant holo applauded KINGSLEY'S PENNSYLVANIA WHISKEY—THE DRINK THAT MAKES YOU DRUNK! Truthful and to the point, especially for brand-new refugees from a hundred Prohibitions. After a couple days in my native land, always more narrow and depressed than I usually remembered, I could use a drink, myself. Even Kingsley's Pennsylvania Crude.

Along the shining concourse, other agents, spies and smugglers, emerged the same way I'd just done, the familiar flash and *pop!* announcing them. Even more departed, laden with equipment, trade-goods, bound for a million secluded phone booths, jungle clearings, and "deserted" warehouses. Elsewhere, automated Broaches fed radio signals and printed propaganda which would appear out of nowhere anywhere from Salt Lake City to Peking Square. Huge freight machines rumbled in another portion of the Terminal.

I'd had a lot of doubts, initially, about the infiltration of my country, and I'm still wrestling with the moral ones. Hell, no one's ever *certain*, but unless all human aspirations are to bog down in a syrupy fog of second guessing, we have to push on. Whatever the consequences may be, the alternative's worse. What bothered me originally was logistics: thanks to Gallatin's successors, the Continental Congress is little more than a ritual, hasn't convened in over a decade, and likely never will again. No taxes, no regulation of any kind (all that got settled, with George Washington's hash, back in 1794), so how do you scrape up enough valuta and person-power to subvert the universe next door?

Well, Kingsley's Whiskey, for example, could use a few billion new customers—it's pretty much a one-time purchase—and so could Laporte Paratronics, Securitech, Ltd., Neova Hovercraft. It's a new twist on the concept of industrial espionage: Confederate entrepreneurhood wants a free market established in America sometime yesterday afternoon if possible. Shucks, this latest caper of mine was for an old respected chain of family pornographers.

Forget "redeeming social value," dirty pictures are *fun*. When I die I want my ashes sprinkled over a nudist camp.

I waved back at a couple of operatives I knew as they vanished into a Broach. Their specialty was stopping counterfeiters—the kind that grind out bushel basketsful on government printing presses. Sure hoped they'd be careful with all those blasting caps.

The less-reasonable satrapies of my homeworld are getting even shorter shrift. I remember reading about World War II, when the Allies dropped millions of crude single-shot "Liberator" .45s to European partisans. Stamped out by General Motors for $1.71 apiece, each pistol came with a bubblegum comic illustrating its operation and purpose: sneak up behind Herr Nazi, blow away his mind, trash the disposable zipgun, and appropriate the enemy's Mauser or P38. We're pursuing identical tactics via Broach, with substantially more sophisticated but equally inexpensive hardware. Next time the Russians "discipline" Czechoslovakia or Afghanistan, they're in for a humiliating shock.

So, for that matter, are the Israelis.

I hopped onto a walkway and rode upstairs a couple of levels into a more conventional underground intersection. Colorfully dressed shoppers gawked briefly at my otherworldly shirt and tie, beat-up felt hat, gray tubular suit, and comfortable brown loafers. (Once a cop, always a cop—had to change before I went out to the club.) Then, perhaps remembering the terminal below, they went about their business, respecting my fundamental right to unmolested eccentricity.

I found a Telecom and punched our combination. Clarissa's a blonde, sort of cuddly and golden, with eyes that are difficult to label: green, hazel, something like that; they change. Her features welled up in three dimensions before the flat white screen, but I hardly got a word in—

"This is Clarissa Olson-Bear, or rather a recording of me. I'm not home right now, and Win's...out of town. Please call our professional numbers for referrals or messages—and if you're a house burglar, you'll be interested to hear we're covered by Griswold's Security."

Brr. I was almost afraid of them *myself.* Their company motto wasn't *quite* "We Don't Take Prisoners," but they gave that impression. Too bad Captain Forsyth, our old Professional Protectives man, had retired last year.

I diddled with the keyboard again, my Neova HoverSport answered with a cheery loyal *Honk!* I gave it some instructions and escalated on up into the Confederate sunshine. Standing at the fancy pastel curbing, I looked over my shoulder. The foothills west, outside the kindly influence of Cheyenne Ridge Power & Climate, were buried under three feet of wet slush. Yechhh.

Given its head, the little Neova's a conservative driver, so I had some minutes to kill. There was a Turner Vendicom right in front of me, its supporting post anchored in the rubbery curbside. I fumbled for a copper, dropped it in, and let the seat unfold, flipping channels randomly as I got comfortable.

Must be news time somewhere.

The little screen seemed to expand before my eyes. "—at radio observatories throughout the System, continue fascinated by allegedly intelligent signals originating in the constellation Cygnus. A spaceship would require hundreds of years to get out there and see what's really going on, but in the meantime, here's commentary on this baffling phenomenon by Channel 1572's resident philosopher, Rod Mac—"

Click! No point listening to that jerk. This stuff was stale news years before I'd come to the Confederacy: inarticulate groanings, mouthings of apparent distress; something like intercepting single sideband on an AM radio, or listening to Dutch or Norwegian—sounds you somehow just miss understanding. But hell, whales often make noises like they're being slowly barbecued, and that's when they're having a party. Ask me, it's interstellar swamp gas.

I turned to channel 1789: "—unethical and imprudent," declared the sober tones of the System's premier newscaster—and self-styled Voice of the Stars. He nodded his fatherly gray head into the camera. "Centuries may pass before the final results are in, but interference with another culture's values, the right of the United States to take whatever course it chooses no matter how we disapprove, endangers fundamental balances no human, simian, or cetacean truly understands. We may have reason to regret such tampering. At least that's the way it looks, Tuesday, February twenty-third, 223 A.L. This is Voltaire Malaise, Ceres Central, good night."

Good night, Voltaire, and good timing. The HoverSport pulled up and I poured myself in. After two days manhandling smelly rubber-tired infernal-combustion Brazilian-made contraptions around on concrete, sulfur, and asphalt-covered streets, it was a relief to set my fusion-powered toy on automatic, feel its electrostatic impellers fluff the skirt out, whisking me home along the green and grassy thoroughfares of Laporte.

I checked the routing program and grimaced. No wonder the car had taken so long. It'd come by way of the McKinley Bypass, whose owners recently had gone on an irrational STAY ALIVE—DRIVE 85 kick. Another week of that and they'd be in receivership. I reprogrammed the Neova and goosed up to a safe and proper hundred and ten.

That's Jeffersonian metric miles per hour.

Voltaire Malaise: funny how the public, even in a country geared to three or four centuries' life expectancy, still associates wrinkles and graying hair with wisdom, instead of what they really are: symptoms of a terminal disease. Easy enough for an expatriated pundit like him to crab about "interference with another culture's values"—he hadn't Broached victims of those values out of torture chambers and "mental hospitals," maimed, broken, Thorazined out of their skulls.

I had.

My world had been a fucked-up mess before the Confederacy butted in: depression, hyperinflation, stultifying regulations, and continuous brushwar to distract the gullible. People fought back: fully half the economy had gone to underground barter, but hysterical government countermeasures—toll-free IRS finklines, highly publicized black-market prosecutions, magnetically coded neobucks, and finally, the feds' last desperate grab, the Value-Added Tax—had ground the wheels of national survival to a tooth-rending halt.

Maybe I even agreed with old Voltaire on a couple of points. Americans needed the help they were getting, but was it right to keep it secret? Malaise insisted the Confederacy's real frontier was outward; he'd gone so far as to move his entire operation to the asteroids. Nowadays, half the folks I knew seemed to be following his example. I even caught myself daydreaming about it.

But hell, I was happy as a clam in Laporte with Clarissa, and my work—unethical and imprudent though it may be—was going to be important for a long while. The U.S.A. wasn't out of the woods yet.

᛭

626 Genêt Place, and home. I tripped out of the shower, fresh and dry, and lasered off a few whiskers, admiring myself in the mirror. Not bad for fifty-nine—in fact, not bad for thirty-nine, thanks to Confederate medicine. The minor bulges here and there lent me a little dignity, I thought. God knows I needed it at five feet seven and an eighth. And a full head

of bushy black hair didn't hurt, either—when I'd blown into this universe, it'd been with a rapidly retreating fringe of gray. So I looked like an underweight Sumo wrestler; Clarissa said I was handsome, and her word was good enough for me.

I changed into conventional baggy pants and poncho, pulled on hand-tooled gaucho boots, and switched my .41 Magnum from the shoulder rig to a wide, comfortable gunbelt. It's an elderly Model 58, a spare, no-nonsense punkin'-roller whose original bluing has long since worn through to a mellow gray patina. Since this was golf day, I pocketed some extra rounds of the special 240-grain load I prefer, grabbed a box of snake-charmers for the tricky shots, and went back down to the garage.

Owl Canyon Country Club nestles at the foot of Cheyenne Ridge where potent unseen thermals from the fusion power plant enhance the protective nature of the hogback nature provided. In another universe, there's often dry footing in Fort Collins when Denver's up to its asshole in dozerbait. Here, as in Camelot, it never snows, nor rains, nor hails, nor even sleets, except by appointment. If the mails weren't electronic, postmen'd have a cushy job.

I found Clarissa and Captain Forsyth at the third green, affectionately nicknamed *El Presidente*. It was just going dusk, but a utility satellite shone brightly on the prairie. Not wanting to disturb my darling pregnant roommate, fetchingly attired in a suitably expanded scarlet coverall, I leaned back against a Greyhound-size boulder, torched up a stogie, and watched her getting ready. At her right, a telecom extension was just winding up its recorded instructions: *"When you hear the tone, the clock will start. Par for* El Presidente *is ten seconds. Take your position."*

Easiest green on the whole course. As the rules demand, Clarissa turned her back to the fairway, lifting her arms above her shoulders. She caught me loitering against the rock, lighted up about a megawatt's worth, with dimples, then returned her concentration to the matter at hand. An .11-caliber Wesley Electric hung at her waist in that goddamned suede cross-draw holster I've been trying to talk her out of for years. Hard convincing her, since she's faster on the draw than I am.

The Telecom went *Boop!* Clarissa wheeled gracefully, pistol materializing in her hands before the man-shaped plastic silhouettes—three of them, in hard-to-pick-up camouflage—finished popping erect.

Pffft! Pffft! Pffft! The linear-induction weapon ripped each target twice, shock waves from its tiny ultrasonic projectiles blasting through the buff-colored plastic. She reloaded in a twinkling of highly competent fingers, compliant to the six-shot rule (despite its basic stupidity—Webley magazines contain two hundred inch-long steel needles), and raked each target twice again. Time: 5.47 seconds, faster than I'd ever seen her; potential motherhood wasn't slowing her down a bit. Score: the Telecom read fifty-six, four points shy of perfect.

"*Oh, shit!*" observed my refined, genteel wife. "Win, you're home!" To negate any possible connection between this pair of statements, she came running before I could caution her not to, and threw her arms around me. I felt her weapon bobble against my shoulder blades where it dangled from her fingers. Forsyth stared discreetly into the distance, a old-fashioned monkey if ever there was one.

We came up for air, and I patted her well-rounded five-month tummy. "I trust you're skipping the obstacle course today?"

"Who's the Healer around here? Of course I'm skipping obstacles, silly, why do you think we're over here on the baby course?" Before I could get in the obvious rejoinder, she added, "Now say hello to the Captain, and take your shot. We'll average scores and spot you ten points."

"Better make it twenty, I've had a hard couple of days. How y'doing, Cap?" I shook hands with the pistol-champ emeritus of Greater Laporte, gin-rummy shark *par excellence,* and one of my oldest, closest friends. He's also a fully qualified chimpanzee.

"All right, I guess." He didn't really speak: chimpanzees can't. Instead he used a wristwatch-size synthesizer that picked up subliminal muscular movements and translated them into speech. "Nobody told me retirement was such bloody hard work! Be glad to get rid of this arthritis, though. Sorry I left it so long. Win, as soon as I'm through rejuvenating, I'm thinking about going back into business on my own. Ceres, maybe Pallas—need a partner, maybe."

"That does it. We're going to have to emigrate if we ever want to see our friends again. How about it, sweetheart, once the baby comes?"

"Why wait? Take your shot, and we'll do it right now!"

"In front of the Captain, here? It's only been two days, honey, and he embarrasses so easily." I waggled my cigar and did obscene things with my eyebrows.

"Oh shut up and take your shot!"

I like a girl who turns that color. I clamped the cigar firmly in my teeth, stepped up and waited through the instructions, back to the targets, hands above my shoulders—*Boop!*—and turned, feet planted wide, elbows locked, left arm pulling back. The front sight rose to the 5-ring.

Blam, Blam! Blam, Blam! Blam, Blam! I thumbed the cylinder open, working the ejector-rod with my left palm. My right hand found a loader at my belt and slammed the fresh rounds home. I gripped again and snapped the weapon closed. *Blam, Blam! Blam, Blam! Blam, Blam!* Score: a perfect sixty. Time...

Eight and a half seconds? Well, you can't have everything.

I reloaded once again, scrounging up my precious hand-imported brass, and stepped to the line to join my companions, who still had their hands over their ears.

"You *ever* gonna trade that plague-eaten noise-maker off?" Forsyth gave me the sourest of looks. "If muzzle-blast was stopping-power, son, you'd be the deadliest gunman in North America!" He stepped forward, limbering up his well-worn .476 Savage, and turned toward us, disregarding the instructions as he waited for the tone. "Bloody firecracker!"

"He never listens on that subject, Cap, I've been trying for years to— Oops! The baby just moved—probably covering *her* ears, too!"

I put a gentle arm around my mate. "Hush, the Captain's trying to concentrate."

"I'll concentrate better when my ears stop ringing! Apologize to your daughter, Win, otherwise she may not want to come into the—"

Boop! Forsyth spun around and drew his autopistol, ripping through six rounds so fast I could hardly tell them apart. He dropped the empty magazine, rammed home a spare, and zipped through another quick six. Score: sixty, of course. Time: four and a tiny fraction seconds.

Arthritis be damned, remind me never to get the Captain *really* riled.

Beep! Only the old chimp failed to go for his gun: I reholstered mine and watched my blushing bride do likewise, sticking out her tongue at me as I reached into a belt pouch for my pocket-pager, the only one in Laporte, possibly unique in all the Confederacy.

"And that's another thing," she told him. "How any civilized being tolerates a nosy, interrupting nuisance like that. . ."

"Then don't interrupt so often, dear." I wasn't quite adroit enough to spare my shin a wifely kick. Forsyth simply shrugged his furry shoulders. He knew me, almost as well as Clarissa pretends not to sometimes, and understands how an old cop's habits die hard. I limped dramatically to the Telecom and undedicated it. There, relayed from our machine at home, was another pretty face. Just my lucky day, I guess.

"Winnie? Clarissa, girl? This here's Lucy!" Only this face hadn't been so pretty when I'd first seen it, splotched and withered, wrinkled with old age and radiation sickness, topped with a mop of snow-white hair and an outrageous paisley sunbonnet.

Lucille Gallegos Kropotkin had lived next door to the house Clarissa and I now occupied, neighbor and friend to a good friend of mine, Edward William Bear—my *own* counterpart in this world. Lucy had gotten well, regained her youth, hitched up with Ed, and moved out to the asteroids. I looked closely now at her warm dark eyes, olive skin, and glossy black hair. Pretty sexy for 148.

"Listen, you two," she advised, "this here's a recordin'—can't wait around fer signals t'get there an' back. I was gonna call anyway, see how th' baby's comin' along an' all, but...well, it ain't gonna be as pleasant as all that, now."

She glanced down at some object in her hand and shook her head.

"I got trouble. Somethin' fishy goin' on out here, an' Ed—th' dummy—started pokin' round, rusty at detectivin' as he was..."

She stopped, squinted hard against a flow of tears that was visibly only seconds away. "Anyhow, he—Win, I hate like th' dickens t'put you out, a daughter on th' way, an all, but—Ed's been missin' fer *days*, an' I found *this* in his desk an hour ago. You'll know what it means."

She held a medallion to the pickup, round, about an inch and a half in diameter, bronze. I didn't have to inspect it to know there was a date on one side, 1789. On the reverse loomed the eerie trademark of the System's foremost enemies of liberty: the Hamiltonian Eye-in-the-Pyramid.

"Win, get out here pronto! He may already be d-dead by now!"

3: GORILLA MY DREAMS

Wednesday, February 24, 223 A.L.

"I am *not!*" Clarissa stamped a foot she hadn't seen in weeks. In the thick carpeting of our gymnasium-size living room, the effect was lost.

"You are too!" I sat, chomping on my cigar, and glowered at her.

"*I am not!*"

"You are *too!*"

Clickety-click-click. "Can I be excused from this colloquium?" My chief assistant and apprentice gumshoe, Koko Featherstone-Haugh, leaned back on a sofa, knitting a sweater for the baby. Koko's a youngish female gorilla, favorite niece of the President of the North American Confederacy.

And they pronounce it "Fanshaw."

"Sure," I growled back, "go on out in the kitchen and peel yourself a plantain. You're on her side, anyway."

Koko hitched her holster into a more comfortable position and took a sip of King Kong Kola, a brand suddenly popular since the recent importation of a certain movie. *Click-click-clickety.* "I am not."

"You are too! Say, this sounds familiar. Did I not hear you, with my very own ears, state that 'mere pregnancy' is no reason Clarissa shouldn't go to the asteroids with me?" I looked closer at her knitting, wondering if I should mention that the arms were getting a bit long.

Click-clickety-click. "Is that a question from my employer, or merely the husband of my dearest friend?" *Clickety-click-click.*

"Waffling already! Look, even without Hamiltonians mixed up in this, space travel's no kind of risk for—"

Clarissa sat down beside me. "Win, I'm a Healer. I'm also a fully grown sapient being..."

I'd seen this independent mood before. Unfortunately it was a major reason I loved the woman. "Yes?"

"I *know what I'm doing!* Maybe they fly around on giant firecrackers where *you* come from—"

"Unfair! Just because my country's economically depressed—"

"And technologically backward." *Click-click-clickety.*

"Butt out, banana-breath! *And* technologically backward, that's no reason to...Listen: how many gees you figure to pull, just getting up to the liner?"

"Hmm. Well, the liner itself starts out at one gee, gradually dropping to a tenth of that by the time it reaches Ceres. That can't be too bad, can it?"

"*You* can it. Answer my question: how many gees aboard the *shuttle?*"

"Uh, six—but there are ways, Win, heart patients do it all the—"

"Swell. You'll qualify sometime the middle of the twenty-fifth century. *I'm* leaving at the end of the week. You think I *like* going off a hundred million miles, maybe missing the baby—certainly missing you?" I leaned over to kiss her and hesitated. "Hey, Miss Simian Collegiate, I thought you wanted to be excused."

"Don't mind me, this'll be terrific for the anthro paper I'm doing: 'Love among the Humans—Ennui or Boredom?'" *Click-click-clickety-clack!* "Dirty bad —I've dropped another...I wonder who *that* can be?"

I got up and crossed to the windows. It was difficult to see in the evening twilight; Confederate tastes run to generous acreage, lots of trees, hedges, miscellaneous bushery. The folks at Cheyenne Ridge had grudgingly let a little white stuff through, not enough to dampen the electrically warmed streets, but plenty for postcard scenery, maybe a snowman or two in the morning. I gave the window knob a twirl, doubling the amplification. Sure enough, through the gate and up the gracefully curving rubber-surfaced drive, a hovercraft skated to a landing and two familiar furry shapes climbed out.

I turned to my companions. "How about something in the fireplace? And kill the fatted whiskey bottle. It's Captain Forsyth—and the monkey's uncle."

⅄

Olongo Featherstone-Haugh, a mountain among gorillas, handed me forty yards of dampened overcloak, unwinding a mile or two of muffler from around his massive neck. "Can't be too careful, old boy"—he wiped an errant snowdrop from his pistol grip—"*awfully* prone to respiratory complications, don't you know."

True enough. Even given current medical technology, no gorilla took unnecessary chances that way. I added Forsyth's ancient yellow slicker to a heap of steaming garments on the stair rail. Upstairs, Koko had a roaring fire started. Clarissa handed the President about a gallon and a half of Scotch.

"Ahh! A wintry evening among friends. Thanks indeed, dear lady."

"Catch your prowler yet?" I asked. Some fool had broken into his office last weekend. Putting in some overtime, Olongo had come back from the john and interrupted them in mid-burgle.

He settled in my biggest chair, arms stretched comfortably across his ample frontage, firelight flickering in his eyes. "Afraid not, old man. Stupid sod that I am, I left my life-preserver in the office when I stepped out. Spot of luck they didn't shoot me with it—had it halfway out of the holster when I threw that wastebasket. Next time I'll be ready for them. Now tell me about this emergency of Lucy's before I perish from curiosity."

"Not much to tell." I pushed my somewhat less-magnificent facade aside to reach into my sporran for a Bic—another popular import—rekindling my cigar. Clarissa wrinkled her nose and punched the ventilation up on the Telecom pad lying in her lap. I passed a tiny datachip across to Olongo. "Been trying all day to get more than this from her, but—"

"I understand." The gorilla nodded. "Something about solar interference."

"Mighty *odd* solar interference," Forsyth muttered as he took another swallow of Kola—he preferred soft drinks, too, a legacy of many years' abstinence on duty. "Wrong time of year, wrong part of the solar cycle. Lucy's right—something funny going on."

"My dear Captain, these things happen." The President lifted a weighty paw and set it down again. There was a distinctly reddish quality to his pelt; I never had the nerve to ask about orangutans in the woodpile. "The cycle's only an approximation, after all." He handed back the chip. "Why not observe for ourselves what Lucy had to say?"

I slid the chip into another 'com pad—we keep several around—the fireplace winked out of existence, and the wall lit up with Lucy's face.

"Winnie! Clarissa, girl! This here's Lucy! ..."

This time I ignored her words, concentrating on the surroundings. A commercial booth. Not her homestead, then, on—what was it?—Bulfinch 4137, a tiny planetoid she and Ed owned outright. Behind her people bustled through a crowded corridor. Ceres, I guessed, first stop on my space-liner's itinerary. But why Ceres and not her home?

The message ended. I turned the fireplace display back on, felt its radiation warm my face again and shimmer softly on the polished wood and metal of the weapons in the case across the room.

"Intriguing," Olongo mused, "if not very informative. Notice how she kept looking back over her shoulder? What do you plan doing about it, Win?"

I watched the fireplace a moment. "Well, I'm booked aboard the *Indomitable Spirit*, leaving day after tomorrow. When you guys showed up, we'd finally decided that Clarissa wasn't—"

"Just a minute, Win Bear!" She looked up from the 'com pad where she'd been telemetering her critical patients off and on all evening. "We never decided any such—"

"Clarissa"—I took her hand and patted it gently—"if it were just the baby, I might not...I mean, I love our daughter as if she were already born, but you can always make another kid."

"That's easy for *you* to say!" This from my shaggy apprentice, sprawled across the floor beside the fire. She ran a pickup down each nearly finished sweater arm, stared at the slip of paper in her hand and at the conflicting data on the tiny screen, a look of simian puzzlement on her face.

"Shut up, Koko."

"Can he talk to me that way, Uncle President?"

"Not when I'm around—*to do it for him*. Shut up, dear, there's a good ape."

Clarissa squeezed my hand. "I know what you're trying to say, Win, but—"

"No buts! I *can't* get another Clarissa, in this universe or any other. I didn't mean to make this a public debate, but what would you be saying if it were *me* who was pregnant?"

She opened her mouth, glanced down at my generously developed middle, and giggled. Maybe a dissertation on married telepathy might do Koko's anthropology grades some good, but hell, let her find out for herself.

"I hate it when you're right," Clarissa sighed. "To tell the truth, I was *wondering* how I'd stand up to six gees. So what are we going to do?" There was that sad look on her face. Any more of this, I'd probably let her come along.

"Be miserable for a while." In all our married years, we'd spent maybe five, six nights apart. "I'll try making it as short a while as possible. Wish I could get hold of Lucy—thought we'd killed off all those Hamiltonian bastards years ago."

The President leaned forward slightly. "Might I offer a suggestion? Although I must confess to certain reservations..."

"Fire away, old primate, I need all the help I can get."

"Very well, to paraphrase one of your greatest statesmen—or was he a religious leader?—take my niece, *please*." His ponderous stomach jiggled in imitation of human laughter.

Koko dropped her knitting and bounded to her feet, resembling a cross between Orson Welles and shag carpet rampant. "Honest? You're not just—"

"No, my dear, I'm not just. But I'm logical: you visited Ceres with me not so many years ago. If you strive to overcome that youthful impetuosity of yours...Come see me in the morning, I'll make all the arrangements."

"Oh, boy! The *asteroids!*"

I shook my head. "Don't get too excited. I want to think about this."

"*Think?* What's to *think* about? Oh, boy! The asteroids!"

"*Quiet!* Unless you'd rather spend the voyage in a cargo hold..."

"Then I *can* go! Gee thanks, Boss! Oh, boy! The— "

"Don't thank me. It's your uncle's idea, and I understand his reservations. On the other hand, *two* investigators might...Say, should we be interrupting your education for a field trip? Olongo?"

"Win, my friend, time is passing this planet by, along with everything it has to teach us. Were it my decision—and it's not, it's Koko's—I'd say go! *And never come back!*" He looked around the room. I knew what he was seeing, I was seeing it, too: furniture, fixtures, nanoelectronic appliances—if not actually manufactured in the asteroids, then made from asteroid raw materials.

"It isn't only consumer goods," Olongo said, "it's the *future*. And, I might add, a considerable portion of the present. Thank Lysander we were able to talk your Propertarians out of their demand for a strict gold standard."

"I wasn't aware that you had! Gold's as important to them as..." I trickled to a stop, unable to think of anything *that* important.

"Win, my boy, in this one minuscule respect, the Keynesians approach the truth: gold has no particularly magical properties that make it the only kind of money possible. A stable economy relies upon a myriad of commodities; you can draw a check as easily from a petroleum account, or on helium, or wheat."

"Yes, yes, but why this sudden allergy to gold?" What little economics I knew were being ripped out from underneath me.

"Hardly sudden. Confederate metals have been declining—relative to nonmetallic standards—for a considerable time. The asteroids, you understand."

I understood. When something gets more abundant, it gets cheaper—Marginal Utility, they call it. The Belt was cranking heavy metals out like popcorn—one advantage to working the debris of a planet that never quite got its shit (or anything else) together. You don't have to dig very deep. No matter, something scarcer would turn up to base our currencies on.

But Olongo was still pontificating: "—down to Earth on a nice, easy ballistic spiral. Your United State will benefit as well, eventually. But the Invisible Hand is going to have to manage some readjustments along the way."

"Great. So sometime next year I can get a black mask and start ordering my bullets cast out of solid silver. People will want to thank me. I—"

"Say, Win, speaking of bullets..." Captain Forsyth stood and stretched a little, wincing at the arthritic pain in his shoulder. He slapped the weapon at his hip. "Were you planning to take that old Smith & Wesson with you?"

Terrific. Time for another ribbing. "Sure. Why not?"

The chimpanzee shrugged—and winced again. "Well, for starters, think what the cold will do to its mainspring: first time you pull the trigger, *crunch!*— powdered steel."

"For that matter," added Olongo, "the entire weapon's steel. Drop it to a few degrees above Absolute, then suddenly subject it to—forty thousand psi? I shudder at the thought!"

"Now hold on a minute, I can have the springs replaced. And it isn't any forty thousand pounds. The custom loads I use—"

"That reminds me," interrupted Captain Forsyth, "those lead-alloy bullets of yours, they're lubricated, right? Little grooves around each slug, filled with some kind of grease?"

"Right, beeswax and—"

"Volatiles evaporate in hard vacuum. Same goes for that antiquated nitro powder, not to mention primers."

"Okay, wise-ass, let's look over the inventory and see what *you* suggest." I rose reluctantly and went to the gun case, Forsyth and Olongo right behind me. The lock yields for only two thumbprints in the world, mine and Clarissa's—three, if you count Ed Bear, who uses the same fingerprints I do. I opened the double doors.

"Well, I suppose this lets out most of my collection." There was the handmade .41 hideout derringer I'd brought with me to this world with the Smith, and almost a dozen other souvenirs of various misadventures since. "Hold on, what about this?"

I reached up and took down a Walther-Zeiss hand-laser. "No ammo to evaporate, no steel. This was made in your world, gentlemen. Think it might do?"

Forsyth took the pistol and turned it over in his hands. "It's proofed for space, anyway." He showed me a tiny stylized spaceship stamped into the base of the trigger guard. "But this overgrown flashlight has some drawbacks, wouldn't you say, Mr. President?"

"Rawther. In the first place, smartsuits are designed to absorb all the energy they can, and reflect any—"

"Smart *suits?*"

"Absolutely *de rigueur,* old boy. A solid-state invention in the form of a tough, lightweight rubbery garment. A bit like ocean divers wear, though infinitely more sophisticated. You didn't imagine we'd still be using that clumsy armor your astronauts—"

"Olongo, we've already had our critique of NASA for the evening. Besides, I've seen these smartsuits on TV—pardon, the Telecom—now that I think of it. Can't get anything these days but goddamned space opera. Anyway, lasers, I take it, are out?"

The Captain rubbed his chin in contemplation. "Well, this toy *might* overload a smartsuit, but you'd really have to bear down—no pun intended, Win. Be like hunting elk with that Browning 9 mm hanging there—theoretically possible, but chancy."

I thought about the years I'd worn a puny .38 as a cop, never very happy in a cruel world filled with .45s and magnums of assorted lethality. "Don't say another word. I get your drift." I stretched and placed the Walther back on its hooks. "So what do you advise—time's getting short?"

Olongo glanced briefly at Forsyth. The Captain nodded confirmation and the President drew his pistol. "I'd be honored if you'd consider taking this."

Across the room, Clarissa peeked up from her Telecom, smiled, and went back to work. She missed my look of helpless exasperation.

It wasn't *quite* the ugliest thing I'd ever seen: a Webley & Scott, big brother to the little electric quick-shooter my wife favored. It was .17 caliber—about the size of pellet guns back home—but I knew it threw its little steel darts at eleven or twelve thousand feet per second—call it Mach 10—enough to mess up anybody's outlook. The magazine was good for a hundred rounds. The handle, shaped to suit a gorilla's fingers, was awkward in my own.

"Let's find the original stocks," Olongo suggested. "I've got them in the car someplace. I also brought some special projectiles you might want to try."

Forsyth grinned. "If you've got any *big* enemies."

"The good Captain refers, in his elliptical manner, to Owen tubes—a hollow contrivance which slips *over* the front end. You see, the drive currents also flow along the outside of the—"

"My God!" I interrupted, looking at the hefty barrel coils. "What would the diameter amount to?"

"A little under two inches," the Captain replied evenly, "just right for putting an ape-size dent in a personal flivver. That's what they use for hovercraft out there, little tiny spaceships that—"

"I *said* I watch the Telecom. Sounds like I oughta invest in some of these Owen goodies. You're sure I'll need a nasty thing like that out there?"

"Oh, it's quite up to you, dear boy. However, with Hamiltonian Federalists involved, I assume you want to be adequately defended."

"I just don't care to think about it so soon after dinner." I started to shut the gun case.

"One more thing, Win." Forsyth reached past me. "You won't want to leave this toadsticker behind. It's a spaceman's knife, or I never saw one before."

"You mean that old Bowie—*Rezin*, rather?" Named after the fellow who invented them in both worlds, Jim's little brother, the specimen in question was another "trophy"; I hadn't more than looked at it in years. Eighteen inches from pommel to point, it had a foot-long blade two and a half inches wide and a quarter thick, razor sharp halfway along the back edge, as well. The alloy was something called Stellite, and the grip aft of the heavy brass guards was long enough for a hand and a half—somebody like Olongo excepted. The damn thing weighed better than two pounds, and gave me the papercut shudders just thinking about it.

"Swords, already. Don't you clowns realize it's almost the twenty-first century?"

"Not by *my* calendar." Forsyth took the knife, ran his thumb along the edge with a casual swipe that made me cringe, and handed it back. "You wanted to know about smartsuits? Well, they *heal up*, better and faster than ordinary window glass. You can't always count on a gun to do the job. Knives make bigger, messier holes."

"And," Olongo offered, "asteroiders have a highly sensible custom regarding personal weapons: pistols, for the most part, are for outdoors; blades are for indoors. Reasonable, when you live in a pressurized environment, wouldn't you say?"

⋏

Friday, February 26, 223 A.L.

You'd think of all the places they'd control the climate, it'd be the airport. For some reason, Confederates don't see it that way. The Lilienthal Aeronautics Building, planted smack in the middle of town, pokes up a couple hundred stories, right into the real weather. We were at the very top, waiting for the shuttle to depart.

I stood shivering with my cloak wrapped around me as many times as it would go, wondering if Clarissa was really dressed warmly enough. Through blowing snow I could see my assistant huddling against her uncle, who had come to see us off. Despite a four-hour briefing the day before, he was still piling on last-minute advice. She looked up at me in silent appeal, then went resignedly back to having her furry little ear bent.

I felt sorry for the old gorilla, too. He'd caught his burglar last night: an attractive young American woman who'd apparently expected the ape to be unarmed again. He hadn't been—his spare persuader's a .375 Nauvoo Browning; she was DOA before she hit the floor, a sawed-off .22 Colt

Woodman clenched in her rapidly cooling fingers. Some people take a while understanding why we have so little crime here.

Others never get the chance.

Now Koko and I were off on some mysterious adventure, while the President had nothing to return to but the same old grind, the continuing subversion of my homeworld. Olongo was personally involved, and for a good reason: his species is damned near extinct back there, getting extincter all the time. In order to survive, they had to be educated to the culture their more fortunate Confederate fellows had adopted. Just considering the human politics in that neighborhood, it was going to be a long, dangerous job. The Voice of the Stars, good old Voltaire, had mentioned it last evening, in a slightly different context:

"The simian population of the other Earth is doomed without our help, but this is little justification for tampering with human affairs in that continuum. Yes, let us lead chimpanzees and gorillas to a better world, but let the established civilizations go their own way. We have better things to do. At least that's the way it looks, Thursday, February 25, 223 A.L. This is Voltaire Malaise, Ceres Central, good night."

Trouble is, nobody could possibly round up all the wild simians. Voltaire hadn't bothered mentioning porpoises and killer whales—the cetaceans of both worlds, civilized for millennia, had gotten things straightened out right away. Likewise, teach a few apes to speak, and in a few years they'd be rounding *themselves* up, and not just to escape.

After all, it's their planet, too.

Koko pried herself away and disappeared into the saucer-shaped shuttle. I turned to Clarissa, who looked pretty, pink, and pregnant, the kind of woman no sane man would be leaving. "Well, I—"

"Oh, Win, promise me you'll—"

"Honey, I'll eat *all* my galoshes and wear my spinach every day."

"Idiot! Take care of yourself!" She threw her arms around me, hot tears trickling into my tunic collar. "I want you back, and so, no doubt, will your daughter...*I love you so!*"

I grinned, nuzzling her hair. "Yeah, and I've been trying to figure out why for years. I was a worn-out, half-senile old—"

"Oh shut up! Three reasons, silly—no, not *those*, well, yes, those, too, but—because you make me think, and because you make me laugh—"

"That was simple. All I had to do was show you my—"

"And because you make me horny! You'd better be back soon, or I swear I'll come looking for you!"

"Clarissa, I thought we had that settled."

"Well, you know what I mean." She bit her lower lip to keep it from trembling. That, and her little red nose, suddenly made her so appealing I almost started crying myself.

"I hope so. And I love you, too—don't ask *me* why, or I'll never get on that shuttle. Now don't stay to wave good-bye, I hate that. And it's cold out here! Take care of our little girl; I'll try to get back here before she does, okay?"

She nodded, wiping her eyes. "Oh! I almost forgot..." She handed me a gift-wrapped package the size and shape of a paperback book. "And the Captain sent you this." Another small parcel, heavier, tied up in plain brown plastic. "I wouldn't let him bring it himself, the cold's bad for his—"

"And it's bad for *yours*, too. Get downstairs where it's warm!" I kissed her hard and turned, not daring to look back. Even in the dead of Rocky Mountain winter, the shuttle's gaily-painted hull shone cheery red and white: LAKER SPACEWAYS ELECTROJET.

Good thing I brought my own lunch. I crossed the catwalk protecting the impeller grid, climbed the three-step boarding ladder, handed Olongo's Webley to the stewardess, who racked it with a hundred other assorted pieces of artillery, and clumped around the aisle to find a seat beside my assistant. She'd brought a brown-bag lunch herself.

"Hey, Boss, want a banana? Frozen clean through, I'm afraid, but I brought an extra one for you!"

The shuttle began to vibrate, lifting slowly. Clarissa stood outside in the cold, obedient as ever, tearfully waving me good-bye.

4: BREAKHEART HOTEL

Six gees ain't so bad, I can take 'em standing on my head.
Which is more or less the way it felt.

Laporte vanished below us in the clouds as the electrojet was driven skyward by an outboard ring of high-voltage impellers, basically similar to those in my Neova, but powered by a ground-based microwave array. Inside, seats were arranged in concentric circles beneath a transparent dome. In the center, a pylon stretched through the roof: elevator or stairs to the control module; on Laker Spaceways, probably the ladder.

Fifteen minutes later, we'd gained a hundred fifty-odd thousand feet, where even anaerobic bacteria have trouble catching their breath, and where the impellers ended their usefulness. The major drag on a bullet, I'm told, isn't so much gravity as air. Presumably the same holds true for spaceships, which is why it pays to use a ground-powered boost before torching off the main machinery.

Spaceships? *I was on a spaceship!* Beside me, Koko munched away, humming dementedly to herself as she gazed in rapture through the ceiling. A stewardess came by to fold our seats back like psychiatrists' couches, tucking us in for a stomach-thrilling moment of freefall as the impellers folded like a cheap flashbulb reflector. Wind whistled past the plummeting hull, then...

Whaaammm! I suddenly weighed more than Nero Wolfe ever dreamed of, my breathing a matter of conscious exercise. Three minutes' acceleration—my features melting toward my ears like Silly Putty—didn't seem much longer than an hour. How time flies when you're having fun. Abruptly, the fusion drives seemed to cut, my seat straightened up, I could breathe again.

Zero gee? *This* I'd been looking forward to: I groped past the safety-webbing, extracted my favorite felt-tip pen, LAPORTE PARATRONICS, LTD. stenciled along its barrel, and held it a foot or so in front of my face. I let go.

It fell in my lap and rolled off onto the cabin floor.

"Gravity and government stop here!" A central panel displayed the daredevil visage of a chimpanzee in a space-black tunic. I folded myself painfully in half, head between my knees, and groped beneath the seat in front of me for my pen, only to discover I was *wedged* in that position. "Welcome aboard Laker's Electrojet service to synchronous rendezvous. Sorry about that lift-off, folks, heh, heh. We'll be pushing along now at a comfortable and convenient one gee for approximately twenty-eight more minutes. Thanks for flying Laker, and good morning."

One gee? *Now* he tells me! *"Koko!"* I whispered in embarrassment.

"What's up, Boss?" She bent and stared down at the veins bulging in my forehead. "View's better through the windows, y'know."

"Get me out of here! Mother didn't raise me to do slapstick!"

"Okay, okay! Move your shoulders a little to the right...that's it. Now, lift your leg and...want me to call the stewardess?"

"For godsake, *no!*" Something went *scrunch!* in the back of my neck, and I was free. The passenger ahead craned around and glared. I grinned sheepishly and tried to straighten a tie I wasn't wearing. Comfortable and convenient? Have to check *that* out with my chiropractor.

⅄

The void around the liner glittered with a thousand fireflies; shuttles like ours, vehicles from Luna, the Lagrange stations, synchronous and near-Earth satellites. But as we swam nearer with little puffs and bumps of course-correction and the giant ship gradually acquired recognizable shape, I knew it wasn't the vessel I had tickets for. According to the tourist brochure, *Indomitable Spirit* was a big round ball, half a mile across, propulsion assemblies sticking out behind like the stem of a pumpkin. The apparition ahead of us was at least four times that size, a collection of giant silvery mailing-tubes glued to a cigar box. As we swept by her colossal drivers, it was spelled out for us in hundred-foot letters:

BONAVENTURA
LOS ANGELES, N.A.C.

A nominal registry, to say the least. This thing would never make it to the surface whole. But what had happened to *Indomitable Spirit?* Were we all being shanghaied or something? There followed a funny elevatory queasiness: zero gee at last—though I wasn't going to risk my souvenir pen (or my dignity) twice in one day. The shuttle aimed for the liner's rectilinear stern, slid into an enormous hangar on one edge, where it clanged gently to a stop. Weight returned; the seatbelt light went out.

Koko favored me with an uninformative shrug.

At the lock, the stewardess was passing out briefcases, umbrellas, and guns. "*Indomitable Spirit* has been chartered for scientific purposes. This is *Bonaventura*. All reservations will be honored. *Indomitable Spirit* has been charted for..."

For scientific purposes? A whole spaceliner? Glad *I* didn't have to pay for it! I followed Koko's waddling bulk into an accordion-pleated tunnel stretching from the shuttle to an inner wall of the hangar. We filed through a submarine-type door that shut behind us with a hiss. Wondering where all this free gravity was coming from, I nudged my assistant and turned back to a window: the passenger tunnel had retracted, the shuttle was buttoning up. Mist filled the hangar, and the electrojet slid outward across the threshold, dropping instantly from view. Now I understood: we were underway!

⅄

The ticket they swapped me said Stateroom 12-22. Koko's, some seventy-seven levels forward, was 89-141. I don't usually cotton to cute little three-foot robots, but this one had wheels and brought back memories of a time and place where Good Humor men were pedal-powered. Besides, it volunteered to carry my luggage. I bade adieu to my apprentice and let the machine show me through the confusing lobby several decks above the hangar, a maze of pathways and irregularly shaped pools where dolphins squeaked and paddled, conversing with humans and simians seated at the water's edge in little oval cocktail bays. Laced about with curving stairs and escalators, a dozen lapping, overhanging mezzanine levels created a bewildering perspective overhead. The suitcase-critter led me to an impressive ochre-hued column, one of many varicolored cylinders that appeared to be holding up the lobby roof. A pair of doors slid open, admitted us, and closed.

"*Ohmygodwhatthefuckisthis!*" The elevator shot past mezzanines and stairways, through the very ceiling, and suddenly the little glassy cage was *outside* the ship, skimming along its leviathan hull. I huddled numbly by the doors, peeking between my fingers with a sort of suicidal fascination.

The little robot emitted a disgusted snigger. I glared at it: "R2, Brutus?" It swiveled its head, staring pointedly the other way.

It was almost a religious experience for me when the elevator surged to a halt and its blessed portals slid aside. I was *indoors* again, being dazedly directed leftward around a corridor to my room. There, another spell of vertigo awaited: one entire wall was transparent from ceiling to floor, riveting my paralyzed attention like a cobra hypnotizing dinner. The bellbot polarized the glass a trifle and waited, humming softly.

With sweating hands I fumbled for a coin—anything round and shiny—and dropped it in the little machine's receptacle. It departed, vibrating a cheerful octave and a quarter higher. I counted my change—I'd given it half an ounce of gold! The architect who built this mind-bending Disneyland for claustrophobes must have been taking payola from the Business Machines' Union!

Polarization or not, there was still quite a fireworks display visible through the wall-sized window. The elevators, four of them from my vantage point—one pair reflected by another silvery tower across the way—were capped with little haloes of blue flame. The damned things had their own rocket motors! Intermittent brilliant flashes sparkled in the greater distance, I knew not why. And, despite acceleration, we were still admitting last-minute shuttles. I watched one from AntarcticAir slide into the hangar-deck below.

Out of the corner of an eye I caught a frigidly official-looking face staring from the 'com screen on the right-hand wall. I turned up the sound: ". . . your Captain, Edwin H. Spoonbill III. Those bursts of color you see to starboard are tests of our debris-defenses. Nothing to worry about, the flying's so clean here that our gunnery computer's had to throw chaff out to practice on. ETA for Ceres: three hundred forty hours—about two weeks—so just relax and enjoy the ride. If you have any questions, our Information Section can—"

Click! The bathroom was at the opposite end of the cabin, as far from those goddamned windows as I could get. I decided I could use another shower. Maybe three or four, if the microminiature bar of soap held out.

⋏

Half an hour later, the sack lunch I'd forgotten about until now demonstrated another verity of space travel, to wit: six gees and soft-boiled eggs mix *entirely* too well. I found a disposal chute and consigned my erstwhile nutriment to the furies of the engine room.

This reminded me of my going-away presents. Captain Forsyth's was right in character: half a dozen fully-stuffed, rechargeable Webley magazines. Good old Forsyth. I plugged a pair into the wall and let their guccione cells juice up on Captain Spoonbill's tab.

Next I carefully undid Clarissa's giftwrapping. (She always saves it.) A paperback-sized brick of the same flat white pseudoceramic Telecom screens are made of. No instruction booklet, no nothing. Just a manufacturer's card advising me to punch the single activating button on the edge, then type out K-E-Y.

Nice trick, without a keyboard.

At the bottom of the card, in her professionally indecipherable scrawl, my wife had added, *Type out W-I-N first!* Same problem, dearest. Oh, well, I pushed the little button. The image of a keyboard materialized across the surface of the gadget. Okay, I touched each phantom letter in succession: W-I-N.

The keyboard vanished. Clarissa's picture appeared, dressed in the same golden-brown outfit she'd been wearing this morning to see me off. She stretched sexily across our emperor-size bed like an aftershave commercial; the fact that she was five months pregnant, and the homey sight of my age-stained shoulder holster hanging from the cornerpost, may have spoiled the effect—for anyone but me.

"Have a good trip, darling, and hurry home. While you're gone, I hope this gimmick keeps you entertained almost as well as I could!"

She glanced over her shoulder as the bathroom door swung open behind her. I recognized the hairy body that emerged, dripping wet. "Did you say something, dear?" The naked figure had a towel draped over his face, rubbing his hair dry. I really do need to lose some weight.

"Bye!" Clarissa winked conspiratorially, grabbed a corner of the duvet, and flipped it over the pickup. Shucks—I'd thought she'd been making the bed. The underside of the quilt lingered for a moment on the screen, then faded.

I was already homesick.

This time I punched out K-E-Y: *"Congratulations!"* congratulated a congratulatory congratulator. *"You* have acquired the *latest* in nanoelectronic *miracles*, the [blare of trumpets, followed by angel chorus] *Helmers Gigacom 67G!* Contained within its sixty-seven gigabyte memories are movies, books, audio recordings, interactive games, and plenty of room for any audio or visual information you might wish to store. The 67G also functions as computer, calculator, encyclopedia, alarm clock, cigarette lighter..."

I let the unnecessary sales pitch run down. Nice picking, sweetheart, and thanks. I punched out I-N-S-T-R and, as soon as I felt competent, very carefully lifted Clarissa's message from temporary storage, where she'd modestly recorded it, burning it permanently into the machine where it would stay like the inscription on a watch.

Thumbing through the contents, I found hundreds of films, thousands of novels and records, a good many of them custom-selected. She'd included all the Mike Morrison movies I'd learned to love, and a surprising number of my favorites from the States: Cornell Wilde's *The Naked Prey; Thirty-six Hours* with James Garner. I conjured up a particularly cherished Maria Muldaur album and let it fill the cabin with weird and lovely music while I finished unpacking. Some call it corn, but others call it heart.

First thing to attend to: alterations and familiarization on the Webley. All I got when I tried calling Koko was an animated cartoon, a little green chimpanzee, antennae and all, informing me the line was busy. Probably out of bananas and calling room service. Next, another try at Lucy. No go. I wired her a note, care of General Delivery, Ceres Central, and called Clarissa. "Hi! It's me!"

"Hi, me!" She was still wearing that hormone-inspiring outfit. "Gee, I'm glad to see you. The house feels lonely already. Like my present?"

"Give a listen to the background—'Midnight at the Oasis.' Where'd you dig up all the American flicks?"

"Jenny Noble, bless her, those Propertarians have quite a library. How was the shuttle ride?"

"Koko enjoyed it. *You* wouldn't have, and neither would our prospective offspring. Olongo get back to his office all right?"

"I guess so, he took off in some kind of big hurry. Listen, do you think our budget could stand it if you called me every day? Why I ever let you talk me out of—"

"Baby, it was *awful* getting up here. You should see my lunch."

"Oh dear, you didn't—"

"I never had the chance. You take care of yourself, now."

"I promise. See you tomorrow, then?"

"You got it, kiddo, every day until the lightlag gets impossible."

Her image disappeared, leaving behind that slightly better/slightly worse feeling you get from such conversations. I holstered my Tom Swift Electric Popgun and went out to find a drink.

⅄

Saturday, February 27, 223 A.L.

It took an amazing amount of shiptime to get the hang of the *Bonaventura*. The layout was simple in conception, all but impossible in practice: take four old-fashioned U.S. pennies—the copper kind, I mean—and arrange them in a square, edges touching a quarter in the center. That's a cross-section of the ship. Now place all five coins on a pack of cigarettes, and convert them into stacks, say fifty quarters and forty pennies high: five enormous towers planted kitty-corner on a blocky rectangular base. The outer cylinders are mostly staterooms, arranged in wedges, so that everybody gets a chance at tossing his acrophobic cookies. The center tower, all seven hundred and ninety-two stories, is services, shops, restaurants, recreational facilities, with a slowly revolving saloon at the top, just beneath Captain Spoonbill's domain, the bridge.

Three elevators ran up and down in tracks along each connective structure between cylinders, a dozen captive miniature rocket ships in all. I didn't discover until the final day of the cruise that there's an internal transport system for us craven yellowbellies. Each residential tower is coded inside, mine gold, the others blue, green, and orange. The center column's white—another thing I didn't notice until a few days out; kept turning the wrong way from the elevators and winding up lost.

One such occasion proved intriguing. Koko was at a beauty shop, getting covered with plastic curlers from sagittal crest to prehensile toes. Killing time before lunch, I misnavigated into the bar on the 790th floor, and when it rotated around sufficiently, I could see Earth dwindling steadily through the glass, and a bright yellow splinter surging gamely toward the *Bonaventura* at what must have been eight or nine gees. Somebody was determined not to miss the boat. I finished my Coke and hurried to an elevator like a Rocky Mountain yokel heading downtown to watch the traffic lights change.

From a porthole above the hangar deck, I watched the speedy vessel come alongside, too big for the liner to take aboard, very long and slender, her reentry-blackened nosecone and glowing pink stern drives contrasting brightly with her yellow-painted hull. Along her fuselage, in striking metallic green, the lettering stood out clearly:

TICONDEROGA
JERSEY CITY, N.A.C.

She locked fast to the outside of the giant ship.

They brought her passenger aboard through the extended accordion tube. Whoever it was—an auburn-coated elderly gorilla, it appeared—he looked the way I'd felt the morning they relieved me of my appendix, lying on a gurney, swathed in pale-green drapery that matched my complexion. His limbs were festooned with plastic tubing and telemetry, an oxygen tent obscured his features further. Going to the asteroids for his health? Maybe the high-acceleration rocket ride had proven more than he'd bargained for. At least it'd be something interesting to tell Koko about over lunch.

I met her, as agreed, at a little hamburger joint two or three overhangs above the lobby floor, where we could watch the finny folk cavorting below. The proprietor leaned casually on the counter, joshing with the customers.

"—so I finally gave up trying to make money," he was telling Koko. "It wasn't worth anything once I got it, and the IRS took it anyway, everything, including the royalties on my books. Learned welding and bartered my services for what I needed." The husky bearded hash-slinger was apparently a fellow refugee. Somehow, he looked familiar.

"Unbelievable." Koko shook her head. "Good thing for you the Propertarians— Win! Karyl Hetzer, this is Win Bear, a United Statesian from Saint Charles Town. Win, Karyl."

"That's Denver, my dear Whatsit. Hey, guess what I just saw arriving!"

"Er, Karyl's got a son who lives in Denver, don't you, Karyl?"

"No, Koko, Laporte—the *little* Laporte, just outside Fort Collins. You know the place, Mr. Bear?"

"That's Win. Yes, I know it—know about *you*, too: *Government, The Mindless Maw*, by Karyl Hetzer. I thought you looked familiar; Jenny Noble gave me a copy. How'd you wind up taking short orders aboard the *Enterprise*, here?"

"Welding. I helped build her, had a little money to invest—for once—and decided to stay on. What'll it be, Win?"

I looked the menu over as it flickered on the countertop. Either of the Jennies would've loved this place. "Think I'll try a Spoonerburger, and pour me out a shot of Scotch and a glass of milk."

"It's your stomach," Karyl observed, punching in the order.

"And a Free System. What have *you* been up to, faithful simian companion?"

"Uh, not much, *kemo sabe*—getting beautifuller, didn't you notice?" She spun around on her stool, showing off her freshly curled pelt. "Never know aboard these cruises, I might run into a handsome young ape who's a captain of industry or something. Say, did you know there are seven hundred and ninety—"

"I read the brochure, too. Here's our food, let's eat."

Monday, March 1, 223 A.L.

A couple of days later, I finally found the gunsmith. He was listed under *Ranges, shooting*. There were also *Ranges, cattle and sheep* (breeding stock for the colonies), and *Ranges, golf*—the kind where you use a little white ball. Never touch the stuff, myself.

The sign taped to his window said:

THERE'S ONLY 24 HOURS IN A DAY
THERE'S ONLY 1 OF ME
YOU CAN HAVE A *FAST* JOB OR A *GOOD* JOB
YOUR CHOICE

The overweight unsanitary-looking character behind the counter folded his muscular arms, cultivating the sour-looking expression creased permanently into his face. "You wanna ruin a fine piece of ordnance, dontcha?"

I've never run across one of these characters who wasn't like this. I think they take classes in it at trade school: Cranky 201, hr. arr. "Look, the customer is always right—"

"Except sometimes." Two inches of ash fell from the butt screwed into the corner of his mouth and rolled down his greasy shop apron. "Friend, you've gotta perfectly good coaxial sighting-laser built into that piece. Just haul up on the trigger slack, and the needles'll land wherever the little red dot is pointing. Iron sights? Downright medieval!"

Koko looked up from a coffee-stained display case where she'd been drooling over some new engine of destruction. "Medieval is right, firmly rooted in the bedrock of—"

"Koko, when I need your help, I'll send up a semaphore—maybe even a *whole* phore." I glowered right back at the 'smith. "Can you put the sights on, or can't you?"

He rubbed a grimy thumb over his unshaven chin. "Well, it means un-shipping the front coil, and I gotta find someplace t'mount the rear sight. Take me at least a week. Wanna loaner?"

"Make it twenty-four hours. And what have you got?"

"Well, how about a nice .14 Edison—one in the back room I got stuck with on a bad debt—you bein' an electric man?"

"I'm a *Smith & Wesson* man. Tell me, what have you got that's *very* small?"

"Small?" He rummaged around in the fascinating debris under the counter. "Nothin' that'd interest you. What's a Smith & Wrestling, some kinda European number? Got a couple of kids' guns here." He handed me a tiny weapon, no bigger than a matchbook, marked Kolibri. "Electric .09—probably got a barrel liner around here'll beef it up to .17, so you can use your own ammo. Single-shot, though. What you want with a dinky little—"

"Ever hear of a holdout gun?" He hadn't. In this whole enormous trig-ger-happy civilization, concealed backup guns were a novelty. I decided to skip it—I could get along for a day or two unarmed. I persuaded him to complete the alterations in two days, but I wanted to get some practice with the Webley first.

"Hold on, what's this?" The gunsmith had the rotor housing off already, peering down the barrel from the muzzle end. He fumbled absently on the bench behind him for a brass cleaning rod.

"Something wrong?" Odd, I'd figured Glongo for a fellow who'd keep his hardware spotless, inside and out.

"Dunno. Let's—" The rod went halfway down the barrel. And stopped.

I took the weapon and sighted down the smooth, shiny bore. Not much to get dirty in there. The .17 caliber needles, magnetically suspended in flight, never contacted the inside walls. A bias in the windings put spin on the projectiles. "Looks okay to me. I can see daylight just fine."

"Yeah, and you'll see *stars*, too, right before the end. There's some-thing—" He put some pressure on the rod. It bent a little, then slid stubbornly until an object popped out on the counter and rolled to the floor. He squatted with a grunt and picked it up.

"*Here's your* 'daylight,' mister." It was a tiny, bore-size cylinder of incredibly transparent plastic, about a quarter of an inch long. "Fella, you pull the trigger on that thing—at eleven thousand foot-seconds—it woulda blown you clean away. Couldn'ta got in there by accident. Somebody don't like you."

⅄

"*El Presidente,*" I told the terminal, turning my back. "*Boop!*" the machine answered. I wheeled, taking up a little on the trigger. A brilliant spot of crimson splashed the target center, followed by a pair of steel needles as I pulled the trigger through. I shifted to the next silhouette, and on to the third. A fast reload, and once over lightly. Score: 42. Time: 9.67.

This was going to take some practice.

I examined the Webley: ambidextrous controls—something U.S. manufacturers had never gotten around to, as if a seventh of their clientele weren't southpaws—the safety fit nicely under my thumb, and, further forward, a lever, marked with three positions. The first was SAFE, the second had delivered one shot at a time, each time I pulled the trigger. Now I slid the lever to the middle BURST position and called for a target.

D-d-dit! Three ragged holes in the plastic. Experimenting with a knob at the back of the rotor housing allowed me to adjust the burst-length anywhere from two shots to a dozen. I set it on five and left it there.

Next lever-position was *full* automatic: an empty magazine (about four seconds) later, and the plastic target looked like a sheet of badly woven lace. I switched back to BURST and called for a solid target, something approximating the fluid characteristics of living tissue.

D-d-d-d-dit! When the ventilators finished pulling steam out of the room, I took a good look at the pseudocarcass downrange, and set the BURST control back to three. No use getting penalized for unnecessary roughness.

I left the Webley with the 'smith, reminding myself to double whatever his bill came to—small payment to the guy who saves your life. Question: was it *my* life the sabotage had been aimed at terminating, or Olongo's?

Koko complained so loudly about my "social nakedness" that I gave in and went up to my cabin for the Rezin. The Telecom was blinking on and off in red—probably my apprentice downstairs hollering at me to get a move on. Strapping the unwieldy knife to my hip, I hurried back down to see the sights.

⅄

One whole tower, the blue, of course, was for porpoises and killer whales. I resisted Koko's urgings that we rent some scuba gear, following the air-filled parallel corridors, instead. We stared at the marine critters on the other side of the glass; they stared right back at us. In a sort of aquatorium, they were holding a class in the use of smartsuits.

Funny, I hadn't thought of smartsuits for the water-walkers. The instructor was a chimp, the same guy I'd signed us up with for later in the week. Floating in the middle of the theater, he was demonstrating the advantages of rubber spacewear, pointing out to the cetaceans that, in zero gee, they could maneuver in a *waterless* environment just as well as any anthropoid. I was tempted to have the engineer stop the train so I could see that, but I couldn't find the emergency cord.

Without much effort, we soon found ourselves turned around and completely lost in a cargo area deep within the *Bonaventura*'s rectangular stern, something like a huge apartment building parking garage, filled from wall to wall with the slumbering shapes of a thousand inert hovercraft, gleaming in the subterranean twilight.

I always thought it was nifty how Apollo took an aluminum Lizzie to the Moon. Confederates, too, adore any contraption that'll move under its own impetus, and they've harnessed every conceivable form (and not a few *in*conceivable forms) of energy to operate them: steam, internal combustion, electricity, flywheels; there've been attempts to run hoverbuggies on enormous rubber bands, spring clockworks, charges of dynamite, now even thermonuclear fusion.

Secretly playing Prussian War ace in a cloud of impeller dust, reading quietly while their computer-guided vehicles whisk them down the Greenway at five hundred miles per, Confederates don't really care very much about the power source. In the portable privacy of their road machines, they've discovered a far greater fountain of energy, a sort of deep contemplative self-reliance which is the wellspring of all their "lesser" miracles.

Then I looked closer: these "hovercraft" had no impellers, no skirts, just fusion-powered drivers, perfect little copies of the monumental hellburners pushing *Bonaventura* along by now at several hundred *thousand* miles an hour. So these were flivvers, miniature personal spaceships which were the asteroid equivalent of the private automobile. Reminded me of an argument I'd overheard in Denver, something about mass transit.

"But that's exactly what we've got already!" insisted Jenny (I forget which one). "And it takes you from exactly where you are to precisely where you want to go, whenever you want, in comfort, relative safety, and total privacy—at a hell of a lot less money per passenger mile than any BART or Metro system. Look it up: I'm right."

I'd looked it up: she was.

Your basic asteroid flivver is capable of sustaining standard thrust—one-tenth of a gee—for a couple of days in a row. I was admiring a big candy-striped 223 Truax, when I discovered something even more interesting under a canvas cover on its port fender.

"What is this heap, Koko, a police cruiser?"

"A what?" She lumbered nearer and saw what I was talking about. "Oh, that—it's just a darling gun."

"And I think it's just the *cutest* thing, myself," I lisped, peering into a cluster of six wicked-looking muzzles in a foot-long pod. "What the hell is it for?"

"A hybrid of the Dardick and the Gatling: slugs from triangular plastic cartridges at maybe twenty thousand rounds a minute. Probably going to a prospector who struck it rich—helps discourage piracy and claim-jumping. Or maybe to a Registration Patrol, who knows?"

I glanced around the hold, suddenly aware that most of these innocent-appearing vehicles were fitted out for Armageddon. "Registration Patrol? *That* has a decidedly un-Confederate ring to it."

"Naww," she sighted along the weapon, squinting a little. "They're just insurance companies, sort of. They travel around making sure their customers' property doesn't get involuntarily transferred. Kind of friendly—sometimes a patrol person is all the company a hardrock miner'll have for months."

Like Sergeant Preston and his dog, Tyge. A small reminder I was headed for the frontier. I slipped the protective shroud back over the cannon and continued looking for the egress.

Instead, I found another storage hold. The light was even dimmer here, blocked off by stacks of crates that threw a million eerie angular shadows. I stopped out of curiosity: three quarters of the loot in this section was invoiced to some character named J. V. Tormount, of Aphrodite, Ltd. The interesting datum was the manufacturer: good old Laporte Paratronics, Ltd., creator of fine Telecommery, electric pencil sharpeners, and refrigerator parts. Also, through the scientific talents of my friends Ooloorie P'wheet and Deejay Thorens, originator of the Probability Broach.

I wondered what was inside these crates, and who the devil J. V. Tormount was. Halfway through my ruminations, I heard a little scuffling noise behind me. "Koko?"

Silence. I turned, slowly, extremely conscious I was armed with only a hyperthyroid kitchen knife. I wrapped my hand around the pommel, then felt silly. Probably a spacefaring bilge rat—or some crewman wanting to know what the hell *I* was up to down here.

Another skittling noise, this time to my left. I tippy-toed in that direction, wondering what made me do these things. Peering down an aisle between two mountains of containers, I saw a graceful ankle disappear around a corner. Something lay on the floor between me and the fleeing feminine extremity. Four or five cautious steps took me to the object: a length of hefty jewelry chain, attached to a—

"*Boss! Look out!*"

A shadow loomed above me, getting larger, fast. I grabbed the chain and rolled forward as something landed behind me with a crash that shook the deck and hurt my molars clear down to my insteps.

Koko shoved her way through the shattered remnants of the fallen crate. Interesting: I'd spent enough time in Deejay's laboratory to recognize loose Broach parts when I see them. "Win! Are you all right?" Her paw was shaking as she touched my bruised shoulder. I patted it.

"Yes, Koko, and thanks. I'm just rattled a little." I glanced down at the bangle dangling by its chain from my own unsteady fingers. "And not just from being dumped on like that." I showed her the medallion. She'd never met an Eye-in-the-Pyramid in person before.

⚓

Naturally, there was no other trace of the person or persons who'd dropped the medallion—and several thousand ounces of expensive paratronic gear. We found our way back to my stateroom, intending to call the purser or Captain Spoonbill, or whoever was in charge of damaged goods, human and otherwise. But there was that red light, still blinking on my Telecom console.

"Win?" Clarissa's voice was strained, I forgot my aching muscles and stripped a mental gear or two worrying about her and the baby at the same time.

"You okay, honey?"

"Yes, dear, I'm fine, and so is your daughter. *You* don't look so good—are you getting enough exercise?"

I let it pass.

"I'm disturbed about Olongo," she continued. "Remember how I told you he seemed preoccupied last time we saw him?"

"Sure. He hurried off somewhere as soon as the shuttle lifted."

"That's right. Well, I've tried several times to call him, and Win, Vice-President Carlson and the rest of the staff finally admitted this afternoon that he hasn't been to work for three days. His secretary can't find him, and neither can his family."

I looked over my shoulder. Koko's eyes were big and round.

"First Ed," said my wife, "then Lucy—now Olongo's disappeared!"

5: THE BLUES MY NAUGHTY SWEETIE GIVES TO ME

"Look, Sherlock Junior, the less you worry about your uncle, the sooner we can start figuring out what's going on." I lit a cigar, rubbing my rapidly stiffening shoulder.

Koko gave up her pacing to plunk down wearily on the floor beside the window, in perfect disregard of the terrifying void outside. "You're right, I guess. Anyway, we don't really know for sure he's—"

"Hold that thought. Now let's see...Olongo's Webley: the only time it's been out of my sight was in the shower, here. *And* once aboard the shuttle craft. Question is, who booby-trapped it, and why?"

She grinned up at me, a lot gamer than I'd have expected, given the circumstances. "Try again, Boss. *Which* booby did they really want to trap?"

"I see what you mean. Okay, maybe it *was* already gimmicked when he gave it to me. But, Koko, he's only the President, who'd want to—"

"Politics just aren't important enough to figure into it." She got an odd look on her face. "Say, you don't suppose this has anything to do with those two burglaries?"

A light dawned: "They were never burglaries, at all! Did Olongo mention anything being stolen? No, but he did catch the first intruder *fooling with his gun.* And the second time around, she walked in boldly, knowing damned well the Webley would blow up in his face! Too bad for her he'd given it to me."

She digested that a while. "Then what about the little ballet in the cargo hold this afternoon? If you *weren't* the intended..."

She was right. Someone was sure as hell trying to kill me now, the medallion obviously bait, and the only connection there was to Lucy, not Olongo. That led to another bright idea: "Listen, was it me or the *location?*"

"What do you mean?" She held a paw across her mouth, stifling a yawn.

"Well, I'd begun envisioning some evil-doer lurking around, plotting to bump me off. But maybe they just wanted that shipment left alone."

"Why bother? There's a regular security detail aboard to—"

"Hell, I don't know. No customs barriers to get around, no regulated substances in this nutty civilization. Kind of puts a crimp in any smuggling theory." I scratched my head. When I'd begun this caper, there'd been too *little* information. Now I seemed to be suffocating under an avalanche of unconnected facts.

Koko yawned again. "O Guru of Deduction, methinks your mind wandereth."

"Don't worry, it's too weak to get very far." My cigar had gone out. I considered relighting it, looked at it again, then chucked it down the disposal. "Back to basics, then: people missing, Ed, Lucy, possibly your uncle, and—hey, don't get me off the subject—what really disturbs me is that crate. Free trade or not, you're too young to remember the last time Broach technology wound up in unfriendly hands. I'd like to know why that shipment's headed for the asteroids. Hell, the only thing the other side of Reality out there is *rocks*—and none of them with good hotels. Aphrodite, Ltd., is it? Well, we've got a chance of pinning *that* one down, anyway."

She watched me belly up to the Telecom. "What you doing, Win?"

"I just happen to have a little pull at Laporte Paratronics—Deejay and Ooloorie, not to mention the Chairman of the Board himself, Freeman K. Bertram, a Hamiltonian, incidentally, until they tried burning his gizzard out with a laser. Let's see what they can—"

"Is that a good idea? I mean, the time-lag's getting nasty now—and they may not like handing out confidential—"

"Listen, Bertram saved my life once, that's how he picked up that laserburn. Ever hear of a Chinese obligation?"

"Is that anything like 'Confucian to the Enemy'?" She yawned again—it was starting to be catching.

"Someday, hairy person, you'll press your luck too far." I diddled keys, waiting for the results to wend their ethery way to Earth.

"Laporte Paratronics, may I help you?" A real-live, real-time receptionist: nice traditional touch, even if she was a chimp. This was company headquarters, north of town, in a huge Aztec-modern pyramid Bertram had constructed before his rigorous and painful conversion to the side of Law and Disorder.

"Sure, extension 4511, please." That'd ring bells down at Laporte University, Ltd., four or five blocks from my place.

Another pause while radio waves got there and back. "To whom did you wish to speak, sir?"

"To Deejay Thorens, that's to whom, or Ooloorie, if her relay's up. Problems?"

"I'm afraid so, sir. Professors Thorens and P'wheet are no longer with the company."

"*What?* Then give me Mr. Bertram. Tell him Homicide Lieutenant Bear—tell him the jig is up and he should—"

"I'm ringing the Executive Suite." I could see her other hand trace out an Ameslan pattern she thought was private: "Tell him yourself, asshole."

"*Win?*" Freeman K. Bertram squinted into the 'com over his antiquated horn-rimmed glasses. "What happened to your eye?" Bertram was a skinny gink, an engineer-type by profession and personality.

I turned around, looking in the mirror. Sure enough, I'd copped a shiner in the cargo bay. "One of your crates fell on me, Freeman, and I'm gonna sue. Seriously, I'm calling from three—make that four—days outbound to Ceres." I gave him an abbreviated run-down. "Now what's this crap about Deejay and Ooloorie?"

He looked mournful, making steeples with his fingers—scratch "engineer" and insert "mortician." "We let them go on a cordial basis, we assure you." The "we" was only Bertram; whether he was secretly a royalist at heart, or a frustrated editorialist, I'd never had the heart to ask. "They had some research they insisted doing on their own."

"Deejay's in San Francisco, then?" Ooloorie made her home there, a big tank of seawater at the Emperor Norton University, communicating with Laporte by various electronic means.

"Why, no. Perhaps this shouldn't be made public, but we weren't happy letting either of them go, and did some quiet checking around. Can you keep a secret?"

"Over several zillion miles of open Telecom?"

"Oh. Well, there are rumors, Win. An expedition to Mercury, attempts to tap the Sun directly, using a modified double-Broach—talk about fusion power! All we know is, they're the foremost experts on Broach physics, and the *Indomitable Spirit* has been chartered, inbound. Neither of them can be reached, their final paychecks came back unopened—you'd think they could arrange to—"

"*Indomitable Spirit?* Well, that clears up one mystery. What do you know about an Aphrodite, Ltd., or somebody named J.V. Tormount?"

"Win where did you get *that* information?" He had a strangled expression on his face. Somehow it suited him, I thought.

"A little bird dropped it on my head. What's the big secret?"

"I—Win, it's a perfectly legitimate operation, and we can't tell you any more. As you pointed out, unsecured communications, and so forth. Sorry."

"I wish you'd reconsider. Maybe I should lean a little harder, but your business is your business. I don't promise to leave it at that."

"There's certainly no harm in asking. Nothing personal, old friend."

"Right." I switched off. "Well, what do you think about that, Koko? Koko?"

She lay, propped up against those goddamned windows, snoring energetically. Well, my shoulder ached, I could stand some z's, myself. I gently got her somnambulated toward the elevator. Room service charged a philosophically impossible amount for the soup and sandwich which arrived a few minutes later. I settled into the sack with my meal and a fresh cigar, noting it was news time out on Ceres.

And somehow, I'd gotten entangled in the headlines.

"Tonight's special report concerns the mysterious privately held company known as Aphrodite, Ltd."

Voltaire was at his authoritative best this evening, lean, gray, paternally disapproving. "Just what *is* Aphrodite, Ltd., and who are its principals? We endeavored to find out." Following was a chronicle of futile attempts to interview one J. V. Tormount at his Ceres office. Or *her* Ceres office—Malaise couldn't even find out that much. Whatever gender, Tormount wasn't in.

Tormount, it appeared, was *never* in.

He'd been a busy little dickens, though, buying up hundreds of homesteaders in the isolated Sargasso asteroid cluster, importing unspecified heavy machinery—and sophisticated paratronics. "The privacy of business is sacred in our society," lamented Voltaire, "yet the people have a right to know." (Where had he picked *that* up?) "Our attempts to penetrate this new but powerful and well-financed firm will continue. It may well be that 'Aphrodite' conceals something sinister in her bosom. At least that's the way it looks, Monday, March first, 223 A.L. This is Voltaire Malaise, Ceres Central, good night."

I wished him better luck than I was having, put out my cigar, set the Gigacom (fanfare, angel chorus) for morning, and crawled between the covers onto my good shoulder.

In her *bosom*? C'mon, Voltaire, that one went out with honest lawyers!

⁂

"*Yaaawp! Yaaawp!*" The Gigacom awoke me—*proximity alarm! A* giant shadow hovered overhead, striking downward. I snatched the descending blanket away from my face before it landed, and lashed out for the wrist—the *furry* wrist!—controlling it, planted a foot in somebody's midsection, and *pushed*! The figure whirled away in a flap of ill-gotten bedclothes, stumbled backward, and rebounded off the windows as I fumbled vainly for the light.

The intruder leaped again, damn near crushing my ribs in the process. We thumped to the floor, thrashing in the darkness, my face suddenly exploding in painful collision with a misplaced elbow. I grabbed a handful of pelt, hoping for an ear or something else to bite. My other hand found the pommel of the Rezin, fallen from the nightstand, and flung away the sheath, to— *Ungh!* The stranger's knee had found a place I couldn't disregard.

I doubled, slashing blindly in confused shock. The blade caught something, sliced and grated. A terrifying scream—and I was free! Light blazed briefly into the cabin from the hall and shuttered off again. I wrenched upright, blood from my nose streaming down my chin, and staggered out into the corridor.

Empty. I glanced at my watch; it wasn't there. Neither were my clothes.

Just as I turned, the cabin door swung shut with a positive *click*. The knob wouldn't move. I wiped my face, left hand coming away sticky crimson. The right still gripped a foot of gory steel. Trying not to drip on Captain Spoonbill's hall carpet, I focused with difficulty: yes, a trail of someone else's blood. I wondered how solidly I'd connected. That *knee* had connected solidly enough; I could hardly stand upright: gas pains amplified a hundredfold.

The naked, sword-swinging barbarian routine has been oversold, I think. Locked out in the middle of the night, gasping, drenched in someone else's blood, I care not what course Conan may take: I lowered myself to the floor against the wall and practiced groaning. A couple of timid passers-by ran screaming at the sight of me, then a uniform arrived, gun in hand, to let me explain what had happened. She passkeyed me in, promising to send a medic, and followed the trail of gore away.

Healer Francis W. Pololo had something absolutely *wonderful* for pain. He also took blood samples from my Rezin as I rummaged around for some nice, easy-fitting trousers, but wouldn't listen about fingerprints. Guess he had that theory filed away with phrenology and palm-reading. Nice fellow, though, and not bad-looking for a gorilla. I thought of Koko, wondering if he was spoken for, and as I gingerly fastened my pants, I thought of Clarissa, too, glad we hadn't made this a second honeymoon. Then I asked the doctor for another pain pill.

入

Full of nerve-deadeners, I didn't want to mix my highs, but the Level 790 bar was a well-lit public place where nobody could sneak up on me, and I wasn't planning to sleep again until I got my Webley back. That infernal gadget of Clarissa's was all that had kept me out of *Bonaventura*'s meatlocker.

A bit slow on the nanoelectronic uptake, though: my assailant had had plenty of time to pull out every drawer in the bureau and empty it on the carpet. Something told me it wasn't just a scavenger hunt.

Despite the nighttime emptiness of the Yellow Tower corridors, the bar seemed almost crowded. "Western Hemisphere" the bartender answered as he poured me out a double—King Kong Kola. "Every-one in Yellow's up from North or South America. Breakfasttime in Green right now, suppertime in Orange."

I sipped my drink; definitely not the Real Thing. "What about the Blue?"

"Whatever time suits their porpoises," he snickered.

I considered throwing up all over his nice clean bar. Instead I turned my back, hitching up my elbows to watch the natives as the sky turned round and round outside. Some were talking, drinking, playing cards or electronic games. Others watched a stage where a young gorilla was taking off her clothes. Seemed like a waste of time, to me.

The place began to fill up even more. More likely *cocktail* time in the Orange Tower. All this joint needed was a big tank for the dolphins, and—

"*Hey!*" The guy beside me stumbled sideways, knocking over his drink. He wheeled on the person next to him. "Whaddyou wanna do that for, sister?" he slurred, peering sadly down inside his empty glass. The pale, sophisticated type beside him turned slowly, gave him a silent sneer down her nose, and turned away.

"Hey! You can't jog my arm like that an' broff it osh . . *brush it off!* Whaddabout my drink?" He extended a wobbly arm and poked her shoulder savagely.

"Take it easy, friend," I said, my tongue doing its own thinking as usual. "Let her alone, I'll buy you another—"

"Who aksed *you*, buddy?" He jabbed me in the chest with stiffened fingers, setting off a number of accumulated pains.

I seized the offending digits, bending them back a little. "*Now, buddy, you want that drink or not?*"

Wrenching his hand free, he drew it back for a punch. "I'll teach you to—" and let fly craftily with his other fist, but I ducked, and he bashed it meatily into the bar. I slid under his second flailing punch and planted my own stiffened fingers dead-center in his solar plexus.

"*Whoof!*"

He doubled, staggering against a chair, and fell across a nearby table, scattering crockery. The occupants jumped up, knocking others down around them in a rapidly expanding circle. Napkins, liquids, curses flew. Somebody threw a punch. In seconds, while my erstwhile antagonist barfed all over the floor, the saloon erupted in a joyous free-for-all, a hundred combatants gaily socking everyone around them. A chimpanzee swung from the chandelier, bombing people with onion dip. The stripper stopped, disgusted at losing her audience, gathered up her clothing, and sat down on the stage, feet over the edge, kicking anyone who stumbled near.

Baap! Seeing sudden stars, I shook my head, swung to grab the shoulder of a tall form looming over me. I raised a fist.

"Whoa...Pilgrim, I'm on *your* side!" He cocked his head and grinned a crooked grin, holding a little chimp—the guy who'd socked me—by the scruff, then casually tossing him out into the riot to fend for himself. "Plucky, but too small—had t'throw 'im...back."

I gave someone behind me an elbow in the guts, snap-kicked a bottle-waver coming at my head, and turned to my now familiar ally. "Say, you're not really..." I recognized this seamed and ugly-beautiful mug, the big Roman nose, and crinkled squint. "Mike Morrison?"

He snatched a pair of fighters, cracked their heads together, and easily side-stepped a wildly thrown chair, which bounced harmlessly off the mirror behind the bar. "Guilty," came the answer in that famous sandy-textured voice, cadence plodding forward in oddly shaped chunks, "but don't tell nobody—headed out t'make m'first...space opera." He shook his head, a sour look passed across his leathery face. "Only thing th' people wanna see, these...days. Feels downright silly 'thout a...horse under me—*unh!*"

Someone brained him with a serving tray. He crossed his eyes and swayed in little circles, a big hand on the bar to right himself, then grabbed the astounded tray-wielder by the lapels. "Mister, somebody oughta smack you fer that." His eyes narrowed in anger, slanted, almost Mongolian. "But I won't, I won't...like *hell* I won't!"

Crack! The unfortunate assailant followed a ballistic curve across the room and landed in a fountaining of drinks and pretzels. Morrison blew on his battered knuckles, shaking out the sting, and sort of looked directly at me, sideways. "Pilgrim, I like a good...dust-up, but let's—*look out!*"

I whirled, by reflex whipping out my Rezin. The pale "sophisticated" lady, composure vanished with a snarl, was shoving something at my face. It snapped into focus—a tiny gun barrel, bullet glinting visibly deep inside the chamber. I slapped the gun aside, left-handed, she lunged, carried by momentum onto my extended blade.

The weapon sank to the guards with a ghastly sucking noise, pommel jammed against my hip. Her eyes, an inch from mine, widened abruptly as if she were just waking up. She gave a tiny gasp, looked down at her midriff, the ultimate despair written on her face, stumbled backward off the blade, and crumpled, her life coursing onto the floor.

Silence swept the room.

I threw the knife aside, her little gun still in my other hand, and knelt beside her in a pool of smoking blood. Not a sound, not a movement. I felt for a pulse—nothing. She was gone. I'd killed a woman, and she was gone.

A huge rough hand descended gently on my shoulder. "She walked right into it, Pilgrim, some kinda...suicide, I'd call it. C'mon, get up outa there." He pried me away from the floor, hooked a chair with the toe of his boot, and slid it under me, carefully extracting the little pistol from my hand and laying it on the bar.

I closed my eyes hard, and opened them again.

Morrison stood slowly shaking his head, hands spread on his narrow waist, a finger curled and locked into the high side of his canvas-like gun-belt. The big, plain military automatic perched where his right hip pocket should have been, rendered tiny by his sheer, larger-than-life presence, its smoothly worn ivory stocks checked and yellowed by handling and hard use. "There ain't much...point, but somebody call a Healer!"

He thrust a tumbler into my hands. I sipped it absently—it burned.

But the Healer was already there, along with security people, alerted by the fighting. He set his bag on a barstool, glanced around the rapidly emptying room, then knelt down by the body, confirming that's what it was. He looked up at me. "Haven't I seen you once already tonight?"

I sat there, nodding dumbly, my hands beginning to shake. "Earlier th-this evening. Someone b-broke into my—"

"So you *said*" answered the gorilla. He stood, glared down at my dripping knife lying on the bar beside the tiny autopistol, then back at the dead woman—girl, really, I could see that now—and gave me an expression I'd never had before from anyone on the right side of the law. "Call the Captain," he instructed the bartender. "Something stinks in here."

Morrison started to speak, paused, twisting the thin gold circlet around his massive wrist. "I saw the whole...thing, *bureaucrat.*" Then he looked at me. "She's the one shoved that *borracho* into ya, an' started this whole...brannigan. Lookin' t'backshoot ya'n all the excitement." He stopped, running a large confident hand through his thinning, crewcut hair, then continued in that relaxed, inexorable, singsongy tone.

"Pilgrim, you gonna play with that, or drink it? An' don't fret s'much. I mean t'see you vouched for with security, at Cap'n Spoonbill's... convenience."

He stepped away, one knee bent slightly inward, a shoulder carried low, then paused and turned back to me. "Pilgrim, you'll be all right. I like your...sand." Then he limped out of my life and into the sunset.

In whichever tower *that* was going on.

⋏

Tuesday, March 2, 223 A.L.

As played out as I was, sleeping soundly that night should have been a cinch, especially with the armed guards outside my stateroom door to protect me from the boogie-person. Though if I'd tried to leave, it might have looked like something else. Those suddenly widening eyes kept coming back to me, but the Healer had a pill for that.

It almost worked, too.

Next morning, they brought me back my Bowie knife, cleaned and polished, along with my victim's tiny gun and holster. It was a Bauer .25, a nine-ounce stainless-steel seven-shot vest-pocket number, of practically no stopping-power.

Made in the United States.

Somehow, I'd been reprieved. With the grisly trophies came a message from the Captain to look him up as soon as I got dressed. I peeked outside my cabin. The guard was still there, but she smiled sympathetically and promised to escort me to the infirmary, which was where the brass seemed to be awaiting my pleasure. The sick bay's down in the rectangular stern, as buried in the middle of the ship as anything can be, and not too far from all those crates for Mr., Ms., or Mrs. Tormount. Inside, Healer Pololo stood waiting, along with Koko and a grim-visaged fellow in Spartan black and gold.

We sat down in the waiting room.

"Mr. Bear," the simian physician offered, "I owe you an apology. I simply figured that no wholly innocent party could be involved in two violent incidents in the same evening."

"Try running a liquor store on East Colfax Avenue sometime."

He removed his wire-rimmed glasses and gave them a self-conscious scrub. "Well, you know what I mean. Captain Spoonbill, this is Mr. Bear."

Sounded like feeding time at the zoo. Spoonbill was an imposing block of a man, conveying in attitude and bearing, rather than literal appearance, the same frozen unreachability as those statues on Easter Island. He shook my hand, striving for the neutral expression that served him for a smile.

"Mr. Bear, concerning your detention last night..."

"That's okay, I'd already done my partying. I take it you've decided I'm 'wholly innocent,' too?" I wondered how they'd feel about smoking in here.

"You have some powerful allies, it appears." He nodded microscopically, indicating Koko who seemed unusually reserved in her brand-new rubbery-looking smartsuit. "Miss Featherstone-Haugh assures me the President will vouch for you unquestioningly. There's also Mr. Morrison—I had a lot of trouble getting off the com with him last night, and several times this morning. He explained how the whole thing happened, though what it means..."

"I'd like to know that, myself. But you're not letting me off on character testimony, are you?"

"Not a chance. Miss Featherstone-Haugh informs me you were a security guard in the United States, is that correct?" Was that approval in his eye or merely gas, as obstetricians like to claim?

I stifled the usual insulting answer. "As close as you can describe it in the Confederacy. I was the fuzz, a pig, a flatfoot—working Homicide detail."

"Then," the doctor interrupted, "you can view a deceased person without..."

"Not too badly anyway." I'd always been a little squeamish, one reason I hate murderers so much. "What's all this working up to?" Koko looked distinctly uncomfortable as she squirmed on the plastic waiting-room chair. Pololo led us to a back room where a silent, supine form lay draped upon a cold titanium table. He folded back the sheet. Koko doubled over and ran from the room, making funny mewling noises. I gulped and took another step forward.

"That's her, all right. I never killed a woman before. Funny, it doesn't feel too different, just sort of sad and stupid."

"More sad and stupid than you may realize," answered the stonefaced Captain Spoonbill. "Tell him, Francis."

The doctor brushed aside a lock of the decedent's hair. "Ever see something like this before?" Curved tightly against a shaved patch on the scalp was a small, leech-shaped transparent plastic object, filled with nanocircuitry. "Brain-bore," the Healer enunciated with disgust. "Given the right drugs and commensurate skill, the perpetrator can create any reality of his choosing inside the victim's mind, a twisted world by means of which the victim's behavior can be manipulated. Maybe—maybe you Americans are right: in this case there *ought* to be a law."

"Forget that, Doc, it's habit-forming." I peeked beneath the little instrument where wires led into a nylon plug through the skull. "You mean this thing made her try to kill me?" And what was that discoloration on her thumb?

"Not exactly," said the Healer, covering the girl's face again. He pulled a small flat tin from his sporran, hinged it open, and offered me a brown Dutch cigarillo. "She could have been experiencing anything subjectively—believing you were Clarence the Ripper incarnate, say, or avenging some fictional evil you did to her or someone she loved." I lit his smoke and my own. "Nothing—no one—*made* her do it, only created some illusionary case of the horrors, some context under which it was a foregone conclusion that she'd try."

And I thought I'd heard of everything that was sickening.

"Seems I'm acquiring a sort of fan club," I observed, "with *real* clubs. First the attack in my stateroom, now this. I'd be superhuman if I could avoid jumping to the conclusion there's some connection." I reached beneath the sheeting to examine the cold dead hand again. A minute drop of dried blood glinted blackly on the thumbnail.

The physician gave me an odd look. "You're the detective, but what connection could there be between a Soviet human female and a gorilla?"

"What?"

"That's what the samples from your cabin say: a gorilla, also probably female, judging by cosmetic residue on the hair samples. And this poor child was Russian or I'll throw my brand-new dental references out and sue the dealer who brought them through the Broach." He started looking absently for a place to flick his ashes, settled on an unused bedpan. "Look, if you ever get to the bottom of this...I'd *love* getting my hands on a brain-tapper, Hippocrates forgive me."

"For my part," said the Captain, "and without prejudice, Mr. Bear, I'll be satisfied just to dock at Gunter's Landing, where you can take your mystery—and the violence that attends it—*off* my ship!"

This didn't seem the time to mention the booby-trapped Webley or the near-miss belowdecks. And, thinking of another nearby Miss, I wondered how Koko was.

⅄

Upstairs, I tried organizing my recent escapades—with an accent on "escape"—for the daily call home. I don't know how other couples handle it—actually, my first wife and I never talked about things that mattered—but Clarissa and I never hold back. It's made for a wonderful life so far, with a few unpleasant minutes, followed by some supremely satisfying ones. Hours, even.

But there was that bit of extra evidence I'd noticed in the infirmary: *wood* is still rare enough out here in space that every scrap is eagerly received. Back home, they make packing boxes of plastic, but goods exported to the asteroids go timber-wrapped by specific request and as an extra selling-point. There'd been a three-quarter-inch splinter underneath the Russian girl's left thumbnail. Must've hurt like the dickens (or did it, with the brain-bore?). It hadn't been there quite long enough to fester, just long enough to give me an idea who'd levered that crate onto my head.

So how was I gonna tell my wife the Healer how badly Confederate forensics need an overhaul? Luckily, I had another call to make first—that little Bauer autopistol and the Woodsman Olongo was attacked with: obsolete U.S.-type weapons, collector-rare in the Confederacy. Why were they showing up over here?

Koko seemed to have other things to do. I was just as happy: it was getting to be perilous in my vicinity, and I still have a few Neanderthal opinions concerning womenfolk and danger, even when the girls're covered with fur and have ten times my strength. I shooed her off to a smart-suit lesson, promising to catch up later, and grabbed the com.

The lag was terrible now, but Captain Spoonbill grudgingly surrendered his strongest beam for a solid hour, at only nominally rapacious rates. Talking through a Broach is complicated by the weird influence it has on radiation, gravity, the very fabric of reality. Try sending regular radio or lasergram through; they wind up, well, twisted, requiring special equipment to hammer them back into sense. I hired the appropriate gadgetry via Laporte Interworld, and punched up a certain broom closet in the good old U.S.A.

"Jenny?" The picture was an informationless gray pudding. "I got a problem you could help me with." I waited through the lightspeed lag, trying to figure out which Jenny I was talking to.

"If I can, Win, but I've got a problem of my own right now..."

"The Fraser campaign—but this—" I stopped; she was still talking.

"We've been ransacked!" They broke in last night, tore the place apart, and set fire to what was left. Even with Confederate fire-control systems..."

"Jenny, something weird is going on all over. Attempted murders, break-ins, disappearances—we've got enemies, and I'm beginning to think they're organized." She didn't much like the details I gave her, but then neither did I.

Finally: "If I get any useful information on those weapons, I'll relay it through Clarissa once you're out on Ceres."

"Right. She's got a little digging to do—no pun intended—to find out if Olongo's burglar was brain-bored." A little more expensive gab and we rang off. The delay connecting with home was somewhat longer than could be accounted for by Dr. Einstein. An elderly chimp materialized: Captain Forsyth, dirty and disheveled.

"That you, Win? Brace yourself, son, there's bad news: someone broke into your house last night. Place is a wreck, though nothing I can tell is missing, except—hold on, son—*Clarissa*. Win, I can't find her *anywhere*. For what it's worth, there are no signs of, well, of blood or anything. I'm doing all I can to track her down, and— You listening, son? You haven't said a word."

What the bloody steaming hell could I say? Ayn Rand and Harry Browne and Robert Ringer can go on Looking Out for Number One: my only reason for living had suddenly evaporated.

Clarissa!

What else could possibly go wrong now?

6: THE MIND IN THE PYRAMID

Friday, March 12, 223 A.L.

We arrived at Ceres just in time for Lucy's funeral. Concerning the remainder of the voyage, perhaps the less said the better. Maybe Lucy and Ed were the best friends I'd ever had, but Clarissa—well, she was *Clarissa*. I was going straight home, if possible at something better than the one-tenth gee *Bonaventura* had tapered down to in the last few days—a stasis-tank aboard a three- or four-gee unmanned freight drone—I didn't care.

Letting others steer me by the elbow, I wandered past the next ten days half-conscious, groping dazedly through the motions. Koko insisted I learn to wear a smartsuit; I argued feebly I wasn't planning to hang around where I could use one; she told me to shut up and march to class. Amazingly, despite a soul-draining ache that never left me, I found the classes mildly interesting, enjoyed myself enough to feel guilty about it, and came to hate that moment each day when the practice sessions ended and I had to go back to my lonely, haunted cabin.

Smartsuits bear about the same relationship to space armor that modern scuba equipment has to cumbersome nineteenth-century hard-hat diving rigs. Everybody's seen them on the Telecom, a rubbery, one-piece second skin, varying in thickness from a quarter to a half an inch, seemingly a frail barrier against the savage rigors of interplanetary space. But space had better look to its laurels—a smartsuit makes that hostile void as comfortable as an area mapmakers once labeled the Great American Desert: Colorado.

Despite appearances, the garment functions primarily as an elaborate and powerful computer. Of all the nanoelectronic miracles available to third-century Confederate civilization, it is the supreme achievement. Each square millijefferson within its multilayered fabric measures the wearer's well-being, making appropriate corrections to air flow, humidity, temperature, half a dozen other nuances clear down to the molecular level. Each square millijeff *outside* selectively absorbs or reflects a hundred different forms of energy, powering the suit and protecting its owner. I guess what finally convinced me was the fact that, as a long-standing tradition, a smartsuit was included in the price of my ticket to Ceres. Seemed like a waste not to try it out. I picked it up at the tailor's and hurried aft to meet my apprentice.

"Mr. *Bear!*" The instructor minced over, limply waggling his simian wrist-talker as a dozen students milled around the airlock, waiting just outside an empty cargo bay evacuated for instruction. "I see you've *finally* acquired your smartsuit. Now, until you're caught up with the rest of us, darling Koko here will help make sure you're properly fitted."

Darling Koko curtsied, twisting a fingertip in a nonexistent dimple.

I carried my suit over my back by its hanger, like a deep-space Frank Sinatra. Heeling my cigar out on the deck, I looked around for a dressing room to change in. "Okay, but won't that cost her instruction time?"

"It's all right, Boss." Suited up, she resembled a life-size silvery-gray Buddha. "I've been getting extra practice after hours with Francis—I mean, Dr. Pololo." You can't tell if a gorilla's blushing, but she lowered her big brown eyes and shuffled a rubber-shod toe.

The instructor smirked exaggerated tolerance: "Don't worry, dear, you're making amazing progress, really, 'extra practice,' or not." He inhaled a perfumed cigarette and blew a sultry puff in my direction.

I shrugged, trying to look as unreconstructably masculine as possible. "You're the teacher. But I think there's something wrong with this suit." I pulled it off the hanger. "I've heard of underwear for the deaf, but this is ridiculous—shouldn't it have a transparent face-plate or something, so I can see where I'm going?"

The chimpanzee grimaced with exasperation, then reached for the hood folded down on his chest. Unlike Koko's suit and mine, his was lavishly decorated in bright lavender and yellow swirls. He stretched the hood up over his face and fastened it at the nape, looking, minus some kind of cutout for his mug, just like a featureless psychedelic story dummy. "You see, the surface nanoprocessors pick up wave fronts, assemble and present them on the inside of the hood." He pushed buttons on one of the complicated keyboards running down each forearm. "Now I can see as well as you can. Better, because I'm making use of lovely ultraviolet, infrared and sound waves, x-rays, radio, you name it."

The decorated surface of the hood whirled and changed. I was looking at his face! "Not really much point to this, you understand, it's just my *image* you're seeing, a simple trick of nanocircuitry. But actors on the Telecom *will* insist, and maybe that's why you've never noticed the absence of a faceplate before. Now, *may* I get on with my class?" He fiddled with more arm buttons, his features distorting into those of Captain Spoonbill, forbidding stoic expression and all. *"And, if you don't let the lock full-cycle this time, Miss Featherstone-Haugh, you'll walk the plank!"* He dubbed in an eyepatch and gold earring, and hornpiped away.

I wound up using a lifeboat, as I'd been expected to suit up in my stateroom. When I was almost dressed, I looked down at Koko, who'd politely turned her back despite the six-inch hull between us. "Hey, amanuensess, this isn't fair!"

I held my foot above the—what, gunwale?—where she could see it through the plastic canopy. It was covered with rubbery material, something like fishing waders crossed with ballet slippers. Instead of feet in her suit, Koko—well, she had an extra pair of *gloves*. She turned, grinning. "That's what you get for evolutionary overspecialization, Boss." She stretched a foot out, fluidly wriggling her toes. I'd caught her that way once, playing our piano back home: Joplin's "Easy Winners," for godsake.

Under the last few days' decreasing acceleration, my reflexes had become a bit uncertain. I climbed down carefully from the auxiliary craft and latched its bubble back in place. I was still unzipped, the garment open from my left hip to my right shoulder. "Quit practicing arpeggios and help me fasten this suit!"

"It's ar*piggi*os, Boss. You know, This little piggy went to market, this'— Boss, what have you got *on* under there?"

I tried to smooth the lumps away. "Under where?"

"Underwear? That's what I *thought!* That means you didn't hook up the catheter and the—"

"God, do I *have* to?" Those extra inner fixtures had resembled the intimidating appliances they advertise in the back pages of *Hustler*.

"Gonna get pretty uncomfortable, otherwise. Besides, you're mixing up the sensor system—see those little red telltales on your forearm panels? Boss, it doesn't hurt or anything, you'll get used to it."

"That's what the proctologist said. Well, back to the lifeboat, then. You're *sure* we're really going to be suited up that long?" Rejecting her rude offers of assistance, I deposited my shorts with the rest of my earthly duds on the seat of the tiny spaceship, got myself resuited, and strapped Olongo's Webley back around my middle where it barely balanced the enormous knife hanging on the other side. I missed my leather gunbelt, too, though admittedly, any mildly hard vacuum would have reduced it to a dry crumbling powder in a very few minutes.

"Catheter and—" or not, smartsuits don't actually take that much getting used to. They seal shut with a brush of the hand, warning the wearer with a number of idiot lights and buzzers if he manages to louse up even this simple procedure. I didn't hear or see any warnings—in fact, with the darkened inner surface of the hood resting only half an inch from my nose, I couldn't see at all, until I felt Koko jabbing buttons on my arm. When vision returned, it was as if the hood weren't there at all.

For damage-proof redundancy and the occasional left-hander, each panel of controls is duplicated on the other arm. They're mostly for minor adjustments which don't override the safer, automated life-support functions of the suit. And they looked so much like concertina ivories, I was tempted to puzzle out "Lady of Spain."

Koko tucked me in all over, an embarrassingly intimate process reminiscent of having your inseam measured by a tailor, making sure the fabric contacted every metric inch of my body. Then we did some careful low-gee bending and stretching to double-check the fit. The freedom and comfort the suit allowed was simply unbelievable. To tell the truth, I felt downright naked, which is how I was supposed to feel, a testimony to the manufacturer's art.

Cautiously she took me through a checklist of the controls. The variety of visual input alone was astounding; our instructor hadn't exaggerated. Images of our surroundings, life-support and other data, even the correct time, appeared and disappeared at the touch of a key, arrayed in border-hugging panels around the field of view, or in multimedia boxes like a TV split-screen display. At one point I discovered I was three feet tall and, even without benefit of runny nose and smelly feet, built upside-down.

"Now you're seeing with your fingers, Boss," Koko explained. "Hold them up."

It was like looking through a periscope. I fumbled over to the lifeboat and poked a pinky under the hatch. Sure enough, there were my baggy pants and poncho crumpled on the pilot's seat. "Nifty. Now how about putting my eyes back where they belong?"

We spent the next couple of hours showing me how to do things like that for myself. Radar, sonar, stereo, back-scratching flagellae, and waste-disposal. She'd been right about the biological functions—the suit took care of those, storing the somewhat disgusting residue and recirculating water and oxygen. I was unwilling to experiment, but Koko assured me you could even throw up in a smartsuit with minimal discomfort.

After a while, we cycled out through the lock and into the cargo bay, Koko so impatient she overrode the outer door with a *whoosh!* that threatened to set me on my fundament. Hanging outside were ropes, ladders, swings, a jungle gym, and various other hardware for risking the integrity of your suit.

"Koko?" Wishing I had interrupted our ground-school indoors for a smoke, I watched her climb a wall under our locally decreasing gravity, using sticky pads she'd activated on her hands and knees.

"What, Boss?" Abruptly Koko's face appeared in a lower corner of my view field.

"That's pretty neat." I diddled with my forearms until she was receiving a similar picture of me. "Now what was it I wanted—oh, yeah; how long are we going to be out here? Even with recycling, these rubber leotards can't hold much— *Careful!*"

She sprang clear of the wall, executed a double backward somersault, and landed lightly on the deck. "Get some *exercise*, Boss, don't just stand around. And you've got plenty of air. Everything with oxygen in it gets broken down, in addition to which, the suit is one big sandwich, lots of layers, millions of tiny, selectively permeable microtanks. Just like the beads in that—that red-tape whatchacallit you were telling me about?"

"NCR paper? But how much air could that—"

"At a couple thousand tons per square— Boss, you've got to be kidding."

No wonder it was so damned hard to puncture a smartsuit. Half its substance was semiconductors, and the other half, microscopic vacuoles pumped rigid with consumables. I jogged in place, then along one wall and back again, reluctant to imitate Koko's advanced gymnastics; it was hard enough just waiting for my feet to touch the deck again between steps. Finally, I parked it on that selfsame deck, observing the rest of the class a football field away, doing their own thing. With sufficient magnification, it seemed like I was there among them. As the light threatened to grow dimmer with enlargement, the area my suit was using for vision automatically expanded beyond the face, until my forearms blurred the bottom of the screen. A little practice, and I discovered I could sit there and scan the wall behind me—eyes literally in the back of my head.

And then the deck below—hindsight, already!

But before too long I began tiring of my new toys, and found myself wondering where Clarissa was, hoping miserably that she was all right. What could have happened to her? Had she gone wherever Olongo, Lucy, and Ed were? Had they all gone the same place, for that matter? Were Deejay and Ooloorie *really* traveling to Mercury? I'd tried to find out, only to be told that communications sunward were being bollixed up by solar flares.

Clarissa! I slammed a helpless fist into the titanium decking. What the *hell* was I doing here, playing space cadet in a suit I'd never have any practical use for? Why wasn't I *doing* something? Why couldn't they just stop this tub and let me off? I don't know how many miserable minutes passed. Incredibly, I caught my chin in mid-nod toward my chest.

"Win...*Boss?*" Someone in a decorated smartsuit stood lightly beside Koko, his features repeated in an inset on my screen next to hers.

"Hunh? Oh—sorry, guess I got lost in there somewhere."

"Boss, this is Mr. Camillus. Mike Morrison sent him."

I stood up. Morrison was turning into a regular guardian angel. The fellow walked over and extended a hand. "Gerber Camillus—call me Gerb—stunt coordinator for Mike's new picture, *Revenge of the Thrint*. Mike said no offense, but maybe you could use some pointers with a blade?" His other hand held a pair of floppy movie knives. I looked him over as much as his suit allowed, a wiry figure, small, but not a chimp—his shoes didn't have fingers. They were decorated, though, like the rest of his suit: black, with mock red cummerbund and sash, white frilly shirtfront and satin tie. To this he'd tacked on a pair of rubbery tails, and, to top the whole ensemble off, a tall "silk" hat above his face-display.

It made me feel even more naked. "Yeah, I guess I could stand a lesson or ten. But not now, I'm right in the middle of a—"

"*Nap*," finished Koko. "Getting comfy with a suit real fast, aren't you?" She glanced at my forearm displays and made a few adjustments. "Oh, I see. If you're going to fret yourself to death, Boss, then override your medication circuits—see, like this. Otherwise, you'll find yourself being electrotranked again." As she lectured, we noticed that the other students were filing back through the lock.

"I guess class is over for today. Not too sure I like this automatic medication jazz. You sure I'll be all right, now?"

Koko nodded.

"Then let's get started," suggested Camillus. "Mike said you were doing some weird kind of hand-to-hand fighting up in the bar."

"Tae Kwon Do," I replied. "Green Belt, though I haven't been working out regularly for a while. Camillus bobbed his head, not understanding a single word. As with the idea of concealed weapons, there'd never been any need in the Confederacy for unarmed combat—nobody was ever unarmed! Also, under a more enlightened North American foreign policy, Japan had remained self-isolated until the 1950s. My detective business had been a little thin at first, and I'd fattened it up giving elementary Korean martial arts instruction. I'd been a Gold Belt, a virtual beginner myself, and after a few bonafide masters from the U.S. and Korea set up real *dochangs,* I'd quit to become a student once again.

And slacked off about twenty-five pounds ago.

Camillus led us back upstairs to a gym. Koko watched a while, then made excuses lamely and departed. "Doctor's appointment," I guessed. Gorillas don't really need much in the way of training for fisticuffs, any-way—they just break their opponents in half and tie knots in what's left.

Starting with a number of fencing and karate stances, we walked through variations allowing for the use of the big heavy choppers com-mon in the asteroids. Mine was typical enough, as was Gerb's, a double-edged fourteen-inch *snickersnee.* We sparred with his toy replicas, however. He showed me a swell trick with a smartsuit, adjusting the surface so the pressure of a blow leaves a visible mark in simulated gory crimson—no arguments whether a touch has really been scored.

But the main thing I learned in that first afternoon was that, all these years, I'd been holding my Rezin upside-down, rather like a kitchen knife, thumb overlapping my fingers in what's contemptuously termed a "hatchet grip." Gerber demonstrated how the short back "clipped" edge is for hack-ing arms and shoulders, and to protect you from the other fellow's blade. The main, "lower" edge is carried upward, thumb behind the quillon like a saber, the long razor-curve slicing into the opponent's belly clear up to the sternum.

No two ways about it, self-defense is just plain *messy.*

I divided the rest of the trip between smartsuit lessons and sword-fighting, with a little target practice on the side. Tactically, the pistol *is* a sword, most effective at a sword's distance, intended for the same primarily defensive purpose, personal protection, rather than as a military or politi-cal instrument (one reason *rifles* are scarce in the Confederacy, and why they're so conveniently immune to political attack in the United States). And, like a sword, a pistol comes to possess for its bearer a unique per-sonality all its own, almost symbiotic with the personality it defends. Say what you will about the mystique of cutlery, the civilized individual's *edge* is the handgun.

The Webley's new sights were perfect, a big square notch in back, a big square post on a ramp up front, coarse and quick-to-center, just like my old S & W. Captain Forsyth's extra ammunition came in mighty handy— I sure as hell needed the practice. I also decided to hang on to the little Bauer .25. In an emergency, it'd be better than *no* gun. But not much.

The *Bonaventura* passed its turnover point (which I spent snugly strapped to a barstool), and continued roaring along backward through the cosmos, acceleration dropping steadily until I was grateful for the heavy padding on the ceilings: I weighed about twenty pounds at the end of the journey, easy weight to throw around with muscles built for ten times that amount.

All the better to smash your head in.

⅄

Seen from space, Ceres is enough to convince you that the *Bonaventura* is a big, expensive fraud. The asteroid shows up as a swirly blue-and-white marble shining in the void, occasional patches of dry land peeking through the clouds, exactly like *Terra Firma*.

"*What the hell?*" I was lounging at a window in the 790-level bar, watching my assistant sipping from a freefall plastic baggie.

"What the hell are you *what-the-helling* about now, Boss?"

I shook my head. "I've been staring at that blasted rock out there half an hour, trying to figure out what's wrong. Koko, *real* planets don't have longitude and latitude lines!" I held a short cigar stub near an ash tray and let the suction carry it away.

She giggled. "Yeah, that's what it looks like. Panels in the atmospheric envelope, that's all." A pretzel got away from her. She snagged it from the air and chomped it down.

"You mean there's a *big plastic bag* around the entire—"

"And every section is just one enormous molecule, holding in the air and straining out excess ultraviolet. Icarus would bump his head long before his wax started to soften." The *Bonaventura* slowly spiraled around the miniature globe, aiming for Gunter's Landing on the north pole, the bartenders spending a final precious hour nailing down anything that was floating loose.

Ceres is green enough to satisfy her mythological namesake, interrupted everywhere by thousands of perfectly circular lakes, a legacy of countless prehistoric collisions. At least I *hoped* they were prehistoric. As the ship swung inward toward the planetoid, it lit up like a titanic Japanese lantern, the "night" side hardly an f-stop darker. I'd been keeping half an eye on the Telecom screen, where Captain Spoonbill was giving a guided tour. Now the electronic point of view swiveled from the asteroid to a dozen giant thin-film plastic mirrors hanging in orbit, trained on the surface below.

Book-type facts don't do it for me, somehow. I knew the miniplanet was a "mere" six hundred and twenty miles in diameter, though there was nothing out the window to give me any real perspective. The Gigacom's built-in *Encyclopedia of North America* states that Ceres has about the same surface area as India—a hell of a lot of real estate most astronomers back in the States are overlooking as "insignificant."

The acceleration warning hooted and the planetoid dipped crazily, setting below the windowframe. Then it rose again all around us, the Telecom displaying an enormous, brightly lighted bull's-eye beneath the ship. There was a *bump*.

We were down.

ⴷ

Ceres is a big, round refutation to the argument that massive projects like dams or highways are too big for little old private enterprise (funny how the Post Office always has to enforce its "natural" monopoly at gunpoint), or that some "necessary" services can't easily be denied to those unwilling to pay and therefore (this is where the steamroller was headed all along, of course) they should be provided "free" by the State.

Hell, *American* corporations—many of which gross better yearly than three-quarters of the *Duck Soup* republics in the U.N.—could stack the pyramids up all over again; Confederate companies run smaller, and they *do* build dams and highways—though they aren't free to steal the wherewithal, an ethical consideration that somehow misses registering on advocates of *government* construction.

We have only one "telephone" at home, but it receives calls from thousands of companies, and delivers the mail, too; parcels arrive via a pneumatic system Edward Bellamy would envy. Cheyenne Ridge controls the weather as a by-product of the highly competitive power-generation business, strictly for PR. If you don't like the flavor they serve, you can either move or have your own climate dropped in—as long as you don't clutter up the neighbors' lawns.

Free riders? Well, suppose you want a streetlight: you either pay for it yourself or get the neighbors to chip in. If one or two surly curmudgeons refuse, well, what's more important, forcing old man Carruthers to cough up his negligible share, or getting the streetlight you wanted? Most likely the old bastard'll demand you keep your crummy photons off *his* property!

Ceres was developed by the same outfit that runs the *Bonaventura*: Harriman, Taggart & Hill. In a daring stroke of capitalism, they organized a transport service to the asteroids, ignoring nit-pickers who pointed out that there wasn't anyone out there to run a service *to*. Staking a claim on Ceres, H T & H modified its orbit, erected the plastic envelope, and offered *homestead* tickets on ships like the *Indomitable Spirit*. Utilities, like atmosphere and mirrors, they sold to other clients, as concessions. The question of who governs never arises: back home we're stuck with what's left of a Congress. Here, where everybody ran his own life from the start, there isn't even anything to *vote* on.

Bonaventura was sitting in an enormous crater surrounded by a mountainous wall. "Gunter's Landing," my apprentice chattered brightly, "ten miles across, a duplicate of Port Piazzi, way down south."

"Right," I answered, zipping up my smartsuit to the collar, "where they have the Leaning Tower. Convenient, having craters right where they're needed."

"Boss, they just kicked the whole planet around until this pair of craters *were* the poles. And I'm going to remember that Leaning Tower remark."

The crater walls described the limits of the airless port; their *outer* slopes served as anchors for the plastic that surrounded the rest of the asteroid. Actually, I'd heard the details before. Lucy had been a project engineer, picking up a dose of radiation in the process.

My bags were on the floor beside my feet. I slid my hood up over my face and sealed it. There was a freighter to catch, departing in forty-one hours. In the meantime, I'd have a modest and preoccupied look around Ceres, and pay my last respects to Lucy. Halfway through the voyage here, her Telecom on Bulfinch 4137 had finally been answered—by a uniformed stranger.

"This is Win Bear. Is Mrs. Kropotkin in?"

His smartsuit was adjusted to a friendly paramilitary appearance favored by firemen and park rangers. "I'm, er, Warden Trayle, of Rothbard's Registry Patrol. Mrs. Kropotkin was one of our clients—you any relation?"

"Uh...brother-in-law." Well, it was almost true. "And what do you mean '*was*'?" There was Lucy's favorite chair, shipped all the way from Earth, a pair of kittens perched up on the back, batting at each other. Above what surely must have been a purely decorative mantelpiece, a bust of Lysander Spooner—Lucy's favorite Confederate President—a pair of her own reading glasses perched on his nose.

"Well, sir, I arrived this afternoon on routine patrol. She didn't answer the 'com, but her flivver was still here. I scouted around, then queried my dispatcher. He said she'd been gunned down Ceres-side. I should secure the property and check the autofeeder for the cats until we figured out what more to do. I was just attending to that, when you—"

"Gunned down?" The idea was appalling. Lucy was nearly as sharp with a shooting iron as Captain Forsyth. "By who—whom?"

"Dunno—wanna talk with my chief? I'll give you his combo."

The cranky little man with a checkered smartsuit and illusory bow tie confirmed it: Lucy had been struck from behind in a Ceres Central public corridor, by a high-velocity projectile through the heart—the first murder in the city in over ten years. Funeral arrangements were such-and-such, apologies, condolences, and Warden Trayle was three hours behind schedule, the bum.

Now, Koko and I took our final elevator ride down to the crater floor, the *Bonaventura* teetering an incredible two miles over our heads. With several hundred other passengers, we hopped a surface vehicle across the starlit, sunny port, winding in and out among at least another hundred slumbering behemoths, none nearly so magnificent as the giant liner.

The shuttle, a buslike affair, headed for the mountains, and the longest tunnel I've ever been through. By the time its massive multiple doors had opened before us and closed behind us a dozen times, the sky was a beautiful bright blue again, with fleecy clouds and green growing things all around, all around.

"Will you be staying in Ceres Central, Boss?" Koko watched the scenery flash by. It didn't occur to me until later to wonder how a hoverbus had operated in the hard vacuum of Gunter's Landing.

"After the funeral? No, I like it better up here in the sunshine. Nivenville, where we're headed, probably." More scenery, mostly flat. I'd traveled all this distance in order to see a pretty fair replica of western Nebraska. "Wish we were going back to Earth together, though."

She shrugged. "Well, there's only weight-allowance left aboard that freighter for one skinny human and his stasis-tank. Besides, this is *Ceres*. Gee, Boss, I'd stay to see the rest of the Belt, too, if—"

"If Olongo weren't missing?" Sure enough, that was a scarecrow we whizzed by. Any time now, I'd be seeing BurmaShave signs.

"And Clarissa. But Ceres *Central*—I've just got to—"

"Forget it, I understand." It was the chance of her lifetime, after all. They really *mean* Ceres Central, a city unique in the System. This asteroid doesn't have a hot and juicy core like any self-respecting planet, so they'd carved a metropolis out of its very heart, possibly the biggest, densest habitation in all of civilization. Besides being an industrial and communications locus (Voltaire Malaise himself broadcasts from down there), there are thousands of miles of busy streets, Hong Kong, New York, Chicago, and L.A. all rolled into one confusing zero-gravity skein, with Pellucidar Gardens, the biggest, weirdest amusement park in the known universe, at the very hub.

Nivenville, by contrast, is just like any midwestern farm community, parched blue heavens over bright brassy fields that Dorothy and Toto would have gratefully come home to. My hotel, *Le Petit Prince*, towers a magnificent three stories above a million acres of marijuana, wheat, and fuelcorn. Koko waited while I checked my bags in the little pseudo-Victorian lobby, then we marched to one of the elevators—the big one in the middle—and took it down.

Real down.

Like about three hundred miles. Halfway there it did a flip-flop in its gimbals, and I almost did another one in my pants. They don't believe in gradual adjustment on the wild frontier. The elevator opened onto a bewilderingly familiar-looking structure. Then I had it—a life-size replica of M. C. Escher's *Relativity*, potty plants, arches, and staircases going every whichway, some people walking up the treads, and others down the risers. Up was where you wanted it to be, and down wherever you chose to fasten your tootsies. It was brain-bending just figuring out which rail to grab in panic.

Ever seen the airline terminal in Las Vegas? The Escher architecture was like that, advertising for Pellucidar Gardens, a pale suggestion, according to the holographic posters, of the wonders that awaited you there for just one thin tenth-piece, all on the inside!

I was seeing plenty of wonders already. At every exit, several dozen color-coded tow cables snaked along briskly, each one headed for a different general destination. Consulting an eyeball-wrenching diagram, Koko and I grabbed the line that promised to take us to the funeral parlor, and let it drag us from *Relativity* to Absolute Astonishment.

Let me put it this way: at any point along each cavernous boulevard, there's room for eight different storefronts. That's compared to *two* in any decent Earth-side community where they've paid this month's gravity bill. In Ceres Central there's one either side of the "street," two more built into the "floor" for people who are thinking sideways at the moment, and the whole mess duplicated all over again on the "ceiling"—that's "floor" if you happen to be walking on it.

The corridors, a hundred feet or more across, are roughly octagonal in cross section, the smaller corner facets serving as sidewalks, tow-cables singing overhead. It's no trick at all to jump a dozen feet and grab a lift, compliments of the Ceres Central Merchants Association. The difficulty's letting go and landing where you want.

Things *really* get complicated when you arrive at an intersection—so many goddamned street corners you don't know which way to look. Let's see, there's back the way you came, and forth. Then there's always right and left. And up and down for folks with stronger stomachs—ever see right to the *core* of a planet, even a small one?

In the center of every second passageway, a monorail provides both high-speed public transportation and a road for private vehicles under computerized direction. Have I left out anything? How about the bridges, up and down the fronts of buildings, connecting one sidewalk to another. I may have missed a few details—tenderfeet never do see all the alligator and buffalo tracks their trusty Indian guides do. And the same guides, lost in a city for the first time, often overlook seemingly obvious items. Little things, like Chicago's Elevated Railway. It really happened once—look it up.

Nikita's Funerium was situated in a classy tunnel just off the business district. I let go of the cable, having stickied up my shoesoles, and nearly broke my bloody ankles coming to a stop. According to the directory, we were overdue in the Grove of Grieving, three flights up and hundred yards back from the street. At least the illusion of floors and ceilings was respected in this place. My inner ear decided it could go to sleep again.

The corridors were heavily carpeted, thick velvet drapings and a satin-cushioned ceiling added to the feeling of a housefly's journey through some Carlsbadian coffin—organ music, stifled sobbing in every doorway—the whole thing dimly lit and anechoic.

Felt like I'd died, myself.

A discreet gold plaque beside the doors announced the Grove of Grieving. I anchored myself to the carpet and turned the knob and—*wild laughter hit me in the face like a lemon meringue pie*. I slid in hastily, followed by an equally perplexed young female gorilla. Bright lights and cheerful ribbonry festooned the walls and ceiling, sounds of merriment and liquid spirits battered at my ears. The place was absolutely packed, at least five hundred various beings yakked and ate and laughed and drank, dancing on any convenient surface to a rock band obviously imported from the States.

Leaving Koko to fend for herself, I shouldered my way through the crowd—no mean trick in freefall— recognizing a face or two from the old days. Captain Geoffrey Couper, Lucy's fellow war-veteran. A colleague from the Continental Congress, Sandy Silvers, hanging from the ceiling. Miners, farmers, engineers, I guessed, most of them in smartsuits. At least I was dressed for the occasion.

I finally ran across poor Lucy, strapped into a velvet casket, eyes forever closed. But happy in the posthumous thought, no doubt, that all of her friends were having such a swell time. An odd mechanical contraption floated beside the bier, conical, about five feet tall, rising to a rounded apex. Well, she'd passed away a week ago. Perhaps some sort of paratronic preservation was required.

I looked down, gently touching Lucy's hand, glad in a way it had happened during one of her young periods. Her skin was beautiful and smooth, she wore a simple Mexican skirt and blouse, hands crossed over her breast holding a fresh yellow cactus rose. Someone had lovingly spread her shining blue-black hair over the satin pillow.

"Poor Lucy...I'm sorry I got here too late. How—" I could hardly speak for the clutch at my throat, the tears blurring my vision. "How could you let this happen to yourself? I promise I'll find Ed for you...only I've *got* to find Clarissa first, and—"

"Hey there, Winnie, boy! How d'ya like this here whing-ding?" The thing beside the coffin stirred, bobbed up and down on its base. "Best belly-whopping funeral Ceres Central ever saw, even if I hadda arrange it fer m'self! *Whoopee!*"

7: TAKE A TROG TO LUNCH

"...*else they're trying to convey, these mysterious signals beg us to recall our destiny, plead that we resist political adventurism, urge us to marshal our resources—not for the unethical usurpation of the rights of others, but for the conquest of the stars. At least that's the way it looks—*"

"Oops!" exclaimed the monstrosity, "fergot about m'radio!" It turned away modestly, performing some adjustment with a pair of mechanical arms, then swiveled back to face me. "Thought I'd listen to th' news. That feller do go on, don't he?"

Brushing an errant Day-Glo streamer from my face, I ducked a wildly thrown cocktail baggie and strained to hear against the party uproar. In one corner, sprouting from a wall, an impromptu barbershop chorus gargled in obscene counterpoint to the band—at the very least, "House of the Rising Sun" seemed in dubious taste, considering the occasion. Cheerful plastic ribbons and sparkling confetti drifted on the ventilation currents. I kept looking back and forth, dismayed, from Lucy, pale and dead before me, to this vulcanized popcorn machine plagiarizing her voice.

"Don't strip yer gears, Winnie-boy." It raised a spindly chromed appendage to pat me on the shoulder. "Whoever kilt me didn't quite finish th' job."

"Lucy?" was about all I could manage, and that in a confused soprano.

"In th' ever-lovin' alloy. That's th' *flesh*, lyin' over there." It fussed proprietarily with the frilly skirting around the coffin, fluffed the pillow up and smoothed a pleat in Lucy's skirt. "Sure it's a shock, son. *I* was all set to wake up dead, *m'self!*"

"Lucy?" I clutched the coffin-edge, trying not to let the air conditioning waft me away. At an inch or so per second squared, I couldn't even execute a decent faint.

Appraisingly, the machine drifted back a foot or two. "Lemme look at ya, boy! So y'finally gave up that antique wheelie-gun. An' there's th' Rezin y'took offa Tricky Dick Milhous. Yeah, it's *me*, Winnie, same ol' lady helped Clarissa carve machine-gun-droppings outa yer carcass th' day y'came t'Laporte. Y'got plastic where yer shoulderblade oughta be, an' a teensie little mole, right on yer—"

"*Stop!*" The telltales on my forearms danced with confused embarrassment. "I don't know how, but you're Lucy, all right." But what else was she? An inverted rubber ice cream cone with a blunted end, covered in smartsuit material broken only by a pair of articulated manipulators—and a weapon slung absurdly from an outsized plastic gunbelt circumscribing her considerable girth. I should have recognized it right away: her Gabbet Fairfax .50.

"Glad y'came t'yer senses." She flicked a sparkle of confetti from the rose in Lucy's hands. Lucy's *other* hands. "Listen, let's get outa here an' talk. Funerals always did depress me." Amidst cheerful waves and inebriated farewells, we took our leave, the other mourners seemingly determined to carry on, guest-of-honor or not, until some nonexistent dawn.

Koko's questioning grimaces went unanswered as we grabbed a tow rope outside and rode it deeper into the underground city. Somehow, watching people strolling on the ceiling wasn't half as disturbing as seeing them walking on the walls. From my perspective, half the monorails were running upside-down, and shrubbery was springing from the sidewalks in any old direction. As if the cavernous boulevards weren't lighted brightly enough by storefronts, the angled sidewalks were fluorescent, and the rails and cables glowed with some internal energy. Lucy wasn't content to let the color-coded ski tow drag her along, but locked a manipulator loosely around it, firing up electrostatic impellers in her base, to zip ahead of us, then bounce up and down impatiently at corners until we caught up.

We proceeded thus, deep into the core of the planet.

She finally stopped before a glaring animated sign across a chasm from the fabled Pellucidar Gardens. Huge holos advertised the thrills available: a roller-coaster roaring along a giant Mobius strip; people diving into a lake-size sphere of water suspended in the center of the centermost cavern. One ride was ominously labeled '"Decompression"—some funny thing to joke about, three hundred million miles into space. Koko gazed with obvious yearning at the System's most famous playground, then followed us reluctantly into the restaurant, Mr. Meep's Cloud Nine. Mr. Meep was another of the many ex-Laporters I knew who'd emigrated to the asteroids. Another chimpanzee, probably a relative, conducted us to a slimmer, many-jeweled cable, which snatched us dizzily upward several levels from the entrance to a well-upholstered niche along one wall. I pulled myself into a seat, fastening the lapbelt. Koko did the same. Lucy simply hung beside the table and clamped a manipulator on its edge.

"Well," I said, looking around, "old Meep seems to have done pretty well for himself." The place was a fantasy, a hundred dusky caves and exotic grottoes overlooking a lushly jungled, many-layered floor. The central cavern was filled with drifting artificial clouds, each topped with a table for two, candles twinkling in the twilight like so many fireflies.

A chuckle burbled up from somewhere inside Lucy's fuselage. "He oughta. Half the population here usta be his customers back home. Here's th' waiter." That worthy helicoptered up beneath a propellor-beanie fastened by a chin strap. He performed a theatrical loop, then a hammerhead stall, fell off on his right shoulder, and swooped to a halt, hovering beside the table and sculling with his hands and feet. He activated our menu and made notes on a 'com pad in his hand.

I asked for lamb chops with mint jelly and a large baggie of milk. Koko ordered a salad and a small hamburger. Lucy—hell, I'd been half expecting her to plug into the wall for a recharge. She surprised me by ordering a small container of beef broth, then produced a stack of datachips.

"Lessee now, steak—rare—French fries, milk shake, spinach...*spinach?* How'd *that* get in there?" She tossed the offending chip over her shoulder. "Guess that'll hold me. Mind if I go ahead?"

I watched this performance, trying to keep my eyes from bugging out of my head. "Datachips, Lucy? Where's the nourishment in that?"

"Fer th' soul, Winnie. Ever heara sensory deprivation? Goin' through th' motions helps t'keep me sane—sane as I ever was, anyway. Th' broth is all th' real fuel I need, that'n nuclear fusion. Guess you'd like t'know what this is all about, hunh?" A chimpanzee in angel's clothing swooped by with a flaming sword—someone was having shish kebab tonight.

"It might help keep *me* sane. It isn't every day you see your friends reincarnated as robots."

"*Watch yer language!* This's hard'nough t'take 'thout wisecracks." She paused, fiddling idly with the salt and pepper gun as it drifted on its lanyard from the center of the table. "There I was, just startin' t'enjoy bein' young agin. If I *ever* got aholda the crab louse who— Anyway, I was out, doin' a little shoppin' not a block from here, when all of a sudden, *Pow!* Next thing I knew, they were gettin' set t'cremate m'pretty little bod. Well, I gave *them* a piece of my—"

"Hold on," asked Koko, accepting her salad from our self-propellored waiter. "If they were going to cremate you, then how—"

"Just th' carcass, honey." She reached down and patted her conical torso. "M'brain's all nice an' cozy down here, now. Pretty scary, though, wakin' up wired to a fare-thee-well, an' floatin' in a pickle jar." She inserted a datachip in a disappearing slot in her chest. "Sesame-seed buns—I love 'em!"

Maybe this wasn't the greatest dinner conversation in the world. Suddenly my lamb chop seemed congealed and greasy, not at all appetizing. I hadn't known Confederate medicine was up to a stunt like this. Clarissa would've loved to—no, I couldn't bear to think about that right now. "If you don't mind a personal question, Lucy old friend, how in the hell did they get all your nerve connections hooked up right? Aren't there millions—"

"*Billions*—by burnin' up half th' core time available in Ceres Central fer sixteen solid hours. Y'oughta see my bills. Good thing th' insurance— Hold on, I see what yer gettin' at. Winnie, there ain't no natural law says a frontier *hasta* be backward. Shucks, all th' brains an' talent's headed out *this* way these days. You're here, ain't'ya?"

"Yeah, but not for long." I explained about Clarissa's disappearance, Olongo's, too, and the pillage of our home and Propertarian headquarters, winding up with the attempts on my life aboard the *Bonaventura*.

"Flamin' frogsnot, Winnie—an' I thought *I* was accident-prone! But look, son, whoever's behind all this, the only hope fer us is right here in th' Belt. Dontcha understand that yet?"

"I'm sorry, Lucy, I can't think of anything besides Clarissa. I *can't* hang around here while she needs me, damn it!"

"But Winnie—"

"My god, Lucy, what do you—"

"Maybe Clarissa needs us both *out here*," suggested Koko.

"Shut up, shut up, both of you, shut up!"

Koko munched her salad, looking hurt. "Yes, Your Redundancy."

"Okay, I'm sorry. But *you* understand, don't you, Lucy?"

"Sure. I'm just as worried about Eddie. Been gone three weeks, an' if it was done as dirty as th' dirt they done *me*..." Her datachip popped out. She replaced it absently with another, this one labeled French fries.

Koko leaned over and gently stroked Lucy's chassis. "You can tell *me* about it, Lucy. I won't bite your head off, like *some* people."

"Guess it started when Mark, our Registry Patrolman, mentioned a fewa his customers bein' outa circulation, 'thout notifyin'. 'Course it's a Free System. No asteroider's gonna ask 'Mother-may-I' 'fore he takes off sunside on a holiday or goes prospectin' Outward. Patrols just wish their clients'd let 'em know more often...Anyway, there was all this Aphrodite hooraw, too—buyin' up all kindsa claims in th Sargasso, where mosta Rothbard's registrees was disappearin' from. Bout th' same time, this Tormount gruboon contacted me, on accounta my engineerin' experience with Phobos an' all."

"Whasha 'gruboon'?" asked Koko around the last bite of her hamburger. Anyone who claims gorillas are herbivorous never looked at their teeth very closely.

"Why, honey, that's a sorry specimen prefers muckin' around th' bottom of a gravity well—half th' population of th' System, if y' b'lieve th' surveys. Don't understand it m'self, but—"

I raised my eyebrows. "You mean you've actually *met* J. V. Tormount?" Leave it to Lucy to succeed accidentally where even Voltaire Malaise had failed.

"That's th' funny part. I'm a pretty fair engineer, usta dealin' with th' front office. But I did all my palaverin' with a coupla flunkies. An *Orca*, called herself Brahoohoo, an' a *Delphinus* name of P'wheet. Figger he'd be any kin t' Ooloorie?"

I shook my head. "She's a *Tursiops*, and besides, if I understand these things, her family name is Eckickeck. Funny you should mention it, she and Deejay are either on sabbatical, or they've gone wherever Clarissa and Ed are." I repeated my conversation with Bertram. "And they're mixed up with Aphrodite somehow, too, I think."

Lucy came to the end of her French-fries recording and cued up a milk shake. "Mercury, is it? Well, I always figgered there were other possibilities to th' Broach. Next thing they'll be scoopin' hidey-carbons outa Jupiter with it."

"How did Ed get involved in all this?" asked Koko. "Was he one of Rothbard's disappearances?" She'd mopped up her lunch and was starting on dessert—the only gorilla I know personally who will publicly admit to liking bananas. I was interested in seeing how she'd handle a banana split in freefall—it's just a little lumpy for the nozzle of a baggie.

"Naw, we're a long, long way from th' Sargasso Cluster. See, we were gettin' ready t'diversify a little out on Bulfinch: giant arctic hares. Been a bristlecone's age since I tasted fried rabbit, an' we figgered it'd be a real commercial item. But we needed capital. That's why I was thinkin' this Aphrodite proposition over real serious-like. Only they up an' broke off negotiations, an' I couldn't even get through to *flunkies* after that."

"Hmm. So Ed started doing a little digging." I had every reason to understand his bump of curiosity. I had one just like it, myself. "Say, do you suppose it's all right to smoke in this place?"

"Why ever not?" Lucy answered. "Could use a coffin-nail, m'self." She shuffled through her stack of datachips again, and popped one into the slot—and popped it right out again. "Nope, smoked that one already."

I fished one of my stogies out from under my suit. "Sorry I can't offer you one of mine, Lucy, or even a light."

"Lemme do th' honors." A tiny flame blossomed from her manipulator-tip. "A regular walkin' Swiss Army knife these days, ain't I? You're right, Eddie couldn't leave it alone. Mebbe he was gettin' bored with home-steadin', or just tryin' t'raise our rabbit money. He let th' truck-garden an' th' goldmine go, started pokin' into th' Cluster disappearances on a contingency arrangement with Rothbard's. Even ordered up a whole mess of expensive Broach-detectin' gear—"

"Hold on. You mean from Laporte Paratronics?"

"Dunno. I was off doin' a little freelance legal work. Before I'd got back he'd took off like a Fed outa Philly, leavin' me a message he'd be home in a few days. Only—only he *wasn't*, Winnie." She stopped for several moments then, collecting her thoughts. It was eerie, listening to her familiar voice in the semidark. The shock was fresh each time I looked over and saw the machine her mind had become imprisoned in.

And I thought I had troubles.

"He musta had some long-haul travelin' in mind, 'cause he left his brand-new Cord at home an' rented a half-gee flivver with oversize tanks.

I got back an' found that Hamiltonian medallion in his desk, gave you a holler, then beat it over here—Eddie's car's faster'n mine—t'try an' trace him through th' rental."

Koko's banana split arrived via "airmail," prepared upon a miniature bed of nails—the kind of thing they use in florists' shops. She lifted the transparent lid, carefully speared a maraschino cherry, and closed the top again. "And what did you find out?"

"Never got a chance t'find out nothin'. I'd just got settled in at th' Admiral Heinlein Arms, when some fluke-infested backshooter up an' killed me."

Step by every other step. I'd laid my plans so far, only to see them demolished by events. Lucy's resurrection had made a shambles of my latest intentions. We finished lunch by trying to figure out who was going to do what, and when. I had a spaceship to catch in something like thirty-eight hours. Koko wasn't too enthusiastic about making similar arrangements for herself. Lucy, who'd counted on our help, was still adamant on tracing Ed.

Meanwhile, the most impressive case of jetlag in at least my personal history was beginning to catch up with me: a journey of a couple hundred million miles, filled with unexpected perils and altogether too much exercise to suit my sessile inclinations. Lucy agreed to escort Koko on a brief exploration of Pellucidar Gardens; it's no fun seeing an amusement park alone. In the meantime, I intended to explore my *own* way back into the sunshine and get a few hours' overdue sleep. We parted at the corner outside, where the park across the way appeared to be an independent floating world-within-a-world—though I understood there were titanic supporting columns elsewhere, linking it to the city. A million varicolored lights and moving signs peeked enticingly through the heavy covering foliage. The Möbius-coaster blasted by, its passengers shrieking gaily.

I watched my friends drift across the canyon, Lucy pulling Koko along behind her, then consulted a map on my face-screen, thoughtfully broadcast by the Merchants Association. Even with its hood down on my chest, the damn smartsuit was useful; I was getting dependent on it already.

When there are at least sixteen outfits doing business at any one street corner, things can get confusing. I took a promising combination of tow cables toward the elevator, getting lost only twice on the way, finally whisked to the surface, where I stepped out into the hotel lobby, happy to have my feet planted beneath me once again, if only at the puny rate of ten pounds per extremity.

I stepped up to the desk. "I'm Win Bear—checked my bags here earlier. I've a room reserved until *Lord Kalvan* departs for Earth." I looked around. After several hours below, the walls and ceilings seemed strangely empty, almost going to waste.

The clerk punched up the relevant data. "That's right," she answered. "Your room is on the third floor, number 313. I also see you have a message, and—hmm, that's odd—the manager wants to see you when it's convenient." She checked the time on the suitscreen hanging down in front of her like a big rubber pocket watch. "He's going to lunch in fifteen minutes —be back an hour after that."

"Let's make it now and get it over with." I let the little chimp lead me back through a hallway, open the office door, and let me in.

Some State-side feminist once cracked that a woman needs a man like a fish needs a bicycle. This wasn't exactly a bicycle, and a porpoise isn't exactly a fish, but she'd better apply for a new metaphor—or is it simile?—anyway: the hotel boss, decked out from snout to tailfins in rubber underwear, was resting in a lightweight wheeled metal frame. "Mr. Bear, I presume. I'm Criickleer Ackackack Sweenie. Please come in and take a seat." His quadricycle rolled forward smoothly, a manipulator similar to Lucy's extended from the frame to shake my hand, then pulled a chair for me around to face the desk.

I sat.

"Sorry to bother you, Mr. Bear, but something odd has happened I think you should know about."

"*Plenty* of odd things seem to be happening to me lately. What is it now?"

The slightest whisper of mechanics, and his arm extended once again, offering a box of cigarettes. I took one, wondering how all this shiny gadgetry was operated. His claw-tip snapped into flame just like Lucy's had an hour ago. He lit one for himself and stuck it in his blowhole.

"Well, I try to run a good house here. So it pains me to admit it, but someone tried to steal your luggage—simply walked by and took it off the rack in the lobby. Our security circuitry noticed, of course, and we recovered it undamaged."

My personal effects, it seemed, were getting more and more in demand every day. First the intruder aboard the *Bonaventura* and now this. Just call me the Man with the Million-Dollar Underwear. "How about the thief?"

"Quite the oddest thing of all. She collapsed spontaneously as soon as we apprehended her. She's in Nivenville Emergency right now, and the Healer there gives her very little hope."

I thought this over. "Did they mention anything about a 'brain-bore'?"

"Let me think—a little circuit box, no larger than a herring?"

I nodded. So did he, in a fishy sort of way.

"Well, they say it'll be some time before...Will you be available for the inquest?" He blew a thin stream of smoke from the back of his head. I hope they won't be quite so anxious to get me buried when the time comes.

"Depends. If the *Bonaventura*'s still at Gunter's Landing, I suggest your local sawbones contact a gorilla name of Francis Pololo. His testimony'll be a lot more valuable than mine. He knows something about brain-bores—enough to hate them thoroughly. As for me, I hate to be uncooperative, but there's an emergency back home, and whoever wants me to stick around here better be faster on the draw than I am. I'd go over to the clinic now, but I'm way behind on sack time, and I gather it'll wait."

"Possibly forever, Mr. Bear, possibly forever."

I let myself out of the office and went upstairs. Maybe I was simply suffering fatigue of the surprise-muscles: suburban ski-lifts; wheeled porpoises; talking garbage cans (as long as Lucy wasn't around to hear it). The room seemed a nice, quiet oasis of familiarity until I realized that this, in itself, was another surprise.

Furniture, for example: given one-tenth gee, the rugscaping ought to be futuristic, spindly. That's the way they show it on the Telecom. But furniture anywhere is built more to withstand bodily wrecking power than gravity. Plunk yourself into a chair, it's still gotta take your full momentum—and it's far easier to high-velocity plunk at lower gees. If anything, I noticed the furniture gets heavier—scoots around a little less that way, I guess.

I inventoried the contents of my nearly purloined overnight bag and briefcase: nothing missing as far as I could tell; peeled off my smartsuit and slid between the magnetically anchored sheets. Then I remembered with a groan that there was still some message waiting for me at the desk.

"That's right," said the Telecom, "you're Mr. Bear in 313." Ever notice how hotel clerks seem anxious to assure you of your own identity? "One minute...here it is. You're scheduled for a stasis-berth aboard the *Lord Kalvan* late tomorrow night? Well, I'm sorry, Mr. Bear, *Lord Kalvan*'s departure has been postponed, indefinitely."

"*What?*" This was getting ridiculous. "How come? Can't you get me another ship? It's an emergency."

"I'm very sorry, but this seems to be an emergency, too, a general warning out for all interplanetary travel: unseasonally energetic solar flares, it says here. No passages accepted until further notice."

I thought about Deejay and Ooloorie. Were they safe, way down there by the fire? Or were they simply little wisps, blowing in the photon wind by now? Wait a minute, could their tinkering have *caused* this disaster? That was a hell of a thought!

And so was this one: Clarissa needed me, and I was *marooned*.

8: THE BRAIN-BORE

The first year we were together, I often wondered whether Clarissa didn't feel she'd married down. Her being a high-powered surgeon and me a two-bit shamus, I mean. I shouldn't have worried: detectives are disgustingly respectable and middle-class in the Confederacy. *Everybody's* middle-class in the Confederacy.

Healers lack the bulge that U.S. doctors throw around: there's a hell of a lot more of them; they have to get out and hustle, make house calls. So things even out.

Now Clarissa could be that *special* kind of physician, even in Laporte, the kind with rich hypochondriacal customers and a solid-platinum stethoscope. She's good enough, got that kind of touch. I believe she could snap the mummy of Ramses II out of his slump, have him up and dancing the mazurka in a week. Three days if he watched his diet.

But what I remember is a hundred gut-bending nights like the one I spent handing her silverware, trying not to look down while she stitched together what was left of a six-year-old neighbor kid who got precocious with a can of pistol powder. Eight full hours, and when that was done and I thought I could crawl away somewhere and throw up quietly, she pulled the well-singed ruins of an alley cat—a ragged little scrap of bloody fur—out of stasis where she'd placed it and repeated the whole performance so the little guy could wake up in the morning with his kitten buzzing on his chest.

Like I said, she's got that kind of touch.

⅄

I didn't take that room clerk's word, but 'commed H T & H myself. Also Pan-Confederate, TransSystem—if there'd been an interplanetary Avis, I'd have tried them, too. Each and every one was sitting tight, hoping the fireworks would sputter down. Outward traffic was still lifting: engine shields in the south end of a northbound hull are good for solar radiation—until turnover—and there wasn't any shortage of cus-tomers or crew willing to bet old Sol'd get over his hiccups in a day or three. But Sunward was a differently complected critter: nary a spacehand in the Belt who'd gamble salary and bonuses against winding up barbecued.

By this time, I was wide awake again. I chipped a note for Koko, learned by trying to reach Forsyth that the 'coms were down for the duration, then decided to see for myself what passes for medical care in the asteroids.

Confederates regard hospitalization as a shameful relic of the past—like whipping the insane or invoking Sovereign Immunity—the worst punishment you can inflict on a sick person. Consider all the interesting diseases gathered there in one location, the inevitable bureaucratically rotten food, continuous disturbances just outside your door, the way they wake you up for sleeping pills.

My one stateside experience as a surgeree—perforated in the wallet muscles by a .22 slug—had been all of that: tottering along the slickly waxed linoleum like Methuselah on his nine-hundred-first, leaning weakly on a treacherously unsteerable IV hanger; the midnight PA operator hollering "*ICU, ICU, respiratory arrest!*", then a few minutes later, "*Nice try, ICU*"; elderly neighbors coughing, snorting, wheezing, moaning in the certain knowledge that, if this wasn't the visit that'd finish 'em off, the next one would for sure; the middle-aged contractor I roomed with, inexorably growing hooked on soap operas; the lilting murmur of Extreme Unction somewhere down the hall.

These are a few of my favorite things.

My first medical adventure in the Confederacy had been different. After Clarissa had stapled me back together, I'd recovered in bed, at home. Probably cut my healing time in half.

Now, I headed for the shower, not especially looking forward to the task. A mere tenth of a gee makes personal hygiene a messy, claustrophobic ordeal. Along the way to the bathroom, it gradually dawned on me that I didn't really need a wash that badly. Strange, when I'd been cooped up in a rubber coverall since morning. Sure enough, on consultation with the owner's program in my suit, I discovered that, in the asteroids, shower stalls will soon be relegated to museums.

Except in hotels for flatlanders.

Guess I wasn't much more scandalized than those first Elizabethans when their vergin' Queen installed a bathtub and started using it regularly, twice a year, whether she needed it or not. This smartsuit business would sure save time; maybe I could teach it shaving too. I wondered whether I could start a fashion trend back home, all by myself.

There's a lot to be admired about small-town convenience and honest courtesy. Suited up again, I stepped out in the sunshine to familiar grass-upholstered streets. A hovercabbie saved me half a tenth-bit by volunteering that Nivenville Emergency was within a minute's walking distance, the small foamed-metal building right between the General Store and barbershop.

Asteroiders must be a healthy crowd; the paramedic behind the counter was asleep. I cleared my throat. He jumped, reflexively extending a hand to keep his brains off the ceiling. "Well, well! *Two* customers today. Don't look sick t'me, Mac. What can I do y'for?" He retrieved a 'com pad from the floor where it had fallen, a crossword puzzle showing on the screen.

"I'm here about your other customer, the one who collapsed in the hotel?" I glanced around at what looked more like a rustic veterinarian's office: a couple of examination cubicles, a surgery, maybe three or four other rooms. The shingle on the door had read "G.A. Scott, H.D."

The paramedic's smartsuit was rigged out in a traveling salesman's horse-blanket plaid. He hooked a casual thumb over his shoulder. "Second cubby on the right," and sat again, pulling a light-stylus from his pocket to resume Man's ageless struggle against 37 down.

Second on the right was an office. His suit display an unadorned surgical green, a Confederate medical circled cross on his shoulder, the Healer hunched over his desk, three different 'com pads displaying textbook data.

"Excuse me, I'm Win Bear."

"Doesn't sound like too serious an offense. You're here about the brain-bore case." Scott, a big, tough-mannered, grizzle-bearded man, his forearms almost blackened by the sun, might have seemed more at home running a jackhammer on a demolition gang—or possibly on horseback, punching giant arctic hares. "Just checking with my reference books. Bet you didn't know we do this before looking at a patient—sort of like cheating on an exam."

I grinned. "I'm married to a Healer; she swore me to undying secrecy. Find out anything interesting?"

"What did you expect? Some bacillus-brain's perverted a basically decent technology, useful in controlling domestic animals or giving porpoises and temporary amputees mobility. I'd heard rumors, but..." He slammed his palms on the desk, pushing himself erect. "Come across the hall and see for yourself."

The room was taken up by an oversize iron lung. Through the plastic observation port a young woman wearing coveralls was visible, a small area on the left side of her skull shaven clean for attachment of a familiarly sinister nanoelectronic device. Scott fussed with the machinery, adjusting dials microscopically with an air of weary concern.

"Stasis, isn't it?" I asked. "She looks just like the other one."

He swiveled to face me, his already angry manner hardening further. "*What* other one?"

I explained about the girl aboard the *Bonaventura*, discovering in the process that I was telling him a lot more about my own affairs than I'd intended. Some Healers have that effect. "So I suggest you talk to Dr. Pololo. Not only does he feel the same way you do about this, but he's probably going quietly nuts with his ship grounded."

He snatched a 'com pad from the wall, punching numbers. Over his shoulder I saw a chimpanzee answer—at Gunter's Landing, the star-filled sky icy black through the broad windows behind her. "Sarah, where do I find *Bonaventura*'s sawbones when he's not busy committing malpractice?"

⊐⊐

She laughed. "Most of the crews out here are still aboard, trying not to overload our transient facilities. This weather's causing all kinds of snarl." She held a thick sheaf of hard copies to the pickup, then threw them back on the desk. "Know anyone who wants forty tons of slightly overripe bamboo shoots?"

"Excuse me," I began, then braced myself for another wisecrack from Scott, "but isn't it dangerous for you people out there in the crater? After all, a solar flare—"

"One of your less-successful operations, Doc, or just a gruboon? Listen, pal, the walls around the Landing are a lot better protection than any plastic atmospheric envelope. Now, how about both of you going away. I'm swamped."

As she switched off, the paramedic dashed in, crossword puzzle dangling from his fingers. "It's an epidemic! Another clown out here wants to see you, Doc. Can you stand the grueling pace, or should I break out the uppers?"

"Show him in, and show yourself out. And Dave, try to keep your knitting out of sight." He indicated the puzzle on the pad screen. "We might as well *attempt* to maintain appearances."

"Anything you say, Chief." He glanced down at the puzzle. "What's a seven-letter word for 'uncouth barbarian'?"

"Y-E-R-S-E-L-F," supplied the Healer.

"Wise-ass," the paramedic muttered disrespectfully. "Hey—that's it! Or does a hyphen count as an extra letter?"

"If you *dash* out of here, right now, I won't tell on you. Git!"

A moment later the rubbery slap of smartsuit feet in the hall outside announced the arrival of a familiar furry form. "Win Bear. We've got to stop meeting like this."

"Francis, I've had enough humor just now to—to keep me in *stitches* for a week. We were just trying to call you."

"Oh? Well, a *Tursiops* at *Le Petit Prince* beat you to it." The gorilla paused, removed his wire-rims, and polished them. "Dr. Scott, I understand you've got another brain-bore victim. The last one didn't survive Win's amateur surgery."

"So I'm told." He pointed to the stasis-tank. "I'm not sure this one's much better off. Suspended this way, I can't operate on her, and the instant I shut the field down, we'll start losing her again."

Francis peered into the chamber over the tops of his glasses. "Young, female, human—exactly like the other. Right-handed, judging from the placement of the bore." He reached into a pocket and extracted his little tin of cigarillos. I accepted, Scott refused with a professionally disapproving scowl. "I've had a chance to learn a little from the necropsy. This is an extremely sophisticated device we're up against, an electronic parasite, really."

"Why do you say that?" I applied my Bic to both cigars.

"Because, said the gorilla, "it's more than just a simple implant. It *grows*."

"*What?*" Scott gasped. I wasn't far behind him.

"That's right, not unlike the way in which a damaged smartsuit heals itself. But this thing leaches iron, trace copper, I don't know what else, right out of the blood, always extending its hold. I found at least a hundred areas of the brain it had connected itself to. Makes me ill to think about it. Did you get pics on this one?"

Scott leaned against the stasis-tank, shaking his head. Beneath his protective grouchiness was a little less professional detachment than I'd guessed. "She was sinking too fast. Those warped, perverted—"

"You can't shoot x-rays, or whatever, inside the tank, right?"

He gave me that *look* physicians cultivate for mere laypersons venturing medical opinions. "Without stasis, we've got perhaps five minutes. Any suggestions"—he glared at me again—"from *qualified* observers?"

Francis answered: "I don't even know what's killing this one, although that blasted thing in there could do it a dozen different ways. What are the indications?"

"Generally depressed everything—respiration, pulse, EEG, endocrine, lymphatic, even bone marrow, for Albert's sake. It's like—"

"Like she was being *shut off*" I barged in. "And don't give me that 'qualified observer' crap. I worked twenty-seven years in a related specialty—*homicide*."

"All right, all right." Scott looked at me with dawning respect, while Francis chuckled, rummaging around for an ashtray. "Any suggestions—from anybody?"

I thought about it. "As long as she's in stasis, she's okay, if you want to call that living. Try and help her, she dies, because that *thing* is ordering her to. It's not the *patient* you guys should be working on, but that goddamned hunk of nanocircuitry."

Scott snorted. "That's a complicated, deadly little toy. You can't just—"

"Who's opinionating outside his professional competence now?" Francis stepped into the office across the hall and stubbed his cigar out in Scott's wastebasket. "I agree with Win. We need a specialist."

"I know a cybernetic engineer," I volunteered, "although she never planned on ending up that way. If we spent one of this girl's last five minutes scanning the device that's killing her, then couldn't you put her back on hold until we figured out how to exorcise it?"

"Your patient, Healer," Francis said.

"No, I'm not," retorted Scott, "but this child here doesn't have much hope, no matter what we do."

⅄

Lucy wasn't difficult to find. The Admiral Heinlein Arms informed me that she'd one-upped me in the pocket-pager department—didn't even need pockets. Three words and she was on her way, my apprentice sulkily in tow. Fifteen minutes later, there was a real crowd around the stasis-tank, the Healers focusing at least half their perplexed attention on Lucy's fascinating condition.

"We're ahead on one count," she observed. "They made the case transparent. All I need's a little elbow room—I got talents them fellers Gray an' Bell an' Edison never even dreamed about."

"Not to mention Don Ameche."

"Shut up, Winnie." She shooed us all into the corridor. Neither Scott nor his assistant appeared too happy being pushed around on their own turf. We piled up in the doorway, elbows in each other's ribs, while Lucy scooted up as close to the tank as her conical bulk allowed. Her "arms" began to telescope until her manipulators rested on the floor. Then, as her torso lifted, she tilted against the observation window, hung there a few moments, then lowered herself to the floor again.

"Okay, ever-body, take a gander." Like my brand-new smartsuit, Lucy's hide had been a plain, undecorated silver-gray. Now it began to lighten, showing some color. I recognized the image of the brain-bore in its plastic shell, magnified thirty or forty diameters. It looked like a transistor radio with its back open.

"See anything looks familiar?" She pointed out a central processor, surrounded by a dozen other chips.

The capacity of this thing must have been enormous. "This here's a Lonestar Instruments 4311-C. An' here's a paira Nanodata 6517s. Tells me plenty, right there."

Francis thrust his way into the tiny room, dug deep in a pocket and held an object, dangling from its loose wires, under Lucy's figurative nose. "For whatever it's worth, here's the bore I removed aboard the *Bonaventura*."

"Well, call me a tie-dyed quark. Circuitry looks about th' same. But then agin, this other one here's still runnin'. That'n of yours is deader'n a democrat." The image on her exterior changed, becoming far more schematic. "Hey, Scotty, gimme fifteen seconds with th' stasis-power off. That oughta be enough t'trace th' logic."

Scott squeezed into the room. "You're sure that's sufficient? I don't want to have to do this twice. And, Mrs. Kropotkin, *don't* call me Scotty."

"Don't call me Mrs. Kropotkin! I'm Lucy—even if I do look like an Apollo capsule. Fifteen seconds oughta be fine—a lot of me runs in nano-seconds these days, an' the rest'll hafta catch it on th' instant replay."

Scott stood by the end of the tank and flipped the safety cover off a switch while Lucy cranked herself back into position. *"Now!"* Nothing spectacular happened; I don't know what I'd been expecting: weird purple rays, maybe theramin music; the Healer flipped the toggle off again and locked the cover down.

"Okay," said Lucy, "stray neutrinos, mag-fields, various other secondaries, comin' up!" A new, indecipherable overlay began taking shape on her illustrated surface, parts of it in colors I don't think I'd ever seen before. One by one, Lucy traced the whorls, isolating elements of the brain-bore's function. "Got it! A minute or two t'dicker with th' thing, an' it'll shut itself down, steada that little girl in there. Anybody got a drink?"

Dave gave Lucy a skeptical look, then glanced at Scott, who nodded. A half-gallon baggie materialized from a file drawer, along with a small stack of metal cups. "The chief has me file it under L," said the paramedic, "because it—"

"Stands for Liquor?" Koko guessed.

"Or Old *Lysander*?" ventured Lucy, referring to her favorite brand.

"Or rots your *liver*?" offered Francis.

"No, because Dave *loves* it so much" the Healer explained. "It takes his mind off crossword puzzles. Tell me, Lucy, how do you intend to drink it?"

"A good question," I agreed. "I thought you relied on datachips to satisfy your vices."

Lucy emitted an electronic harumph. "You boys'd better mind yer manners. An' get me an eyedropper, Dave. I ain't equipped t'handle cups." She accepted a careful drop or two, then modestly turned her back. "Guess I'm a cheap date now. Ah! Right in th' old nutrient solution!" She turned around to face us once again. "Say, what's th' matter, ain't anybody else drinkin'?"

⅄

I never did understand the brain-bore's circuitry, just that it could be reprogrammed in a relatively short time once Lucy started "talking" to it. The real break was a radio link through which the victim presumably received occasional new instructions.

"Hold on a minute." I grabbed Lucy's arm as she and Scott and Francis headed back for the stasis-tank. "Doesn't that imply that whoever tried to kill me through a conditioned assassin might have been aboard the *Bonaventura* in person? I mean, after the first attempt failed..."

"Dunno, Winnie," answered Lucy. "Lemme think on that a bit. I ain't convinced it was the same party tried t'get you all three times."

That was a wrinkle I hadn't considered.

"Of *course* it was," said Koko. "Who else could it have been?"

Francis looked up at her a moment, then dismissed the argument and shifted his attention back to the patient in the tank.

Scott's proprietary manner had returned. "She'll be weak, you understand. If we can shut the bore off, she's going straight back into stasis until I get a recovery system set up. This is going to be one sick little girl for a while."

Lucy stood before the tank and Scott beside the switch as Francis and Dave prepared to lift the lid. The word was given, the toggle thrown, and, as the mechanical coffin opened, a flood of signals began passing through the eighteen inches between Lucy and the diabolical device on the girl's head. Slowly the fatal tension appeared to drain from her sickened body, a bit of color returned. She began breathing evenly, and Scott, consulting vital signs, looked satisfied.

Suddenly the victim lurched upward on an elbow, confused terror brimming in her eyes. I took an unconscious step forward and she fixed on me, shrinking backward into the tank. Scott sprang to her side, trying to make her lie down. The look of wild horror on her face intensified, she kept her eyes riveted on me.

"*You!* I have to— What is this? Who are you people? I have to— Don't you know what's happening? Aphrodite doesn't know what it is, *but it frightens the voices falling from the stars!*"

She collapsed. Scott and Francis checked her signs as Dave prepared an injection. They gave it a few seconds to work, then closed the lid and switched the stasis field back on.

"I think she'll be all right, now," Scott observed. "You sure that bore is thoroughly deactivated?"

"Like a doornail," Lucy answered, "except fer reabsorbin' its intrusions in her brain. Give 'er a day or two outa stasis, an' likely it'll just fall off."

"What do you suppose she meant?" asked Francis. "Did that rambling mean anything to you, Win?"

"Some of it. Her disorientation was plain enough."

"As was her residual conditioning against you." He scrubbed his glasses once again and set them on his nose. "Aphrodite, voices falling from the stars—what was *that* all about?"

I thought about it. "You've seen more delirium than I have. Voices from the stars—those mysterious *signals* they've been picking up. And Aphrodite—well, at least we know the real villains, now."

"Or do we?" asked Koko. "Win, I have a scary thought—or maybe just a silly one. You guys said the brain-bore has a radio circuit, right?"

"Right, but—oops! Koko, I *hope* that's just a silly idea."

"So do I, Boss. I don't like to think we're being invaded from interstellar space. And by remote control!"

9: ONE BORN EVERY MINUTE

"**W**innie, you been *nekkid* long enough!" Lucy grabbed my arm and started pushing smartsuit buttons.

"What do you think you're doing?" I snatched my arm away, but not in time to keep my feet from turning orange. I looked at them and shuddered. We'd returned to my room at *Le Petit Prince*, leaving the medical types to map out my suitcase burglar's convalescence. Koko leaned back in a chair now—gorillas are another reason extraterrestrial furniture's substantial—watching a movie on my Gigacom.

Bedtime for Bonzo, probably.

She looked up at me. "Lucy's right, Boss. You need a little decoration, a little flair, like me." Her smartsuit was pretending to be the uniform of a Revolutionary officer—Continental Army, naturally. Her sleek and ultramodern Whitney .464 spoiled the effect a little; it should have been a sword, or at least a flintlock.

"Look," I said, "if *you* want to go around dressed for Halloween, that's your business. Leave those alone, will you, Lucy?" She'd pushed another half-dozen buttons while I was arguing with Koko, turning the rest of my suit a glossy black. The feet were still the color of a pair of tangerines, now with just the slightest trace of webbing. They clashed with the pink carpet.

I sat down on the bed, trying to get them back to normal.

"Aw, c'mon, Winnie, lemme finish. Cross m'heart, you'll like it."

"You left your heart down in Nikita's Funerium." I turned around and looked in the mirror. "This white part on the belly, Lucy, what am I supposed to be, anyway?"

"It's a surprise. Now gimme yer arm." She started pushing buttons again.

"Listen, if you like decoration so much, how come your own precious body remains unsullied? Sorry, cancel that. I didn't mean to—"

"That's okay, Winnie. Now I think on it, you're right." Her skin began to lighten up at once. Suddenly she was swathed in her favorite pattern, a riotous yellow paisley, lots of different shades of green and blue. It made her look like a giant tea cozy. "There, how's that?"

"Friendship compels me to reserve comment." I looked in the mirror again. "Now tell me what *this* is all about." My suit had become a solid shiny black, except for orange feet and a snow-white "bib" down the front. I pulled my hood up suspiciously. Sure enough, a pair of beady little bird-like eyes—and a beak.

"Appropriate," said Lucy, "seein's how we're takin' off fer th' South Pole."

"Sure, and if we were going back to Gunter's Landing, I'd have to wear a Santa Claus—*the South Pole?* I have a freighter to catch, Lucy, providing it ever takes off."

"Winnie, I got Eddie's flivver parked down t'Port Piazzi. Won't getcha back to Earth, but we'll all be a lot more comfortable on Bulfinch."

Koko sat up abruptly. "We're gonna see another asteroid? *Oh, boy!*"

"Well, so much for the charms of Dr. Francis. After all, who can compete with the Wild Frontier?

"Hold on, Lucy. How can we leave Ceres, with that solar flare and—"

"I'm plannin' t'lay on extra shielding. Ugly thing t'do t'Eddie's brand-new Cord—a '23 Ad Astra, as pretty as they come. But it'll get us home. Until *Lord Kalvan's* primed t'lift, we can go over his notes an' records, mebbe figger out what happened to him."

"Oh, no you don't! You're not going to sneak up on me like that. I'm staying right on Ceres until the flare warning is over, then I'm going straight back to Clarissa." I folded my arms across my chest and glared at her.

"Clarissa's *also* missin', I'll remind you. Winnie, what's wrong with comin' down t'Port Piazzi? Th' smaller, independent vessels gather there, mebbe you could find somebody willin' t'risk th' passage early."

It made a sort of weird distorted sense. The bigger, more cautious companies would wait until there wasn't a stray photon out of place. Worth looking into, anyway. But not as a penguin. I erased Lucy's artistic efforts, then discovered I no longer cared for the plain, undecorated look, either. I summoned up the operator's manual on my hoodscreen, and started pushing buttons for myself.

"How do you like it?" I examined the results in the mirror: basic blue on blue, with a double-breasted row of brassy buttons down the front. Now if I could only find a helmet. "A policeman's outfit, circa 1890—that's 114 A.L. to you anarchists—see the badge? Properly, I'd have a billy club, and—oh, yes, I forgot." I programmed in a golden chain across my stomach, mimicking a pocket watch.

They were both speechless with admiration.

Only after I began packing my bags did it occur to me I'd never gotten any *sleep* in this hotel. Now *there's* a problem with ignoring night and day—you keep on putting off going to bed. Wonder how Alaskans handle it. Neverthless, something here on Ceres seemed to agree with me; I felt just fine, although it took Lucy's superior mechanical strength to squeeze my suitcase shut—at one-tenth gee, sitting on it doesn't work at all.

"Lucy, how does it feel to—I mean, when you lift an arm, for instance, does it feel like you're really lifting your arm?"

"Sure. Wouldn't make much sense, otherwise, would it?"

Koko shut off the Gigacom—reminding me that I'd forgotten to include it in the suitcase. I stuffed it in a pocket. "How about walking, Lucy? You move just like a...well, a hovercraft."

Lucy's bulk lifted slightly off the floor, drifted a couple of feet, and set back down again. "That felt like one step. Hadda concentrate, though, 'cause this rig blends 'em all together t'smooth out th' ride. Yeah, an' I seem t'hear with ears, an' see with eyes. Watch this—"

A fine, three-sided slit appeared in the space between her arms, became a sort of trapdoor that pivoted downward, stopping at the perpendicular. Resting on the inside of the door was a metallic cylinder, its half-dozen muzzles gleaming hungrily in my direction.

"Pardon my aim, Winnie." She turned slightly until I was out of her line of fire. "No sneak-uppity backshooter's gonna eighty-six *this* ol' lady agin!" She patted the Gabbet Fairfax at her side. "I got this, too, but mainly fer window-dressin'."

"Uh, Lucy, if it feels like you're taking a step when you glide forward, how do you go about unlimbering that Darling gun?"

"By stickin' out m'tongue, nosy. T'start th' fireworks, I just give 'em th' raspberry, wanna see? Didn't think y'would." She folded up the weapon. "Well, let's get outa this gruboon fleatrap."

Honest Whatshisname, the hovercab driver, was waiting for fares outside. He looked us over and folded away the second pair of back seats for Lucy. The vehicle whooshed forward as she told him "Port Piazzi," gained speed as we passed the couple of remaining blocks out of town, and curved around to intersect a huge overpass. Suddenly, we did a motorcycle stuntman's loop, and found ourselves traveling upside-down along the highway's *underside*. I gulped, shutting my eyes against the sight of thickly planted fields whizzing overhead.

"Gruboon?" asked the cabbie. I nodded weakly. "Well, circular velocity on Ceres is a couple hundred miles per hour *short* of what this buggy'll do flat out. You wouldn't care t'wind up orbiting in an unpressurized vehicle—the atmospheric envelope folks wouldn't like it, either."

I indicated tentative agreement and peeked out at the countryside. It was like riding in a small airplane.

I've always *hated* riding in a small airplane.

"We'll do a little better when we hit the main road," the cabbie said cheerfully. "Have you in Piazzi in thirty minutes, or you can ride for free!"

Ulp! We didn't ride for free, but by the time we sighted the side slopes of the south polar crater, I couldn't even *think* of sleeping—and I wasn't very hungry, either. I paid the modest fare and we caught a bus out into the port.

Gunter's Landing had been an enormous, Spartan bowl, ringed with cavelike offices and service facilities. Port Piazzi was much the same, except that, where only a few dozen giants had rested on the crater floor, here were thousands of smaller vessels, and a more informal atmosphere.

Or is that a more informal *vacuum*?

As we climbed off the bus, a bright sizzling flash caught my attention. I increased the magnification, tickled the contrast-enhancement, and there he was, five hundred yards away, clinging like a spider to an exposed swatch of skeleton on a small freighter, welding torch splashing over its hull. The registry read:

PROMETHEUS UNCHAINED
THE SOLAR SYSTEM

But somebody'd chalked it over, changing it to *Sitting Duck*.

"Karyl? Karyl Hetzer?" I had to try several frequencies before he answered.

"Win Bear, Private Eye—and Koko!" He shut his torch off and hopped three dozen feet to the ground, kangarooing over to meet us. "Introduce me to your friend." He shook manipulators with Lucy, patted Koko's head (to her annoyance), and clapped me on the shoulder.

"Whatcha doin' refittin' th' old *Duckie*, Karyl?" Lucy inquired. "I'da thought she'd be sellin' fer scrap."

In my suitsereen, Karyl's bearded image grimaced. "Practicing entrepreneurship, Lucy. She'll do fine, running stasified food to Titan. And it's *Prometheus*, unauthorized graffiti to the contrary."

"*Prometheus*," Koko mused, "wasn't that supposed to be—"

"Th' System's first *starship!*" snorted Lucy. "*There's* a project Deejay an' Ooloorie won't do much braggin' on. Got three-quarters into construction when a little problematic glitch they were *sure* of solvin' failed t'unravel on schedule."

Karyl chuckled. "They finally towed her out of Earth orbit, and she's been squatting here gathering micropits ever since. Cost the backers a pretty piece of change. I picked her up for a song—and that a quarter-tone off key."

Koko's image was a portrait of chagrin. "Yeah. Uncle Olongo was one of those backers—now he'll have to wait a few more years to reach the stars."

"How come?" The little ship certainly looked unprepossessing, something like an upended onion, loose cablery and stanchions sprouting from the top.

"Well," began Lucy, and it was clear by her tone that she was unlimbering for a lecture. I regretted the pair of innocent words that had started her. "Theoretically, Winnie, *two*, as they say, is a ridiculous number. Zero's fine, an' even *one* ain't strainin' things. But shucks, wherever there's *two* of anything, there oughta be more—somewheres between *n* an' infinity."

"That's interesting," I lied. "Like Loch Ness monsters—there has to be a herd of them or nothing. But what's that got to do with a used starship?"

"*Unused*—that's th' point. Winnie, when the United States got discovered, it created problems: suddenly there was *two* universes—an' there oughta be either *one* or some silly number with a lotta zeros. Get it?"

"I admit I've always wondered why they hadn't discovered more alternate probability worlds. It'd be pretty interesting, wouldn't it?"

"Now yer talkin'. They *have* run across at least *one* more, an' mighty strange, at that. See, in theory, all these universes laid out end t'end—accordin' t'their well, sort of *likelihood*—oughta form a big multidimensional bell curve. *Statistics*, unnerstand?"

"Go on," I dodged, hoping for something in the next few paragraphs I *did* unnerstand.

"Well, each universe got created when some event, major or minor—they don't really know how big a change it takes—caused it t'diverge from th' universe it started out identical with."

"Sure. Like Gallatin winning the Whiskey Rebellion caused this universe to diverge from the one Karyl and I were born in."

"Or *losing* the Rebellion caused *yours* to diverge," offered Koko.

Karyl laughed out loud.

"Whatever," said Lucy, ducking a swell fight. "Anyhow, 'way at th' end of th' curve, there's this teensy little continuum where th' very *first* event sorta fizzled out 'fore it got started."

"The Big Bang?" I asked, with sudden inspiration.

"*Little* Bang. Natcherly, the laws of physics are a mite different there, which makes that universe plumb easy t'detect with instruments. An' that's what Deejay an' Ooloorie did."

I thought about it. "Swell. So what happened then?"

"They built the *Prometheus*," Karyl answered.

"Persuaded my uncle and his friends to," Koko corrected. "The idea's that the Little Bang universe is so tiny—just a pinpoint, really—that traveling across it is easier than traveling across ours."

"A few cosmologists'd swaller their gum t'hear that explanation, dearie, but y'got th' high points. Fer each location *here*, there's a theoretical correspondin' one *there*." Lucy drew a diagram in the crater dust, corrected it, corrected it again, and finally gave up, erasing it with her impellers. "Just go from point A— Earth, fer example—t'point A-prime in th' Little Bang universe—"

"Via Broach?" I asked.

"Right," said Karyl. "And since all points are *common* by geometric law in the Little Bang universe—"

"Yer *already* at point B-prime—say, th' location correspondin' t'Alpha Centauri...Who's tellin' this, Karyl, you guys or me?"

87

"Call it a cooperative venture, Lucy. Anyway, all you have to do is emerge at point B, and you're already automatically where you want to go—*without traveling the invervening distance in our universe.*"

"I see what you mean—*hyperspace*. What went wrong?"

"Hy*po*space, more like," said Lucy. "An' since all them geometric points are common in th' Little Bang universe, *there's no way t'tell 'em apart.* Y'might wind up 't Alpha Centauri—or y'might's easy wind up over in th' next galaxy somewheres!"

"Or fifty thousand years in the future," added Koko. "Works with time, too."

"Hmm. That's a problem, all right. And they never solved it?"

"Else we'd be havin' this conversation on Beetlejuice XVII, or somethin', wouldn't we?"

"We wouldn't be having it at all," I answered.

"Since we are," Karyl said, changing the subject at long last, "how do you like Ceres so far? Oh-oh, you were heading back for home, last time I heard."

I nodded. "It'll be a while, now, with this solar-flare thing going on."

He glanced around as if making sure he wasn't overheard—a futile gesture over the radio. "*What* solar flare?" He tapped the indicators on his forearm accusingly. "There hasn't been a whimper on *my* counter, or anybody else's I know of. Win, I believe we're being *hoaxed.*"

Lucy slid forward, exhaust gases from her impellers freezing instantly and drifting to the ground. "Whaddya mean, *hoaxed*? This holdup's got to've cost billions already. Nobody'd stand fer—"

"And likely to cost billions more before it's over," interrupted Karyl. He slapped the Guccione welder into his palm. "Why do you think I'm back to *this*? *Bonaventura's* going nowhere, and taking my restaurant with it. Something *big* is going on in the Belt, I wish I could find out what."

"I don't believe any of this," said Lucy. She skimmed away and started gaining speed toward an empty area of the crater floor. "Port Piazzi, this here's Lucy Kropotkin, puttin' in fer clearance fer a semi-static test run. Call it twenty thousand feet."

A new voice filtered through my suit receiver. "This is Port Piazzi, Lucy. Give us your transponder. Which ship are you in down there?" I scanned the walled horizon, trying to find the window in the cliff above us that was Port Piazzi's ground control. Karyl saw me, pointed to a light high on a peak.

"I *am* my ship, dummy!" Lucy answered. "Can'tcha see me wavin' at ya?" She was well clear of us now, enveloped in a cloud of dust. Suddenly she lifted high above it, gathering momentum, growing tinier with distance. A moment later, she was almost out of sight. I stepped up the magnification, and there she was, beginning to drift backward. Plummeting, she finally checked her speed, alighting gently on the rocky floor from which she'd taken off.

"Well, as I live and breathe!" She skimmed up close to us and halted.

"Lucy, you haven't drawn an honest breath in weeks!" I looked her conical volume up and down. "Do you call *that* living?"

"Beats th' pox outa mosta the alternatives, Winnie. Karyl, you're right. It's safe as houses out there. Somebody's pullin' our leg. I'm gonna get to th' bottom of this if it kills me all over again. Letcha know how it turns out, okay? An' thanks fer th' information."

We waved good-bye to Karyl and followed Lucy, threading our way among the grounded flivvers until we reached a large white streamlined racy-looking specimen with a boat-shaped tail and chromium venturis. She pushed a series of buttons in a certain sequence and the starboard door swung open.

"Don't stand out there all day, you two. I wanna pressurize th' hull." We ducked inside the tiny cabin, dogging the door behind us. Lucy folded the driver's seat away and stood before the fancy woven-metal instrument panel. There was a hiss, and then a rushing, rumbling sound. The indicators on my face-screen said it was safe to take my hat off.

Koko and I sat down as Lucy played with the wireless. "Hello, Navigation Rock? Lemme have th' weather report." She turned to me. "They're one of Ceres' natural moonlets, fifteen, mebbe twenty, thousand miles out."

Bubbles floated upward past the pickup as a killer whale's head swam into view. "This is Navigation Rock. Solar flux continues strong and erratic according to our instruments. I advise against departing any time within the next ninety-six hours unless you're outbound and heavily shielded."

"In your hat," said Lucy. "Where you gettin' yer skinny these days?"

The giant porpoise bobbed up and down, momentarily nonplussed. He'd probably never *had* a hat. "Why, from— Wait a moment, let me check." Something mildly repulsive with a lot of arms drifted across the screen. Abruptly, the image faded.

Lucy waited patiently, then started pushing buttons again. "Hello, Navigation Rock, you still there?"

Silence.

"Somethin' funny goin' on—agin." She readjusted her controls. "Hello, Port Piazzi, what th' dung's got into Navigation Rock?"

One of the rare orangutans who'd decided to join civilization appeared on the console. "Hello, who am I speaking to?"

"Cord Ad Astra 4137—Lucy Kropotkin. Listen, I was talkin' t'Navigation Rock just now, an' they pooped out alluva sudden."

The orang consulted his dials and knobs. "LOS, 4137, not even a carrier. That's unusual, they have at least a dozen relays. I'll try another channel.

Hello, Navigation Rock, Port Piazzi calling. Do you read me, Navigation Rock?"

Nothing.

"Just a minute, 4137." There was a long pause while he conferred with an associate, another, even longer pause. Then, "I'm sorry, 4137, we'd send somebody up to look, but there's the solar storm. We don't seem to be able to raise any of their competition, either. Anything I can do for you while we check into it?"

"Sure, gimme their coordinates."

"But, 4137, uh, Mrs. Kropotkin, it's *dangerous* out there."

"It's gonna be a lot *more* dangerous down here without you give me those coordinates, pronto. Whaddya think I pay m'landing fees fer?"

"Very well, it's a Free System." He reeled off a list of numbers while Lucy programmed the Cord's computers and cleared for takeoff. The flivver began to vibrate subtly.

"Hold onta yer helmets, kiddies!" She stabbed a button and the crater floor fell out from underneath us. Suddenly we were bathed in bright sunlight. I cringed, thinking of the radiation sleeting through our bodies.

"Lucy, I thought you'd ordered extra shielding for this thing!"

"Wasn't time, Winnie, but don't you fret—lookit this gauge." She pointed to the image of a dial on the screen. Whatever it was measuring, it wasn't measuring much of it. "See there, hardly a worm-wiggle. We been hoaxed, right 'nough, there *ain't* no solar storm. Wait'll Port Piazzi hears about this!" She started re-establishing contact.

"Slow down, Lucy!" That was Koko. "Whoever's behind this—they've even interfered with Navigation Rock, somehow. I don't want to be interfered with the same way—until we find out what's going on."

"She's right, Lucy. Let's sneak up on them, okay?"

"Yer both right, you two. Must be gettin' senile 'r somethin'—mebbe just undernourished. How about a bite t' eat? We'll be a coupla hours gettin' there."

I declined in favor of reclining. There wasn't room enough to stand inside the vehicle, but there was plenty to stretch out in. I guess it amounts to the same thing in freefall. Part of the extra space came from the orientation—"down" was toward the fusion burners (at one-tenth gee, it didn't matter very much), the paired seats flanked a ladder lying on the "floor." A minijohn and microkitchen rested on a supporting shelf behind, and aft of that, a firewall or bulkhead for the engines, generously upholstered for snoozing.

I unbelted my weapons and strapped them down, removing the .25 from the inside of my suit and wedging it into an extra ammunition pouch. Some gun. The hissing of the engines made a lovely, soporific veil of sound. In disconnected snatches, I could hear my friends discussing the solar flare.

There were plenty of weather-predicting companies, and no single outfit should be able to fake a storm-warning on a scale like this. They'd be paying restitution well into the next *eon,* at least that's what Lucy kept insisting. Koko seemed crushed, disappointed in what had seemed the Promised Land to her, and unjustly disappointed with Lucy for being unable to account for the anomaly.

I wondered—and worried—about it myself. This whole situation was getting more complicated by the minute: people disappearing, others trying to knock me off, electronic zombies wandering around loose. And above all, Clarissa, always Clarissa. Like that dream where you're running, trying to reach the one you love, and, in all the confusion, somehow never quite able to.

I slipped from fitful doze into a solid, if occasionally troubled, sleep, vaguely aware at turnaround, then back into the warm, friendly darkness behind my eyelids.

I almost missed it when we reached the asteroid known as Navigation Rock.

10: SWIM THE FRIENDLY SKIES

Sunday, March 14, 223 A.L.

Find a little asteroid, drill a little hole, *plant a little bomb.* Heat the whole mess cherry-red in an induction field generated by orbiting construction drones rented for the occasion. When solid rock has acquired the consistency of incandescent bubble gum, the explosives puff it up into a larger, hollow shell.

Old stuff, right? Then tunnel in and plant your trees and grass—don't forget the animals and air and topsoil.

Wrong.

Instead, try filling half the mile-wide cavity with water. A modest spin will plaster your captive lake around the inner surface, shallow at the poles, deeper at the equator. Top it off with an air system like the aquarium in your living room—an aquarium whose denizens make their mortgage payments by furnishing unprecedentedly accurate navigational information to half the civilized Solar System.

If I'd been in a position to appreciate the situation—a longtime inhabitant of the Belt or seasoned space-traveler—a falsified solar flare report and the subsequent cutoff of Navigation Rock's transmissions would have been my greatest shock so far. It certainly seemed to be affecting Lucy.

Her final approach was downright paranoid, one "hand" carefully caressing the controls, the other locked rigidly on the trigger switch, prepared to unleash the Darling gun on the flivver's starboard fender. One nervous twitch of her tongue, we'd be minus a windshield, courtesy of her own built-in quick-firer.

At one pole of the asteroid a gigantic bay was brightly lit and open wide: invitation or trap? Lucy chose to hang us out in empty space, politely waking me before she depressurized the hull. I'd been sleeping with my hood down, so I appreciated the thought. I sat up groggily, feeling worse after my nightmare-ridden nap than before. We were once again in free fall, hell on equilibrium, but otherwise welcome as I runged my sleep-stiffened way toward a jumpseat in the nose. Beside me, Koko seemed unusually awed and quiet, but our chauffeur was simply full of cheerful trivia.

"Tried t'raise 'em on a dozen different bands, Winnie. They're clammed up real good." She pointed toward the bloated rock drifting beyond the windshield. "Guess *that's* why."

I squinted myself into tears before remembering to adjust my suit-senses. On the cracked and pitted surface below, four broken stubs of well-scorched alloy thrust a feeble foot or so into the flivver's spotlights. "Antenna mast?"

"Usta be half a mile of it," Lucy answered, goosing us into an orbit that suited her minutely better. "Somebody done that *deliberate*. Loosen up yer ordnance, *amigos*—time we got t'gettin'" The cabin thrummed; a little yellow light on my forearm warned me it was now completely full of vacuum. She pressed a few more dashboard buttons; a scarlet panel lamp blinked on and off, then died. "A little surprise fer anybody tam-pers with Eddie's car!"

She opened the door, swung herself outside, and hung there without visible means of support, waiting. Finally I stepped out onto nothingness, clinging with acrophobic trepidation to the door handle as Koko followed and Lucy took us each by the hand. "You two just let *me* do th' maneuver-in'. Gonna leave 'er ajar, case we need a fast getaway." My fingers tingled momentarily as she left the open frequency and trans-mitted through our suit-skins: "Somethin' happens t'me, don't try startin' th' engines without you flush th' toilet an' turn th' kitchen water on—cold. Otherwise, it'll be th' Second of July, all over again. That's th' way I got it rigged, *comprende*?"

"Flush the toilet, water cold. I get it, Lucy." I was also getting sicker by the second. *Try* not looking down when it's that way every direction.

"Unh! Er, toilet and water," Koko acknowledged after a second prod in the ribs. This must have been her idea of heaven, the goddamned fuzzy space cadet. I clutched fearfully at Lucy's chassis, trying to keep my right hand on the butt of the Webley. She produced a brief, quick-frozen pro-pulsive flurry that nearly jarred me loose, and we began drifting slowly across the hundred-yard void.

At least I tried to *think* of it as "across."

Navigating by the seat of her impellers, Lucy compensated for Koko's greater mass by shortening up her left manipulator, while extending her right, the side I was on, as far as it would go. It wasn't quite enough; together, we made a lousy spaceship, but the warm, buttery light of the lock kept getting closer all the same. Finally our pilot pivoted passengers and corpus around her axillae and gave one brief, carefully calculated blast. We slowed and bumped into gentle contact with the sabotage-blackened rock.

I stickied up my shoe soles and Lucy let me go.

"Stand by a moment, kids. Somethin' I gotta find out." She grabbed a broken cable sprouting from one fused and buckled tower leg. "Hello, Navigation Rock, any of you mudpuppies still there?"

At this range, even Lucy's arm made a passable antenna. A blurry, snowfilled image seeped into the bottom corner of my suitscreen, the same Orca, I think, that we'd talked to back on Ceres. *This is Navigation Rock, who are you?*

"This here's Lucy Kropotkin. Any reason we shouldn't come inside outa th' cold?"

Koko turned her back to watch the Cord as it hung a hundred yards away, lighted by the open lock beside us.

"We're quite secure, Lucy. However, we can't persuade the outer door to cycle shut See what you can do, I'll meet you at the inside entrance to render such assistance as I can." As before, some indistinct squirmy horror oozed across the viewfield, and the killer whale rang off.

We picked our careful way to the lock over a highly uneven suface. The ground seemed broken, tortured, cracked, and fractured like the bottom of some drought-sticken river bed. Evidence, I supposed, of the heroic modifications made to this submoonlet.

Stretchmarks.

Thanks to the artifically imposed rotation of the asteroid, keeping my feet glued to the ground was a problem. Against a negligible native gravity was pitted an inexorable outward pull—approximately the same tenth-gee that had held me down on Ceres—threatening to propel me into space. It was a long walk home. I never watched my step so carefully in my life. The lock itself was a smooth-hewn hangar-size rectilinear proposition, filled with friendly yellow light, but not much of anything else. Lucy left us teetering at the edge in double-ended vertigo, and hovered her way over the abyss, somehow maintaining what amounted to a synchronous orbit.

"Win, c'mere an' take a gander. An' bring that toad-sticker of yours."

Not being outfitted with engines, I crawled reluctantly around the well and over the lip like a housefly. Lucy was investigating the edge of an enormous sliding door. Fragments from the shattered antenna tower had spattered this end of the lock, one six-foot metallic splinter penetrating the gasket like a broom straw tornadoed into a phone pole, neatly nailing the door to its frame. She reached across for my Rezin.

"Hey, don't mess up my knife! Probably won't cut that supersealant, anyway. Just get Koko over here, and we'll help you wiggle it out, okay?" Maybe *okay* wasn't the word; it was beginning to dawn on me that, where any direction can be "up," the longest, most dizzying direction inevitably seems "down." I swallowed and tried to think of this wall I clung to so desperately as a *floor*, while Lucy casually fetched my assistant. The pair drifted easily across the chasm, Koko holding Lucy's manipulator, and grabbed hold of the six-foot fragment. I shoved, then Koko shoved, with Lucy pulling "upward" at every stroke. Back and forth we sawed, Koko scarcely breathing hard, while I, with merely human muscles, began to worry about my suit's capacity to absorb sweat.

Finally the stanchion lurched free, taking the three of us with it. Lucy blasted, snatching us up into the lock as the door began abruptly sliding shut. She stomped a red emergency panel and we hopped out of the way as another set of doors, an inch or so behind the first, closed up as well. Grateful for the double floor beneath us, we walked over to a handhold in the wall and waited for the air.

Suddenly an elephantine gout of water bashed me on the head, nearly tearing me from the strap. In an instant it was boiling around my hips with a violent swirling motion. A second more and it washed my shoulders, lapped its way past my head and filled the lock completely. A trapdoor in the ceiling far above us slid aside and I looked "up" at a fascinating scene.

Overhead reached a broad tunnel into the rock. The roiling water made it hard to judge distances visually, but the sonar in my suit said half a mile, brilliantly illuminated every inch along the way. Lucy seemed serenely unperturbed, and Koko continued uncharacteristically silent. I gulped and concentrated on viewing this thing as a horizontal tunnel, but my brain was gibberingly convinced it was the bottom of a well.

Ever *been* at the bottom of a well?

Then Lucy was off again with a churning, whizzing sound, taking both of us in tow at a respectable submarine clip. At the far end of the tunnel, I had another queasy reorientation to perform, mentally transmuting what seemed to be an endless abyssal cliff side into a shallow sea bottom, clothed in weeds of a hundred colors, shoals of shiny rainbow fish dashing in and out among them. The floor was white and sandy, the surface not far overhead, alternately sunny and reflective. There to meet us as the waterlock's inner doors rumbled shut in a cloud of well-stirred silt were a dozen killer whales, their striking black-and-white markings disguised by partially fastened smartsuits, as if they hadn't entirely trusted the damaged lock. Good judgment, in my estimation.

"Howdy," Lucy opened. "Got a place a body can set a spell?"

The largest of the creatures swam toward me, its suit a delicate complex of geometric patterns. "Greetings, Lucy Kropotkin. It is I, Reeouhoo, come to welcome you to Navigation Rock." Apparently Lucy had neglected to switch over to acoustic communications. I got her off the radio and we straightened identities around. Reeouhoo, an old acquaintance of Lucy's (and who wasn't, from the asteroids to Burbank?), was dismayed to learn about her injuries. Koko was duly introduced, and so was I—learning in the process that there had been a perfectly good airlock for land-dwellers down at the asteroid's south pole.

"Well, no harm done," chattered Lucy. "An' anyway, we got the waterlock workin' again. Saw yer broadcastin' tower, too—what's left of it." She'd settled to the bottom where a miniature submarine sand dune began collecting on her lee side. Koko was paddling around like a giant frog, while I, never the most enthusiastic of swimmers, peered up at the surface, a broken, fluttering mirror only a few yards above our heads. This would be one of the shallow ends of the pool—Lucy had mentioned depths as great as a thousand feet at the equator. "Gonna tell us how it happened?"

The giant porpoise hesitated. "We have yet to sound it out, my friend, and it is a murky situation indeed. I believe it would be best if you accompanied us to a place of rest for land-dwellers. There we can relate to you as much as we know."

Suddenly he whirled and burst into a welter of eardrum-splitting clicks and screeches. Dimly in the distance, an alien swarm appeared, unporpoiselike, and coming toward us fast.

Some inner reflex made me backwater in mounting horror as the nightmare shadows overtook us. They swirled around us in a rapidly narrowing circle and closed in. Dozens of glistening hungry tentacles enveloped Lucy first, then Koko. I whirled in shock to discover a pair of the squishy, horrifying things behind me, fended off a sucker-studded arm, and fumbled desperately for my knife.

11: A FRIEND IN NEED

Tuesday, March 16, 223 A.L.
Koko flapped her wings and giggled.

Thirty feet below her, stretched half-asleep on the sun-baked roof of the *Oahu Wahoo*, I ducked, too late to avoid the slithery missile she'd released from her toes. The sunfish hit me with a slimy *smack!* and lay there across my stomach making stupid mouthings. I shuddered and tossed it over the side, planning revenge.

The furry bombardier above me gained altitude, banked on a plastic wing, sculled fiercely for balance, then swooped to a hasty, amateurish landing on the houseboat. As she stumbled past, I contributed a strategic foot to her confusion. She followed the sunfish over the rail with a dismayed shriek and an enormous slow-motion splash. In Navigation Rock's minimal pseudogravity, there were still droplets in the air when she regained the surface, airfoils drooped in a disheveled tent around her.

"There is," I informed her placidly, "justice in the universe *after* all."

Koko spat out a salty mouthful and raised her wrist talker above the waves. "You got my pretty new wings all wet! Wait'll I tell Lucy!"

Said personage rose with a blast from the lower deck and settled beside me. "Tell me what? Say, *muchacha*, yer supposed t'be *flyin'* with them things, not swimmin'!"

The moment somehow shrank a little then, as it occurred to me how much Clarissa would have enjoyed it. I reached into my sporran on the deck, extracting a cigar: the killer whales, always looking to make an extra tenth-piece, had gene-spliced up a nicotine-producing strain of kelp. Being a generous sort, I was helping them test it. "Our aqueous aeronaut needs to practice touch-and-goes—though I suppose carrier-landings have their own peculiarities. What have you and your fishy friends been up to all morning, Lucy?"

It was going on three days since our arrival. The welcome we'd received had been expansive—if a little startling—beginning with a hair-raising jet-assist to landling territory from a squadron of Reeouhoo's pet *Loligo paelii-plus*. Maybe "pet" isn't the best word—try "artifacts," or "tools"—most sea-folk I knew well were chess pros, theoretical physicists, even opera singers, content with purely abstract strivings, and mildly derisive of the materialistic culture their fellow sapients have erected on the land. *This* delphinoid gang was different, following a pronounced mechanical bent that made them oddballs among *Cetacea*.

Reeouhoo's people were determinedly making up for the dirty evolutionary trick that had equipped them with a weighty and complex brain while depriving them of any manipulatory faculty by which they might accomplish something tangible. Thus they'd made peculiar and brilliant use of giant squid—and of that same brain-bore technology I'd classified as irredeemably disgusting only days ago.

Giant squid? Well, maybe there are monsters in the depths of Earth's great oceans who can lay better claim to the title; there's plenty of evidence for horrors hundreds of squishy feet long. Navigation Rock's were giant enough for me: four to six feet in length; just about right to make a swell pair of *hands* for killer whales. "Intelligent" peripherals. The nanoelectronics were anchored to the mantle of each cephalopod, tuned to the ultrasonic wishes of its Orca master: *tote* that barge; *push* that button and *scratch*...that's right, a little lower and to the left...*Ahh!* At cetacean frequencies, an amazing volume of information can be conveyed in a short burst. What I'd first taken for Reeouhoo's panicky shrilling had merely been ultrasonic marching orders for molluscs—I'd never have heard it at all if it weren't for my smartsuit.

We'd been whisked away by the armpits to the normal receiving area for folks with legs, a sort of south-polar high-rise, with a flivver-dock and airlock in its basement, jutting several hundred feet above the shallows that surrounded it. Naturally, this land-dweller's motel is in freefall, being at the center of rotation, and the trouble with the sea—or rather, the horizon—is that there isn't any. It keeps on going up and up and up until it's hidden in the clouds. On a clear day, you can see the north pole.

Having enjoyed my fill of weightlessness for the nonce—possibly for several nonces—I soon transferred to one of a string of houseboats tethered permanently at the equator. *Oahu Wahoo* was bright red with a phony sternwheel, a couple of potted palms on deck, and a little kitchen where I scrambled dinner for Koko and myself. (In return for which she daily hunted down the only fresh comestibles in twenty thousand miles. *I* had to do the gutting and scaling—she's even more squeamish than her boss. Yechh.) I got regular sunburns up on the roof.

Okay, technically they were *radiation* burns. The fusion torch, stuck high atop an impossibly tall and slender mast on the penthouse of the south pole hotel, had a slowly rotating cowl, so the lights went out every "night" and came back on every "morning." During the dark periods, its reflection on the ocean surface high overhead provided a handy surrogate moon.

Nice engineering.

Once or twice a day, owing to hurried business requiring a shortcut—or maybe simply out of sheer high spirits—a killer whale would erupt explosively from the depths, surge high into the mist, and then, instead of splashing down again, keep sailing skyward with the spray until it plunged spectacularly into the waves on the opposite side of the world, gouging out a foamy bullseye. A mini-tidal wave raced and rang around the hollow sea until it lapped against my boat and rocked it gently half an hour later.

The gap seemed impossibly wide, the trip often taking its passenger perilously close to the "sun," but the asteroid's gravity was low and an *Orca*'s aim unerringly accurate. They don't call it *Navigation* Rock for nothing.

Actual business was carried on far below in a series of peculiar offices. Yesterday, I'd hailed a passing *Loligo* and gone to take a peek, my apprentice tagging along. We descended until the gauges on my arm began complaining, and hovered a few dozen feet from the bottom, looking down at a sort of prestressed concrete floorplan: low walls delineating different areas of the operation; roofless cubicles filled with giant Orca-designed instrument consoles and desks. Everywhere squid were dusting away the steady rain of silt, skittering across pilot-lighted panels pushing buttons and twiddling knobs, typing, filing, hurrying plasticized memos back and forth, dodging stands of kelp, and batting at pesky fish who trespassed freely through the busy complex, often—mostly lunchtimes—to their startled demise.

Every half-hour or so, one of the cetacean technicians or supervisors would rise abruptly, rocket to the surface for a breath of air or a snack taken on-the-fin, then dive back to its post, measuring, calculating, sending, and receiving vital data from all over the System. Somewhere, I knew, a marine accountant in a cluttered cubicle would be toting up the cost and mailing out the bills—computerwise, there's no such thing as a free crunch.

Lucy had helped erect a temporary north polar antenna. Reeouhoo and his colleagues were in the dark concerning the original's destruction, an act of sabotage that hadn't been limited only to broadcasting equipment. This we'd learned that first day as we lounged on a lower, open level of the southern residential tower, enjoying drinks beside a glass-topped table and chatting with the finny folk who relaxed upon a watery shelf at our feet, washed by coriolis currents.

"Well, I'll be a wall-eyed wallaby! Them stinkers took us all in, fer fair!" Lucy had just returned from outside, accompanied by thruster-powered technicians. She'd discovered a second surprise package, about the size of a shoebox, at the *south* pole. She held it before us now, dangling by a number of carefully loosened wires.

"So it would appear," answered Reeouhoo. He sent a casual, many-tentacled "hand" racing over the waves behind him, seized an unwary surface-basking perch, retrieved it, and munched reflectively. "Of course we can repair the material damage, but I fear heartily for our reputation. Who would *do* such a thing?"

"*Hamiltonians!*" I answered, "or maybe Aphrodite, Ltd."

"Could amount to th' same thing," Lucy advised.

"I still don't get it." Koko was having trouble adjusting the straps of her wings, another experiment the enterprising Orcas hoped would stimulate a modest tourist trade.

I raised a finger. "Let me try—just to see if I've got it right, myself. It would seem, loyal assistant, that someone wanted all transportation in and out of the Belt suspended for a while—"

"*Belt? Suspended?* Boss, this conversation is going to *waist!*"

"For what reason, we do not know. Sometime in the past few months, they planted that device near a sensor array. At the right time, it began making noises like a solar flare. Nobody noticed until a later package destroyed the transmission antenna." Subsequent cross-checks with the

Rock's seventeen or eighteen major competitors—those who were back on the air—had revealed a System-wide pattern of treacherous sabotage.

The Orca gave a sort of wallowing nod. "I am chagrined. There are only a handful of artisans capable of deceiving the instruments we employ. I can think of no one among them unethical enough...The damages to System commerce alone..."

I stoked up a seaweed cigar and leaned back in the wire frame to which I'd strapped myself. "What I *don't* understand is why this little goodie didn't self-destruct when the rest of the fireworks went off." At least a dozen minor explosions had shaken the asteroid, shattering communications, crippling the small fleet of private flivvers belonging to the residents.

Lucy chuckled, a weird synthetic noise I still wasn't used to. "It sure as shingles *tried*, Winnie. From th' looks, I'd say it's been out there *more*'n a few months—it's pretty peppered up with micros." She turned the dust-pocked gadget to display a particular module. "Got a little bitty metallic rockette right here, wedged 'tween th' chasis an' th' receiver—kinda shorted out th' bang button."

"So," I mused, "we have a sophisticated, intelligent enemy doing long-range planning—but who didn't foresee a little item like the micrometeorite density in this region. Somebody who isn't from the Belt?"

"Good deducin', sonny. We're gonna *need* that devious mind of yers from here on out if we're aimin' at crackin' this scheme."

Reeouhoo whistled for another snack and nodded at me again.

ᛘ

Even such a puny effort of deduction jarred me badly: I was very well acquainted with at least one pair of Reeouhoo's tiny handful who might be technically capable of faking a solar flare, two missing friends possibly involved with the apparent opposition, Aphrodite, Ltd.

What's worse, it made me realize how out of practice I'd become. Clarissa's disappearance, assorted other traumatic events, the weirdly changing scenery, had combined to reduce my little gray cells to ineffectual sightseeing mush.

Reeouhoo wasn't the only one who should be chagrined.

Even more, I was shaken by the way I'd been taken, by friend and foe alike, for a fucking *sleigh ride*. Since leaving Laporte, I'd been harried and railroaded, steamrollered and run-around, always *re-acting*, never initiating anything. I'd been out of self-control and under the thumb of seen and unseen movers, as surely as if I'd been brain-bored myself.

It was time to change my *modus operandi*, seize events, and try to figure out exactly what the hell was going on. This asteroid seemed a perfect place for it, so I dug in my heels and stayed to sit and think and *plan*.

And get live seafood dropped in by a flying gorilla.

Okay. Item: a number of good people, particularly my wife, were AWOL. Possibly, I reminded myself, for a variety of different reasons. Possibly not.

Item: I myself had been the object of numerous, highly varied assaults upon my dignity, property, and continued longevity.

Item: some of this seemed connected to Aphrodite, Ltd., and its elusive entrepreneur, who possibly had Hamiltonian motivations. Possibly not.

Item: none of this made very much sense; if there was some conspiracy percolating, it was pretty disorganized. Take those attacks: somebody'd tried to eighty-six me with a tampered Webley (unless they'd been after Olongo), then sicced an undergunned and brain-bored pistolera on me in the bar. But smack between two murderous attempts, they'd rifled my room while I was sound asleep, without harming a single cilium on my defenseless pate—until I woke up and made a fuss.

It sure as hell complicated things, but the only rational conclusion was that there were actually *two* conspiracies, one group a bunch of rats who clabbered other people's brains and dropped shipping crates on mine. The other bunch, for reasons of their own, hesitated to kill but not to burgle— the chickens.

The Chickens and the Rats, that was it.

Fair enough: could I sort out all the things they'd done, determine which was done by whom? It might tell me what each group wanted, give me a clue to who they were. If the Rats had Ed, I'd probably never find him—better hope it was the Chickens. Olongo's pistol? The Rats, though his disappearance presented the same unanswerable questions as Ed's. The crate was a Rat-type notion, too, but it seemed sort of off-the-cuff, which clashed with the long-range attitude the solar-flare hoax implied. Did that mean the hoax was a Chicken job?

Finally, Clarissa: same questions as Ed and Olongo, to tell the uncomfortable truth—reinforced by what they'd done to our home and Propertarian h.q. So: Chickens searched people's rooms and planted fancy electronics on Navigation Rocks. With any luck (though I honestly doubted it), they also kidnapped people—*and took very good care of them.*

Rats were arsonists, used the brain-bore, attempted murder—and, yes, left Hamiltonian medallions lying carelessly around. And that, I was afraid, was another point against Ed and Olongo.

And Clarissa.

For the hundred-thousandth time, I regretted bitterly making her stay behind. My reasons had certainly seemed good enough, and went far beyond the daughter she was carrying for us now.

This wasn't the first time we'd tried. And failed.

Despite a medical technology that, from my viewpoint, borders on necromancy (or perhaps *because* of it), the Confederacy tends to bow to nature and let these tragedies happen as they will. Clarissa had suffered through three miscarriages, and I'd suffered right along beside her with all the guilt and shame and anger that's normal, despite what each of us knew professionally about the psychology of the thing.

We never came even remotely close to splitting up, as sometimes happens, but there was a strain, there was one *hell* of a strain.

And then the Healer in her seemed to take over, tearfully stubborn and cold-blooded in the oddest of circumstances. That was when she informed me flatly that she'd been keeping tissue samples from the beginning. When I finally caught on to what she was saying, I—well, I couldn't bear to watch her do the sections, but stared with fascination at the micrographs as she savagely hunted down the common genetic misprint at the center of our grief.

Then she turned around and *built* us a daughter, chromosome by chromosome, searching for and banishing every weakness she could find, taking half from me and half from herself. She made *me* flip the coin—insisted it's the father's job to determine the sex of a child.

Sentimental to the last, that girl.

⅄

That afternoon I shared my inconclusions with Lucy. Koko was off aerial spearfishing; the Orcas were busy mending interplanetary fences. She shoved a cigarette-cassette into the appropriate slot. "Don't know as I share yer reasonin', Winnie. F'rinstance, one group coulda nabbed Clarissa, an' another blew yer place up. Shows how bad things are when *that* seems like positive thinkin'."

"Yes, two separate outfits might have burgled Olongo and made *him* disappear—which implies the Chickens and the Rats are in conflict. You know, they *could* have blown up Navigation Rock altogether, if they'd wanted. That practically *proves* that—"

"These Chickens of yers are only benevolent by *comparison*, boy. This hoax has cost us Belters zillions in lost opportunities alone."

I stubbed out my cigar. "Agreed. But what's next? I *can't* go home, now, you've got me about convinced that the answer's out here. Lucy, it's time I *did* something. Problem is, I can't figure out what!"

"Well, back when th' taxpayers was involuntarily supportin' you, what would you have done?"

"Oh hell...There's Tormount—a dead end. Even Voltaire Malaise couldn't—"

"Yeah, but Malaise sure knows more'n he can broadcast—always that way with newsies: lawsuits an' so on."

"Chalk it up as a possible lead. What else have we got?"

"A solid line right to th' kidnappers. Ed found 'em, didn't he?"

"They found *him*. If I retraced his steps, how could we avoid getting grabbed ourselves? Shit: loose ends scattered all *over* the System. A thousand detectives couldn't—"

"No, but how about a thousand *ex-Congress critters*? Looks like Hamiltonian trouble—betcha we could holler up a *passel* of help over that. Can't do it from here, though. We're too modulatin' vulnerable, an' I'd wanna use m'own I S & R jimcrackery, anyway."

"Information Storage and Retrieval—you mean on your own asteroid?"

"Good ol' *Bulfinch*—'thall th' gods an' goddesses they were namin' rocks after, figured I'd just finish off th' list in one swell foop. It's *real* well defended, Winnie—if I'd stayed home, I'da never got gunned down in th' first place."

"Now you're talking. Let's collect Koko. You start rounding up the cavalry, and I'll follow Ed's leads—*very* carefully. I'll even brace Malaise and find out what he's not telling civilization. How's that sound?"

"What I wanted t'do all along—only you were all fer hightailin' it Earth-side."

I gathered my belongings and flagged a squid for transportation to the Airlock Motel while Lucy sank sedately beneath the waves to inform our hosts. She also put out a call for Koko.

Seven hours later, my assistant *still* hadn't shown up. The Orcas stopped looking when they found her wings folded and tucked beneath a submarine bush of some kind, and held down by a rock. A counter at the northern lock said someone had cycled it roughly two hours before Lucy and I decided it was time to leave.

Ed's Ad Astra was no longer in orbit around Navigation Rock. The only person besides the two of us who knew how to start the engines without being blown to confetti was my loyal assistant. In its place was a standard distress transponder flashing idiotically, its radio voice silenced by a slash of the sidecutters.

Inside was a note, written on the kind of thermoplastic paper used inside the aquatic asteroid.

Dear Boss and Lucy:

I wish I could say how Sorry this makes me, but there really isn't any choice. Some Things take precedence over others. If I could only tell you more—but the Cause I'm working for is Important and we must have Secrecy for a while yet. Someday you all will be able to forgive me. At least I hope so.

Koko

12: THAT'S THE WAY IT LOOKS

Half an hour later the south pole airlock irised closed behind a spaceship twice the average flivver's tonnage, which practically dismantled itself regurgitating Telecom equipment, makeup people, rewrite artists, flunkies, and technicians of at least four different species.

And—last but not least—the august personage himself, Voltaire Malaise.

August or September, the Most-Trusted-Newsman-In-The-System would've stood out in a crowd like that one, if for no other reason than that he alone, of all the participants and spectators (Lucy and me among them), disdained to wear a smartsuit. He stepped down in his legendary brown beat-up serape and battered gray Stetson, beneficently surveying the worshipful throng with visible satisfaction.

Patton could have make an entrance like that. Or Alice Cooper.

Bestowing upon his admirers one final noble gaze, he took the nearest elevator into the asteroid, and the crowd evaporated in a sort of reverential hush. I signaled Lucy and we drifted to the lift ourselves, half-expecting to be following a trail of rose petals.

Five cigar butts and a fish sandwich later, I found myself staring down at my own business card, being returned to me in the service corridor where I'd been kept simmering for hours. One Roger Benton, a fellow with a permanently worried look, chief accomplice and weekend pinch-hitter to the Voice of the Stars, tendered his apologies. "Mr. Bear, I didn't even get a chance to bring it up. He's got a touch of bronchitis—the humidity in this impossible place—and needs a rest before beamtime."

Lucy was the smart one—she'd stepped out for a lube job or a henna rinse or whatever she was getting these days. "Look, did you say I was investigating Aphrodite, Ltd.? He did a couple of pieces on the subject not too long ago and came up pretty empty.'" There've been U.S. Presidents more accessible than Malaise was turning out to be.

The System's best-known bridesmaid swallowed and looked at his watch. "Tell you what: come on down. We're setting up in the lobby. Try and stay out of the way, maybe he'll give you a minute after the 'cast. Will that do?"

"Guess it'll have to." I lit another stogie on the same attention-getting principle that generates deliberately annoying commercials—maybe they'd give me what I wanted just to get rid of me—and followed him to the elevator. Downstairs it was a regular Pentagon fire drill, tangled-up machinery, technicians snarling hysterically, more trailing cable snaking across the carpet than you could swing a whole jungleful of Tarzans by. And, no matter how technology progresses, TV people still feel the need for enough light to bleach the hairs inside your nose. I found a darkened, relatively quiet corner and parked myself.

The whole asylum suddenly fell silent as the Journalissimo manifested himself in a ten-ounce smoky-silver tunic, tastefully selected to match his eyebrows. Or perhaps the other way around. He paused ceremoniously here and there, dispensing pleasantries and personal advice upon those who couldn't defend themselves, made his way to the focus of all those bright lights, draped his jacket on the back of a complicated, gimmicky chair, and sat down in his pinstriped shirt-sleeves to pass judgment on a stack of hardcopy some humble scriptperson had laid before him.

He looked up just once, directly at me, an odd perplexity in his gray-blue eyes, shook his head, and returned to the stopwatch in his hand. Occasionally he'd slash the copy with a stylus and read it softly to himself, stopping frequently to suppress a lingering cough. Seen this close, he remained the same stern grandfather North Americans had grown up watching and believing for half a century: sandy-gray—was it a hairpiece?—bushy salt-and-pepper eyebrows; a gritty little semivisible mustache that made him look just like a branch manager of Confederate Mutual Life. Beneath the wise and weathered face, he favored neutral, conservative attire—a swell trick in this particular corner of the universe. Even his deep midwestern voice had the same sandy-gray quality, an inexorability that had become the standard for Confederate enunciation. In a culture almost totally devoid of authority figures, despite the competition of a thousand other networks, his word carried the weight of divine revelation.

Earlier that morning, when Navigation Rock first got wind of his intentions, I'd taken time to look him up in the *Encyclopedia of North America*. Born in 140 A.L., he'd been a print reporter long before going electronic just in time for the 1957 War Against the Czar. "He'd landed with Confederate volunteers in Antarctica and parachuted into the Kingdom of Hawaii when the Russian-supported Hamiltonians were driven into the sea. He'd been with Admiral Heinlein, a fellow Missourian, at the Battle of the Bering Straits.

Impressed by the Confederate Lunar colonists' use of propaganda to finish off the Czar, he became an enthusiastic space advocate, although it had taken him nearly thirty years to get out here himself. Now his daily programs from Ceres Central were a fixture. To many, Malaise was the very soul of credibility, a veritable walking catalog of Boy Scout virtues, the single most convincing and authoritative person on the 'com. To some few curmudgeons, he appeared brisk, remote, self-important gravity personified. It was rumored that his rivals called him Titanpants.

Well, you can't please everybody.

Abruptly now, he set aside his stylus, stretched, and slickerseamed his jacket. An attendant brought him mouthwash in a baggie. He gargled, spat, and sat again, precisely at the instant that a chimp wearing a headset pointed a hairy finger at his solar plexus.

"Good evening. Twenty thousand miles above the golden face of Ceres hangs the nerve center of interplanetary transportation, Navigation Rock. We're here tonight to report a series of bizarre events that..."

From there he told about the installation's failure, the evidence of sabotage, and what was being done about the damage. A 'com screen behind him flashed with views of the asteroid's inside-out ocean, the killer whales responsible for the guidance and safety of half the System. Regular news followed; Malaise introduced each segment, and in between, with the studio cameras off, conferred in quiet tones with his assistants, touching up his notes as he received the latest on a dozen different developing stories.

⅄

Tuesday, March 16, 223 A.L.

At last, the famous sign-off: "That's the way it looks. This is Voltaire Malaise, good night."

Then they did the whole thing over again for relay to those planetoids out of range on the "other side" of the sun. When the lights finally went out, somebody brought Malaise a towel and a sandwich that would have been architecturally impossible on Earth. I saw Roger Benton whisper something urgently and point in my direction across the expropriated lobby. Malaise frowned, gave Benton a few sharp words, and vanished into the next room, rubbing his back and coughing.

I'd been robbed. Again.

The System's number one second banana sadly shook his head all the way over to where I was sitting. "Mr. Bear, I—"

"Bet you say that to all the detectives." I got up and relit my cigar, trying to think how Humphrey Bogart would have done this: "Look, sweetheart, I'm gonna see him, one way or the other. For the time being, I'm asking nice, see?" (Was that a little Edward G. Robinson sneaking in there at the end? Nyahh.)

Benton fussed and fluttered in a way that had me wondering. I was just a P.I., after all—*I'd*'ve told me where to get off. Suddenly he brightened. "Er, uh...wait a minute, I've just had an idea!" With this he practically ran out of the lobby. When he came back fifteen minutes later, he looked positively reprieved. "It's all set. I remembered what you said about your flivver being stolen. Well, *we'll* take you and your friend back to Ceres. Voltaire gets rather bored unless he's piloting himself—which the network's insurance won't allow—maybe he'll find it diverting to talk with a real detective for a couple of hours. How's that?"

"Friend, I was ready to kiss this marble good-bye hours ago. Meet you at the south pole—I'll be the third penguin on the left." I started to walk away, then stopped: "And Roger, we're all rootin' for you. Old Voltaire can't last forever."

♠

"*Stop, smiling—we don't do 'happy news' here!*" Malaise took another pull at his baggie, then folded his arms across his chest. Hoarseness had crept back into his voice and his back was apparently still bothering him. "Drives me out of my excretion-coated ever-loving mind. Blast it, why didn't somebody *tell* me you were taking a shot at Aphrodite? You'd think they all work for another bloody network!"

I grinned, reluctantly liking this irritable shirt-sleeved Scotch-drinker who inserted what serves Confederates for profanity into every off-camera sentence. Old Voltaire wasn't so bad after all, and neither was his whiskey. Lucy had absorbed somewhat more than a drop or two through her internal nutrient system and settled down in a comer by the bulkhead behind us, making soft humming noises.

Just resting her eyes.

Malaise pointed at the autopsy report I'd been carrying around since the *Bonaventura*, along with terrifying holos from Dr. Scott. "Read me that again, the part about the woman self-destructing. Great Albert's ghost, how long's this technology been kicking around without anybody noticing?"

Once aboard the network cruiser, I'd begun filling him in on recent history, bits and pieces he immediately decided added up to some "grand conspiracy against Civilization." Lucy's somewhat hyperprosthetic condition had added a certain amount of credibility. He'd reported her "assassination" himself, the night it happened.

"Which shows I'm right," he concluded bitterly, "and the network's wrong. We have to be more incisive, do more checking. If this'd been caught by another net...I'm going to get on it right away, and Bear, let this be a lesson to you: I'm not an unimpeachable authority on anything. But plague take me, as long as I'm managing editor of this madhouse, I'm going to bloody well *try!*" He twisted painfully and shouted back over his shoulder, "Do you people hear me, *we're bloody well going to try!*"

That's one thing his staff seemed to agree about in private: Voltaire Malaise was trying. He'd done a sort of double-take when I stepped aboard his cruiser, as if wondering where the hell he'd seen me before. God knows I'm used to it; I've got a sort of standard-issue mug. Then he'd quieted down, folded his arms, and listened off and on for a solid hour, nodding here, shaking his head there, as I reeled off my adventures.

There were continuous interruptions: the guy had been *born* asking "what's new" and was foully impatient at even the small degree this excursion (the net's idea, he grumbled) was keeping him out of touch. Every other minute he got updates, drafts of pieces planned for the next beamcast. He'd read them, making corrections: "Soften that ending a little" or "That's bullshit, and everybody knows it."

I was surprised at the ruthless way he screened his personal opinions out. He was a pro—insisting on the title "managing editor" and no other—and told me there were only two kinds of people in the world (I agree: those who say "there are only two kinds of people in the world," and...), professionals and amateurs. The Confederacy, in his view, was history's first *amateur* civilization, and he didn't much like it.

"They all think they can casually switch from farming or mining to construction, banking—Constitution take 'em, even to *newscasting*—any time the mood hits 'em. Bloody dilettantes don't understand a division-of-labor economy, specialization. Nobody respects *credentials* any more! Maybe it's true after all —the public's a great beast and shouldn't be allowed even to vote."

I laughed. "Well, we're very nearly there. Nothing left to vote on, really." And much the same was true back in the States—except that it'd been accomplished differently: only about 10 percent of the electorate were expected to turn out next year. Propertarians thought it was a good sign.

"We could be *moving*," answered Malaise, "on the march, outward to the stars. Instead, precious time and energy get wasted, dissipated, fiddling around in a country that hasn't anything to do with us."

"The States? I wouldn't exactly call that a waste. I wouldn't be here without that 'fiddling.'"

Abruptly, Lucy took an interest in the proceedings. "The stars are mighty patient, sonny, an' anyway, that time an' energy you're reallocatin' so casual-like belongs t'private individuals. Shucks, they may think goin' to th' *stars* is a waste, mightn't they?"

The newsman glowered. "Which only proves the limitations of amateurs. Blast it, woman, they're *wrong*, somebody needs the authority to make them see it!" He slammed his half-filled baggie to the floor, where it lay wiggling like hospital jello.

"Hold on there, boy! As I recall, we had a Revolution or two settled just that little point."

"What if we did? Circumstances change. Times are different now, and—What's that, Roger?"

Benton had come up behind him with a Telecom pad emitting groans and whistles of a particularly repulsive nature. "It's those signals, sir. The ones from interstellar space. They've started up again."

It was hard to say for sure, but for some reason Malaise seemed a touch paler. "You *know* I don't report on crap like that. It's stale information, and won't be relevant again until the signals are translated—if there's anything to translate there. They haven't been, have they, Roger?"

Now I saw why Benton looked unhappy all the time. He stared down at his feet and sighed. "No sir, this is just a new—"

"Then take that thing away and don't bring it back until somebody can tell me what it *means!*" He turned toward me as Benton slunk away. "*Amateurs!* Sometimes I think that kid'd be better off hustling used flivvers."

I eventually got through to the end of my story, more or less in sequence. I finished up with Koko's—well, defection you might call it.

"Featherstone-Haugh, you say?" He seemed genuinely startled. "First the President of the Confederacy—we should have known about that—and then his...?"

"Niece. I don't know what the hell is going on, but— Listen, those space signals really give me the willies, too, I—"

"Bear, I misjudged you. You have a professional's eye for detail, and you're not too bloody bad at doping out the angles. But we're going to have to cut this short." He readjusted the straps of his special chair, the same one he'd used for the beamcast. "My back is killing me, and I'd better try to get a little sleep. You and Mrs. Kropotkin, here, help yourself to the bar. I'm going aft."

And that, as they say, was that.

ᛉ

Wednesday, March 17, 223 A.L.

Next day, Lucy and I were outbound again from Port Piazzi in a borrowed Tucker Thracian, heading for Bulfinch 4137. It was going to be a longish trip, and I'd been watching movies on my Gigacom for about three hours when I noticed it was newstime. I tuned the flivver's Telecom, wondering if Voltaire would mention anything I'd told him yesterday. The picture blossomed into life and there was the *wrong* familiar face:

"—Roger Benton, substituting for Voltaire Malaise. At the top of the news, Voltaire Malaise, 83, veteran fifty-year journalist and Managing Editor of the Ceres Central Evening News, *has vanished without a trace.* Network security police report signs of a violent struggle in the missing beamcaster's apartment."

And speaking of violent struggles, that's exactly what Benton was going through now, trying to suppress his sheer, undiluted glee.

13: BASALT OF THE EARTH

Bulfinch 4137 was a chunk of carbonaceous chondrite whose main excuse for existence seemed to be holding about a billion assorted craters together. Call it an incompetently squashed-out hamburger patty two miles across, maybe half that thickness; eight thousand acres that Lucy and Ed (when he was in) called Home Sweet Homestead.

One face was splashed by an enormous impact crater, fully half the asteroid's diameter, around which rambled their makeshift-looking house, a miniature landing port, and the Mine All Mine, surrounded by nondescript heavy machinery. The obverse of the little world, sporting four gigantic silvery water storage tanks, was carpeted in nitrogen-fixing corn and wheat, hemp, and Lucy's cash crop, opium poppies.

She nosed the rented Tucker toward the plastic atmospheric envelope, aiming for a big red-decaled bull's-eye: "Won't be a minute now, Winnie. Watch out th' window."

There wasn't much to see until we made gentle contact. Then, the target-marked portion of the envelope became a bulging funnel under our engine's steady pressure, sweeping backward from the hood ornament to swallow us up until we were hanging only a few hundred feet above the rocky surface. Behind us, the plastic funnel was closing in, the bull's-eye shrinking to a dot. Suddenly, the material beneath us ruptured, admitting our little spaceship without losing a single cubic foot of precious atmospheric gas.

And now I knew what an amoeba's dinner feels like.

Lucy hovered a while to let me watch the plastic stalactite shrink skyward like silly putty in reverse.

Then she put the nose up and set us neatly in a landing area gouged out beside the big crater.

"Now listen, boy, don't let the pretty scenery deceive ya—ain't 'nough gravity out there t'anchor down a postage stamp. Step out too smartly, you'll wind up bumpin' yer head on th' sky. An' it'll snap y'back hard enough t'break yer whatsit. Use yer sticky feet, an' have a care."

I nodded absently. Through some optical chicanery, the sky was a beautiful rich blue. The asteroid's unimproved surface was a dirty grayish-brown, but in scattered crater bottoms, bushes, grass, and at least a hundred spindly, ridiculously skinny trees relieved the eye. We slipped out of the flivver and began picking our way toward the house, which was bigger than I'd thought, at least a hundred feet on a side, and even then, dwarfed by a pearly dome that stood behind it.

Lucy went walking on her hands, along a chiseled stairlike trail to a broad landing. There an odd three-legged contraption rested, a Thorneycroft utility Rockhopper, according to the nameplate, painted, to suit mine hostess's lack of taste, a garish yellow paisley. It was parked before a cluster of rugged concrete structures and a more finished-looking translucent hemisphere, which together made up the ranchhouse.

"Started out with that there pour-fab," Lucy said, pointing toward one of the massive cement cubes. "Hadda cast it centrifugally in freefall an' set it down real gentle-like. Lived there fer three solid years. It's a barn now—an' there's m'Stairway to th' Stars!" An impressive metal tower on the barren crater's central peak seemed to reach up even through the atmospheric envelope. "Usta mount th' shackles fer th' Drexler lightsail that drug this rock into our orbit—"

"*Your* orbit?"

"Sure. Shucks, Winnie, so many planetoids out here, they're practically free fer th' takin'. It's the good *locations* cost money. I was gonna use that tower fer an elevator an' dockin' platform, but they went an' invented dilatin' plastics." She chuckled. "Been thinkin' of upholsterin' the crater in tinfoil—gimme th' biggest sun-powered barbecue in th' System."

"So that's why you haven't done any landscaping out there. Looks like the backside of the Moon." Lunatic image of our satellite mooning the rest of the System—maybe I just needed more sleep.

"Well, it wouldn't do t'make *everything* look like Earth, would it, Winnie? All th' same, someday they're gonna figger out how t'localize gravity, an' when they do, that crater's gonna be m'*lake*. Be real pretty, don'tcha think?"

More visions, this time of trout bumping their heads on the sky, but I kept them to myself.

We entered the house through an ordinary door, but there was gasketing around its edges and an emergency canister of oxygen hanging on the wall beside a fire extinguisher. This room, one of the concrete blockhouses, had a transparent ceiling and seemed to be a greenhouse or conservatory. Lucy stopped suddenly. I avoided bumping into her, but wound up flailing around in the air until she fished me down.

"What's the matter, Lucy?" I shook my head, trying to reorient myself.

"Shh!" She glided forward cautiously, drawing her .50 caliber pistol. I slid my Webley out of its holster and followed her example, creeping softly. There was something wrong, all right: half the plants, petroleum-bearing cousins of the latex tree, were uprooted from their beds and plastered in a dried-out tangle against the ventilation grillework. Even where the giant "seedlings" were still in place, the soil and its retainer-netting had been gouged out brutally.

"Some uninvited worm-turd's been diggin' fer treasure!" Lucy patrolled the aisles, grumbling angrily to herself as she pushed the freefalling greenery aside. At the end of fifteen minutes, she hadn't found anything to shoot at, so we repeated the performance two short flights of stairs higher, weapons at the ready.

Here, in the dome, the clutter and destruction were only a little less organic in character. Furniture, bric-a-brac, plastic documents floated everywhere in the negligible gravity, stirred up by our passage. A skeletal steel framework divided the plentiful space into several lofts and levels, the bottom being the living room where we had entered. Immediately above our heads were the library computer and Lucy and Ed's office areas.

Which is where I found the body.

Now I've been finding bodies all my life—or looking at them after other people found them. That's what a homicide cop gets paid for. That, and finding out who done it. I've seen them in every state of post-demise, from warm and pink to green and gooey; every single one of them made me want to throw up.

I often got my wish.

In that respect, this customer wasn't any different; the only thing keeping me out of a state of reverse-peristalsis was thinking about the mess it'd make in a thousandth or a millionth of a gee or whatever this was. The guy was hanging, face to the outer wall, by a nail or screw where his open smartsuit hood had caught as he'd gone sailing by it. No blood, but his cranium was sort of squishy, the result of violent contact with an anvil or some reasonable facsimile. What made him unique was that he was a *cop*, or as close as asteroidal anarchism comes to it: I recognized the tannish program Ranger Trayle's suit had worn. The patch above his breast pocket said "Rothbard's Security Patrol."

"Lucy? Put that sofa down somewhere and get up here."

"Sure thing, Winnie." She didn't bother with the spiral ladder. As she passed my level in a snowstorm of magazines and sheet-plastic, she shot an arm out and grabbed the railing. "Whatcha got now, Winnie—Oh, my lights and liver!"

"It's more a matter of *who*, Lucy. Recognize this guy?"

She dragged herself inboard and took a closer look. "Why, that's Ranger Trayle, Win. Somebody's stove his head in—with a real stove, looks like. An' he was such a nice young feller."

"I'll take your word for it. This isn't the Ranger Trayle I talked to. If the body weren't so fresh, I'd guess he died just a little before my conversation—with an impostor—well over a week ago."

"No takers. Yer fergittin' his smartsuit, Inspector—though a good pathologist could still...Oh, well, guess I better call th' Patrol. Reckon they been wonderin' about him." She slid toward the edge of the balcony.

"Reckon. And take a lesson learned the hard way—make sure you really know who you're talking to. Rothbard's a plump, curly-headed little guy with—"

"With a chuckle like a horny-toad in heat. Gotcha."

Call me sentimental, the main thing on my mind was what a space-going ambulance would look like. Make that a hearse: this former person was way beyond the talents even of Confederate medicine, and only his smartsuit was keeping him from making an olfactory spectacle of himself.

Ain't science wonderful.

Customs being what they are, I had no legal obligation to leave things as I'd found them. Besides, I was as good at this sort of thing as any Confederate pseudocop, and considerably more experienced, given the comparative crime rates of the U.S. and the N.A.C. I gave the deceased a once-over. In the pockets of his suit (which garment, eerily enough, had begun fading back to neutral silver-gray), I found his patrol ID, a little hard money (the richest kind), and various personal effects uninteresting to anyone but his next of kin. The weapon on his hip, in my opinion, marked him for something of a tenderfoot—which made some sense of his present lamented condition: a plasma gun, the very *latest* thing, and by all accounts not entirely accurate or reliable. No matter, he'd never even had the chance to take it from the holster.

Lucy made the call and was again attempting to restore some order to the mess we'd found downstairs. I hollered at her not to tidy up the evidence too much and did an Errol Flynn over the rail to give her a hand. Four hours later I concluded sadly that if there were any clues to be discovered in this place, they'd been repossessed by the finance company. Our intruder hadn't smoked while he was here—a novelty in a culture unafraid of cancer—or drunk, or even, as far as my modest abilities were able to discern, used the bathroom. Maybe he was royalty. Or a movie star. Or Superman. Or a ghost.

Or the ghost of Superman.

Another thing struck me: much as I hate to think about it, I've seen about a hundred instances where some little old lady's been toes-up for days without the neighbors noticing, and, given forty-eight hours or so without his Alpo, little Spot or Rover winds up munching on his erstwhile mistress. I wasn't sure about cats, but Lucy's hadn't touched a morsel. Maybe it was the smartsuit. Or maybe felines think they're citizens, and eschew cannibalism. It was probably that automated food supply in the kitchen.

I draped myself on a chair in a corner to mull things over. Speak of the devil, it wasn't too much later that old Lysander, Lucy's venerable roommate, hopped delicately into my lap.

I rubbed the thinly carpeted spaces in front of his ears as he squinged his eyes and hummed the lyrics. "Well, old-timer, if only you could talk. You watched the whole damn thing, I saw you on the Telecom. What's the matter, *human* got your tongue?" He gave me a disapproving look and proceeded to launder his toes. I could remember when he'd had a preference for perching on my head and was glad he'd finally given it up—freefall had been entirely too good for him, he massed twenty pounds if he massed an ounce.

"Cmon, Lysander, who wasted our gallant Ranger?" Lysander switched to his other paw, offsetting a tendency to drift by digging his hind claws into my leg. Another reason to be grateful for smartsuits. "Hey, Lucy?"

That worthy was across the room shoving plastic hardcopies into some kind of machine. "Just a minute, Winnie. You 'bout ready fer somethin' t'eat?"

Above my head somewhere, Ranger Trayle's body was still cooling off. "Uh, not right away." I excused myself to the cat, lifted him gently and set him in my place in the chair. He went on washing his paws as if I'd never existed in the first place. "I was going to ask you, out of morbid curiosity, about Lysander's sanitary arrangements, here in, oh, call it 'semifall.' Must be pretty messy."

She stopped feeding flimsies for a moment. "Go on back in th' utility room an' see fer yourself—-my own ingenious invention, if I do say so, as shouldn't—but gimme a hand with this donkey-work first, will you, son?" So I wound up stuck there for another hour and a half, handing printed plastic sheets to Lucy: correspondence, bills, all kinds of other stuff. She inserted them one at a time into the machine to be digitalized, filed, and cross-indexed, and at the other end—my favorite part—shredded and conveyed to the plantrooms for mulch. *Sic semper* paperwork. This would be a popular export, once we started trading openly with the U.S.A.

"Been meanin' t'get at this fer months. Here's one of Eddie's workups on th' disappearances." She slapped it into the machine.

"Hey wait! I wanted to see that!"

"Sorry. Call it back again on one of th' 'com pads over there." She gave me the reference coordinates; I disturbed Lysander once again and sat down. Naturally, he wanted to park himself in the middle of the pad, so I picked him up and hung him in midair where, if I was patient enough, I could watch him fall and even hit the floor—in a half-hour or so. He curled up comfortably on nothing and shut his eyes, well content to sleep through the excitement.

What Lucy had shredded was several sheets of handwritten notes on unexplained disappearances among the asteroids over the last year or so. Even sorting out the normal background occurrences, the list was impressive—and I'd never quite gotten used to seeing someone else's doodlings in *my* handwriting. "You know, I think we've been wasting time scouting around for *positive* clues. Whoever dug up your petrol trees was looking for something. Have you found anything missing around here?"

She swiveled, fixing me with invisible optics. "Now how could it be missing if I'd found it?"

"All right, wise-ass, you know what I mean. Anything at all?"

She paused. "Haven't really thought about it Could be a thousand things in all this mess. Anything useful in them notes of Eddie's?"

"Yeah! For example, why did he order several hundred ounces worth of Broach-detecting gizmology? Did he ever get it?"

"Couldn't rightly say. Remember, I was gone at the time. Oughta be an invoice or somethin', less'n it's scattered out with all these other papers. One thing I hate, it's messy burglars."

"*Murderers,* Lucy. Burglars have a little more class." I climbed back up a level, past the remains of Ranger Trayle—when were those blasted "authorities" going to get here?—and found my way to Ed's desk, a heavy piece of metal furniture with a built-in swing-out stool and Telecom peripherals. The main drawer had been nixoned open, crushed down with some kind of power lever that tore it out of its tracks. Amidst the scattered paper clips and erasers, I found a yellow plastic invoice, just as Lucy had predicted, acknowledging shipment from one of Mars's industrial centers in the big, continent-long canyon where they say the air is actually getting thick enough to breathe.

If you're a virus or a cockroach. Progress marches on.

"Lucy, can you spare a minute? I want to find out if the stuff actually arrived here."

"Be up in two shakes of a shaman's rattle." Ten seconds later she was clucking electronically over the noncomputerized rat's nest Ed had allowed to build up. I don't know what his excuse is. My desk at home looks just the same because I'm always afraid I'll entrust something important to the 'com and not be able to summon it up again.

"That's funny."

"Lucy, very little is *funny* when there's a stiffening corpse floating six feet from your left shoulder and you're going over the contents of a burglarized desk."

"I ain't *got* no shoulders right now, an' I don't mean funny ha ha. I'll tell you what's missing; it's that Federalist geegaw I showed you on th' Telecom. I left it where I found it, second drawer down, an' now it's vamoosed."

Interesting. That might explain why the bottom drawer had remained undefiled. "You know, an awful lot of mayhem has been associated with these little medals over the years." I reached down into a pocket and extracted the medallion from the *Bonaventura.* I still hadn't decided whether they'd dropped it accidentally or left it as bait. "Damn eye in the pyramid, always gives me the creeps. Say, I never noticed before: the knurled rim is actually a separate piece and turns around the rest of the— Lucy?"

"*Urrrk!* Greeshbobble n'frammish glork, Winstead!" With that, she started spinning, whirling dizzily in larger and larger circles. I looked down at the coin and a light suddenly dawned. I gave the rim a quick quarter-turn back to where it had started just as Lucy crashed through the flimsy railing and toppled over the edge.

"Great thunderin' balls afire!" She blasted her impellers, righted herself, scattering half the papers we'd sorted out below, and, regaining equilibrium, thrust out a manipulator. "Gimme that thing afore y'ruin me!"

I reached out gingerly and handed her the medallion, which she clutched defensively to her nonexistent bosom. "What's going on, Lucy?"

"Nothin' special—*I just totally lost control of m' whole body!* Win, when we were lookin' at that infernal brain-bore, back on Ceres, we were only seein' *half* of what was goin' on. This medal here's th' other half. *It's what gives th' orders!*"

14: SOUP OF THE MORNING, POISONOUS SOUP

How Lucy ever trained the kitty to a freefall litterbox...It was sort of a half-gee miniature cement-mixer with an open end so Lysander could climb in and out. Every now and again, an automated vacuum cleaner would whisk the contents out through the dome wall into a farm-bound trajectory and replace them with fresh-ground asteroid.

But that wasn't half as interesting as the hole above it in the paratronic deepfreeze, precisely at heart level and punched cleanly into the enameled metal surface. Inside, the slug had stopped in a plastic carton of quince yogurt: full copper jacket, about 130 grains, .356 in diameter, as American as pizza pie.

There were only three commercial cartridges I knew with a payload like that, one of them nine decades obsolete. The other two were military-issue .38 Special, one an oddball bastard with a cannelure, or crimping-groove, around the middle of the slug to hold it in the case—and insufficient powder to drive it even halfway through that freezer door, and the other a much more efficient, autoloading item originally designed for Treasury agents who wanted something that'd get into gangsters' armored limousines. Six grooves, lefthand twist. This penny-colored goodie rolling around in the palm of my hand hadn't come from any revolver. Unlike the otherworldly weapons I'd encountered so far, it was a professional's choice. Maybe they were calling in their first string.

Which, I reluctantly concluded, made it necessary to re-examine the late Ranger Trayle and reconsider this head-injury business. Lucy watched; the body turned easily in the absence of even *dead* weight, its opened smartsuit exposing, as I'd expected, an ugly purple-puckered hole in the lower right chest. The suit had sealed up and tried to treat it, but the high-velocity projectile had virtually exploded the liver—a certain death wound—but none too quick, and very painful. Trayle had been on the run; his massive skull fracture had come in a chance collision with Ed's desk or something of that sort. Given the circumstances, it was probably a blessing. A little careful snoopery turned up hair and dried blood along the rail of the mezzanine.

My appetites and aptitudes don't generally include post-mortem augury, but the size of the wound, smack on the nine-millimeter mark (allowing for the skin's elastic properties), was all I needed to see: Confederate weapons either run a lot bigger or a lot smaller (and commensurately faster) or, like lasers or Trayle's own Flash Gordon blart-and-bonkus blaster, leave even uglier wounds, if such comparisons are possible.

A .38 Super Automatic, then, a Hartford Colt: either a Government model or the short, lightweight Commander—with a Spanish Star or Llama as extremely marginal alternatives—made in U.S.A. The suit had absorbed the blood and other body fluids, trying to save its wearer, but now, in some nanoelectronic sense, was dying, itself.

By the time I'd had enough and decided to leave the rest of the carving to whatever medicos finally arrived, Lucy was ready to conduct another experiment. She'd cobbled up something she called a Franklin cage, grounded it on a balcony rail, and placed the Hamiltonian medallion inside. "Okay, Winnie, turn th' plague-blasted thing on—I wanna see if I can take it." She handed the infernal instrument to me and slid a few feet away.

"Lucy, you're either going to fry your brains or wind up bashing into something, very possibly me." I looked at the medallion in its hastily spot-welded container. "Why don't we send for some proper test equipment?"

"We got company comin' any minute now. 'Sides, I gotta whole workshop fulla gear downstairs if I thought it'd tell us anything useful. You ready?"

"No. Brace yourself." I reached between the bars, careful to avoid the neck chain Lucy believed was an antenna, and clumsily turned the edge of the coin.

"Nothing—give 'er another twist."

"It's your funeral."

"Already used up m'quota of *them*. That thing just ain't gettin' through. Twist it all th' way."

I fumbled compliantly; Lucy shuddered a little. "Well, my visualizin's 'bout half occluded with snow, like fringey Telecom reception. Feel a bit contrary in th' joints, too. Step a coupa feet closer, will ya?"

I didn't like that slur in her speech, but shrugged and sticky-footed over as far as the ground cable permitted. "Feel anything now?"

Silence.

"Lucy, *say* something!"

"*Some. Thing.*" Otherwise, she didn't move.

"Uh, raise your right, er, arm, please." How was I going to live with myself if she was permanently injured by this thing? Her right manipulator cranked slowly ceilingward. I twisted the rim back to its original position and placed it on the floor like some kind of poisonous snake. "Lucy, are you all right?"

"*Bet yer lice-infested crotch* I am!" She snatched the cage and all but tore it apart getting at the coin. Turning modestly, she opened her built-in gunport and tucked the medallion into a recess beside the artillery. "Nobody *else* gonna start pullin' m'strings while I got somethin' t'say about it!"

I tried to repress a shiver. "What was it like?"

"You asked me t'say somethin' an' plague if I didn't come back involuntarily with a bad joke. Then y'asked me t'raise m'arm, wasn't nothin' I could do but...*obey*, Winnie, *me*! That thing's *dangerous*. Give th' bureaucrats a cartonload, they'd have us all marchin' around like little tin soldiers inside a week."

"Looks like Ed was on to something really nasty. What did it *feel* like, Lucy, I mean while the thing was operating?"

"*Terrible!* I was madder'n a nesta riled-up yellerjackets, Winnie, coulda kilt you cheerfully. A body under th' influence *knows* it, hates it, an' can't do a flea-bitten thing about it. Second most horrible thing I ever went through!"

Now I knew she was all right—and I wasn't about to hand her a straight line for free. I pulled a cigar out, lit it casually and enjoyed a puff or two. But she outlasted me, after all: "Okay, what *was* the first, dammit?"

"The first what? Oh, that. You don't wanna know. I'll just say th' next bastard nominates me fer th' Presidency better be faster on th' draw than I am. Was a pretty near thing—'None of the Above' beat me only by a single vote: *mine*!"

"I'll decide later whether to believe that. Any idea why this medallion gets only to you, and not to me or the cat?" Lysander had taken off like a scorched tachyon when Lucy started acting funny—funnier than usual, that is.

"Winnie, you disappoint me. Anybody with th' brains of a finely diced planarian could—"

"*Thanks*, Lucy."

"Y'see, what's keepin' me alive is basically th' same technology as that brain-bore thingummy. Shucks, ain't even a choice of control-frequencies—that's all determined by th' neurophysics of th' situation. Anybody wired up right's a sucker, plain an' simple, get it?"

I got it, but didn't have to like it. At least there were some limits to this; we weren't all going to wind up zombies day after tomorrow. I gave some thought to sleeping in a football helmet for the next few years. At that moment the doorbell started squawking—well, a little adrenaline's good for you—announcing the impending arrival of what passed for the authorities. They were asking for permission to come aboard.

In twelve years, I *still* hadn't gotten used to polite cops.

Lucy went to answer. I finally found Lysander anchored to the ceiling by his toenails, batting at a small shiny object he'd discovered. I kicked myself into orbit, admiring my new-found dexterity at such things, to see what had taken his fancy. Three midcourse corrections and a pair of barked shins later, I had it, an empty, pinky-size, semirimmed, nickel-plated brass cartridge case inscribed: CDM .38 AUTO. Interesting. Confederate cases are all mild-steel or titanium.

ᴧ

We found Ed's Broach-detecting equipment spread out in the work-shop where he'd set it up during Lucy's prolonged professional absence. Once the local Civil Liberties custodians had appropriated the Ranger's body and taken depositions from the both of us, we hurried down and Lucy started twisting knobs and throwing switches. Neither of us was surprised when the dingus on the bench reported noises where there shouldn't have been any. "Where is it coming from, Lucy?"

"Gimme a second...sure as corruption's comin' in strong. Yep, that's what I thought: somewheres in th' Nomad group—parta th' Sargasso Cluster. Buncha nonconformist rocks sorta wander in an' outa the ecliptic steada stayin' neatly put."

"Sounds like an ideal place for anarchists. Anybody out there?"

"Must be *somebody*, with a signal like that. Coupla minin' outfits, a few dozen homesteaders. Mighty lonely stretch of sky, till Aphrodite start-ed buyin' in. Sure is a humdandy of a signal—mebbe Tormount's fixin' t'Broachify th' Rock of Gibraltar in or somethin'."

On one of my infrequently productive hunches, I extorted Ed's notes from a nearby Telecom pad. "How many of these Sargasso disappearances would you say are in that Nomad clump?"

She took the pad, punched in some instructions, and waited for the results. "Two thirds, could be three quarters. Hard tellin'—folks ain't too consistent or original namin' their rocks sometimes."

"Lucy, my semimechanical *compadre*, I think we've finally got a solid lead. Maybe it's time we hit the road."

"Gimme a chance t'rinse out a few unmentionables an' wind th' cat. Mind you visit th' little boys' room— I don't wanna hafta stop an' let you out by th' roadside."

ᴧ

It wasn't quite that simple. For one thing, there were half a dozen very carefully worded Telecom calls to make, nailing down certain individuals I wanted to interview. The object would be to follow Ed's investigations as far as we could without ending up among the missing ourselves. According to Ed's records, a neighbor, discovering my friend's Earthside background, had pressed him to look for a pair of daughters who'd left home to stake a claim among the Nomads. When word began to circulate, other folks with absent friends and family had added to the pot. Ed found himself tempted by more valuta than he and Lucy could have scratched out in years of ordinary pioneering.

What made it complicated was that Belters turn up missing all the time: there are something like two billion of them scattered through the System, and anybody foolish enough to try taking census or demand identification numbers is a likely candidate for early retirement—and burial.

Everyone's a refugee from something. Take that neighbor's daughters, out to make an independent place for themselves. Thousands of former Czarists, Hamiltonians, cryptoauthoritarians of a hundred different stripes were welcome out here as long as they minded their manners, although they were well advised to change their names. Similarly those who fled from tyranny in *my* world were flocking to the asteroids, often winding up cheek-by-claimstake with the very characters they'd fled from, driven out by Propertarian progress. Add millions of American embezzlers, alimony-duckers, income-tax evaders, *Confederate* criminals fleeing restitution obligations: a mighty difficult population to analyze and reduce to statistics. People were getting a new chance out here—sometimes two or three new chances—and often failed to leave a forwarding address.

Still, Ed's computations indicated a rash of vanishings unexplainable by such cynical and mundane considerations. Something big and sinister seemed to be going on, centered, at least statistically, on the wandering clump of minerals known as the Nomad Cluster. If there was a difference between my cosmic twin and me, it was that he's more methodical—at least on paper. I keep my investigation schedule in my head. The last time he'd logged in with the computers here on Bulfinch, he'd decided to take off for the Nomads post-cliché.

And then he'd disappeared.

Our first stop would be that original trouble-making neighbor, a rancher of some description named Schroeder. Proximity in the asteroids is a figurative sort of thing; Lucy told me the trip "next door" would take six hours at a standard tenth-gee. Accordingly, I gave my Webley magazines a thorough charging and checked to see there was an explosive-tipped round in the tiny chamber of my confiscated Bauer. Then I hardcopied Ed's notes and we actually did take care of the cat and go to the bathroom (at least I did—I don't even want to *know* what Lucy had to face in that department), then bade farewell to the old homestead. Lysander wanted to come along, so I found myself squeezing ridiculously past him through the front door and shutting it quickly behind me—I think I bent a couple of his whiskers.

Strapping myself into the seat of Lucy's flivver (we'd sent the Tucker home on autopilot), a Stanley Flitemaster painted her usual vomitous shades, I watched her laying out the course. "Hey, isn't that a little out of the way? If you plotted it across this empty-looking stretch, we'd save at least—"

"Don't tell grandma how t'suck eggs—a revoltin' turn of phrase if I ever heard one! Winnie, that's straight through Charlie's Cloud; we'd get holed, fer sure. You *like* breathin' vacuum?"

"Charlie's Cloud?"

"Named—posthumously, acourse—fer one Charles Cato Montgomery, its late lambasted former owner."

"Somehow I sense another shaggy story in the wind."

"It's them egg-salad sandwiches y'had fer lunch, boy. Seems as how, when we first started enterprisin' this section of th' Belt, a buncha San Francisco greenies—some say exiled Hamiltonians, mebbe old Nortonians, I dunno—declared themselves th' Guardians of th' Asteroids. Swamped about a thousand frequencies announcin' they were gonna git things all neatened up an' *organized* out here. Told us t'git ready t'receive Cato's Edict Number One."

"And what, pray tell, was that?"

"Never rightly found out. That rock ol' Charlie'd settled on just sorta blew up one night, spontaneous-like. Right before his big broadcast. Bullets, lasers, rockets, every kinda deestructive whatnot zeroed in from so many directions at once, we never did figger out who th' culprits was. All that's left of Charlie an' his gang's a great big swarm of little bitty pebbles. We gotta do some maneuverin' t'avoid 'em."

"Sounds like plain old-fashioned murder to me. How many of those 'destructive whatnots' were *yours*, Lucy?"

"Further deponent blabbeth not. *Did* run plumb outa ammonium nitrate that season. Near cost me th' whole poppy field. It was a fair bargain: government's a vice best left—if anywhere at all—back where it started, on Earth."

"I see, and if this volunteer government had been accepted by a majority of asteroid-dwellers, what would you have done then?"

"Found some *more* ammonium nitrate. *Nobody's* got a right t'start a government, Winnie. We left that—*and* typhoid *and* cholera—back on Earth when we came out here. An' everybody's got a right t'stamp it out. Simple self-defense."

⚔

Thursday, March 18, 223 A.L.

Six hours, two Gigacom movies, and a pong tournament later (I think Lucy beat me nine out of eight), our instruments reported contact with a target still too far away to be directly visible. Of course, decelerating as we were, we'd have had to use rearview mirrors, anyway. By the time we'd matched velocities, it was big enough to take me by surprise, an enormous, swollen, rotten-looking apricot of a world whose bilious coloration made even Lucy's yellow paisley look downright tasteful.

I was good enough with the instruments by now to see that the thing's apparent size was mostly an illusion, exaggerated by the plastic atmospheric envelope whose contents were noxious-looking green and yellow soupy gases. Lucy maneuvered us to one pole, where a metal tower pierced the plastic bubble, and set us down on a landing pad. I zipped my hood and drew the Webley to check its charge again.

"Hold on there, Pecos Bill, leave that hogleg in th' car." She began unbuckling her own gunbelt, a sight I'd never thought I'd see. It left her looking sort of lopsided.

"Lucy, are you leaking nutrient solution? I'm not going into that muck without—"

"You wanna wind up just like Charlie Montgomery? This here's a *bugranch*, Winnie, one big nasty anaerobic crudsy-culture. Touch off a round in that atmosphere, an' it'll go up like—"

"The Second of July. Okay, you've convinced me. Where do I hang my belt?" I started unbuckling.

"Th' peashooter, too, son. I saw you tuck that little .25 inside yer suit. Don't matter how big th' spark is, the bang'll be big enough to—"

"Okay, okay! Should I leave my Rezin, too? And where do I check my fingernails and teeth?"

"Don't get testy! I don't like this any better'n you. Pox, I'd leave m' Darling gun, but it'd take half an hour to unship, an' anyway, I'm a stabler personality type than you. Keep aholda yer knife, that alloy won't spark none. *An' mind yer suit integrity*—one whiff of that junk in there, it'll be plantin' time fer Ma Bear's only son."

Said suit was relaying an automated permission-to-land signal. At the end of the elevator ride, a warning flashed in lurid colors and about twenty-seven languages on the inside of the door, reminding us this wasn't any health-resort. Except maybe for bacteria. We waited for the lock to cycle. "What's this bugranch business all about, Lucy, some kind of glorified Confederate ant farm?"

Her arms retracted and emerged again, thinly sheathed in rubbery smartsuit material. "It's th' very latest thing, Winnie. Specially invented microwigglies out there, crawlin' around, breedin', eatin', goin' to th' little teeny toilet—burnin' rock an' metal into mush that can be refined an' distilled: metal, chemicals, pharmaceuticals. Watch yer step, now."

The door slid aside and we sticky-footed out onto a plastic-coated catwalk that branched in half a dozen directions before us. I looked up at the "sky," a view of Jupiter, inside out. Twelve feet below the catwalk, plopping, bubbling, and smoking, it looked like the final scene of *The Magic Christian*.

I preferred the sky.

"Eventually," continued Lucy as we made our way along the grillework toward a small, piling-supported dome, "they'll collapse the envelope, irradiate th' whole shebang, an' bake it sterile in an induction field fer months. Then they'll introduce new strains of bugs, a few million nightcrawlers, an' this'll be th' nicest little north forty y'ever did see. Sure wish they'd thought of this when Eddie an' I got started. Woulda saved a passel of elbow grease. As it is, I been expectin' 'em t'try it out on Venus fer years, but no one—"

We'd reached the dome, apparently a terrestrial refuge from the noxious atmosphere, fronted by a special decontamination lock. Judging from his slashed and tattered smartsuit, that was Farmer Schroeder, the guy I'd planned on talking to, lying in the outer door, keeping it from sliding shut. You *had* to go by the smartsuit; what was left of its contents were semiliquid, bubbling and steaming, humping with germ-infested hyperactivity. Something crawled as I tried to tear my eyes away from the glistening remains, and I realized it was my stomach.

"Lucy, I'm going to be sick. How do I—"

"*Urrrk!*" Lucy shook all over, lurched, and started going round and round in circles. She bumped against the catwalk's guardrail, dangerously bending it outward, circled round again, and hit it in a slightly different place, where it groaned and squeaked with strain. I cast about in desperation, snatching at my absent holster.

Suddenly, behind me, a smartsuited figure screamed out a challenge. I whirled just as he lunged, the glint of steel naked in his hand.

15: CUT OF A THOUSAND DEATHS

Somehow I squirmed aside, and once the shock boiled away, settled into that icy, slow-motion clarity of mind I've learned to call "second-order panic," an exhilarating stupidity which, if you live to tell about it, is always impossible to explain: smugglers, downhill racers, shoplifters, parachutists, nod their heads and grin—*they* know. My hands were steady now, fingers curled around the Rezin's grip without memory of its being drawn.

Maybe a head taller, my antagonist was lightly built, with not too much advantage in the way of reach—and that little offset by the greater length of my knife. His smartsuit was a lustrous pale gray, the face sealed in anonymity. But a Hamiltonian medallion glinted openly around his neck, removing Lucy from the picture. He seemed to understand the ground rules here, showed no interest in using the pistol strapped to his waist, and took not a martial artist's stance, but that of a fencer.

Something, anyway,

It wasn't much. I kept thinking: I'm fifty-nine years old, already out of breath, twenty pounds overweight at a charitable estimate. In this sort of ceremony, victory—and life—are to the swift; the first guy to get in and out again leaves the other fellow leaking.

He circled, a short dagger extended in his left glove, making tiny distracting figure eights in what passed for the air. Grateful for the practice I'd inflicted on myself, I stood my ground, let him bring the fight to me, unwinding from a reflexive Korean walking-stance, turning with him, holding my weapon raised halfway before me, its tip level with his throat.

He *lunged*, knifepoint streaking at me! I pivoted, *kicked*, let him dash himself against a solid heel to the short-ribs. His suit took most of the grief; as he shook himself alert again, I saw a transient glitter in his *other* hand, a second blade tucked defensively along the forearm. If I'd known about *that*, I might've canceled the sidekick. Sure enough, there was a whitened scuff along my shin.

Given the climate, I'd nearly bought it, right there.

Okay, we'd felt each other out. The question's always which side of your blade the other guy'll come in on, especially with southpaws. I made his decision for him, shifting to a diagonal guard, his right shoulder lined up with my bowie tip. Now he'd *have* to come in on the right.

So I told myself.

He circled, shadow-fencing in the air beyond my reach, then *lunged* again, straight for my midsection. I began a parry, somehow sensed the insincerity of his thrust, and barely blocked a low strike he'd essayed with his other blade, just saving my groin.

Idiotic thoughts about the *nick* of time. I'd seen that putrefying cadaver in the doorway: it wouldn't take much; one good cut, the hellish environment would finish the job—clear down to the bone. Abruptly, something *slammed* me hard against the catwalk rail. It was Lucy, quacking mindlessly. I nearly lost the knife as pain surged through my legs from hip to toe, my opponent closing for the kidneys. With a grunt of agony I twisted, half a tick from flopping into bottomless corrosives. He leaped, both knives extended like the swords they poke at fighting bulls, *and struck!*

Supported from the armpits by the guardrail, I snapkicked; he took it squarely in the crotch, lifted off his feet, but I was busy regaining mine and couldn't press the minimal advantage. He stumbled crookedly away, preoccupied. Somehow, he'd connected, too: the right sleeve of my suit was deeply sliced, not *quite* through the fabric. Edges stirred, trying to reseal. They wouldn't stand much more strain.

The guy must have been made of stone. He outclassed me all around, and he had two blades—he wouldn't fall for any more dirty footwork. *I rushed him.* He stepped back just in time to get run down by Lucy on another careening circuit. As they crashed, the knife in his left hand went flying and vanished in the muck with an evil hiss and a wisp of yellow steam.

I charged again, blocked a right-hand cut, and gave him pommel and quillon in the face. He slashed blindly, blade skittering across my suit controls. I chopped two-handed, aiming for his neck. The blade arrived off-center. I felt his suit's resistance, the greasy parting of flesh. My edge grated to a sickening halt in green shoulder bone.

He screamed, scrabbling for the cross-draw holster on his hip. Desperate, I recovered, *lunged.* The Rezin disappeared into his body, his blood bubbling and boiling around it with a thick cloud of oily smoke. I wrenched the blade out as he fell, then snatched his medallion, crushing it on the rail with the pommel of my knife.

Lucy gathered up her senses in an instant, grabbed the guy's uninjured arm, half carrying him to the air-lock. I wasn't much help: the exertion had about finished me off—and not a little smoke was rising from my own sleeve now. I slapped a palm across the tear and stumped along behind her, blind with pain and exhaustion. The assassin died as we were cycling the door.

⅄

Decontamination *hurt.* Half the little telltales on my arm were blinking hysterically as my exposed flesh, scalded by the caustic spray—and probably infected with a billion voracious artificial microbes—was screaming for attention. Maybe even amputation.

Finally I passed some psychological limit; when I woke up, Lucy had stashed my assailant in stasis—just in case we'd diagnosed wrong—and peeled a portion of my suit to examine my injured forearm. She spent fully as much time on the goddamned damaged sleeve. "Best thing for it, Winnie. If we can hurry th' repairs along, it'll repair *you.* Hold still!"

"*Jesus X. Bushman!* Try keeping your fingers out of the hamburger, please! Damn near killed me out there, now you're trying to finish the job." To make things worse, I'd broken three cigars I was carrying. I trimmed and lit a reasonably undamaged half, dribbling sparks and ashes all over my lap.

"Least I crashed th' opposition, too—can't say I ain't fair." She sprayed on tissue-sealant—the kind that's illegal, Stateside—from the shelter's copious *materia medica*, and returned her attention to my suit. Apparently our late host had actually *lived* down here in the slime: we were sitting in a comfortable, well-appointed living room.

"Yeah, well, you're supposed to be on *my* side."

"Which I am, when I'm m'self. Thanks fer smashin' that medallion, Win. One more go-round, I'da ended up in th' swamp. Ugly way t'die." She put my sleeve aside. "Guess you'll mend now. Soon's yer pressure-tight agin, we can get on outa here."

I grunted. "We sure won't be interviewing Ed's former client, will we? I shouldn't have called ahead, Lucy. You suppose I've killed the others I Telecommed, too?"

"Don't be a ninny. That hatcheteer was after us. We must be gettin' close t'somethin'. Sure wish I knew what th' plague it is. Seal yer suit an' let's make like a hockey team."

I looked down at the sleeve, which hung there good as new—more than I could say for my plastic-coated arm. "I want a look around, first. The Civil Liberties Association is going to love us—we're starting to leave a trail." Something else occurred to me: "Lucy, about this bugranch business—how come I haven't come down with acute Andromeditis or something?"

" 'Cause them microcritters ain't designed t'chew on people. It's their metabolic byproducts does th' damage. An' we ain't callin' *no* Civil Libertines—time we got discreet. That feller in th' lock ain't gonna mind none, an' th' one in stasis, she's fixed up as well as anyone can fix her."

"*She?* A brain-bore victim, I presume." Lucy nodded. "At least the other side's consistent—a highly overrated virtue, if you ask me. Say, how come the medallion around her neck didn't scramble her *own* circuitry?"

"It was all done with mirrors, Winnie. That suit of hers had an extra layer of shielding. That's why I said they're after us, specific-like. Otherwise—"

"Right—why the extra medallion? You win, but let's at least leave a message for the Patrol." I slid my arm back into the suit, braced for even greater agony. Surprisingly, the pain completely vanished. I tried the limb out every whichway, and it seemed all right. "You rustic types certainly pioneer in style," I commented as I poked around the room. "Don't think they had a piano as big as this one, even aboard the—*Sonofabitch!*"

Lucy turned. "Thought you came out here aboard th' *Bonaventura*. Whatcha got there, son?"

I turned the holoframe so she could see it. A hand-written inscription floated in the air below the double portrait: TO DADDY WITH LOVE, HIS GIRLS.

"Ain't it th' one on th' right tried t'steal yer luggage on Ceres?"

"Yeah—now in stasis at Dr. Scott's." I consulted Ed's notes. "Disappeared shortly after staking claim with her sister—guess where. Maybe we should *skip* the rest of the interviews and go directly to the heart of the matter."

"Th' Cluster?"

"Wherever that Broach-noise was coming from. Ed seemed to think—"

"But not often enough. One thing, though: how'm I gonna keep from gettin' poleaxed by ever Tom, Dick, an' Alex got one of them medallions? It's getting downright monotonous!"

"I just stomp 'em, Lucy. You're the technician."

⅄

"Stop foolin' with that *antique*. Gonna ventilate us both fer sure." We'd just finished turnover on the first leg of our journey. I was examining the weapon she'd taken from the knife-happy hit-lady.

"Lucy, this could be important: Olongo was assaulted with an American .22; I nearly got shot with an American .25. . ."

"An' Trayle blown away with an American .38. There's yer pattern—it's them pest-ridden countrymen of yers!"

"Country*women*. That's what I thought, but, Lucy, CDM is a *Mexican* headstamp—*Cartouchos Deportivos*, or something like that, and the .38 Super Automatic is a hell of a lot more popular there and in Central America than it is Stateside. Now there's *this*—"

"Another little bitty beanshooter. So what?"

"So it's a *Russian* beanshooter, to be specific, a 9-millimeter Makarov, and to get one, you have to have the right initials: KGB. *That*'d be a hell of an alliance, my world's Soviets, and your very own Hamiltonians!"

"*Smile* when y'say that. We fought two wars provin' it ain't so. Mebbe it's just somebody collects little tiny guns. Don't like t'hurt folks *too* much." She patted the monstrous Gabbet Fairfax safely reinstalled at her side.

"Be serious! This means there's a *second* secret channel to my world, somebody who uses brain-bores and makes people disappear. Somebody—"

"Stupid enough t'plant a Broach out here where nobody in *your* System's *reached* yet. Winnie, yer deducin' yerself right over th' brink. Wait'll we see what's what 'fore y'start theorizin.'"

"Oh, yeah? Well, tell me, Lucy, what did they get *you* with? What caliber?"

A long pause. Then: "I been afraid you'd ask that, son, it's downright humiliatin': .309 diameter, 71-grain copper jacket. In other words..."

"A .32 ACP—the only machine gun *I* know of that uses it is a Czechoslovakian antique, the Model 60 Scorpion. Lucy, I'm going to go right on 'theorizin' ' all I like. Clarissa's *missing*, and I keep thinking about her with a brain-bore fastened on her head, being *used*." Neither of us spoke for a while.

"Winnie, how about findin' us a movie on that Gigglycom of yours. One of them East Clintwood things y'keep tellin' me about."

⋏

Friday, March 19, 223 A.L.

Twenty hours later, we stopped to take on more reaction mass and life-support supplies at another puffed-up asteroid similar to Navigation Rock. Instead of just one explosion, *thousands* had been set off at the right stage of plasticity, creating a vast, complicated "apartment house" of foamy rock, a myriad of interconnected bubbles.

Inside the planetoid, in addition to fuel-storage and reservoirs for air and water, there were artificial environments as varied as the many Earth provides—plus many more invented simply to please and amaze (and collect hard money from) the passing traveler. The last couple of thousand miles, the proprietors of this astroknott's berry-farm had beamed their Telecom brochure our way: forests, jungles, deserts, icecaps, Martian rills and crater bottoms, depths and shallows suited to marine voyagers.

Lucy had noodled with the flivver's transponder on the theory that *we* didn't *want* to advertise. She paid for our supplies in blessedly anonymous cash. I didn't hear any complaints from the management. We hadn't any choice, however, about deflivvering while the cabin was being serviced. We went inside, determined to maintain as low a profile as we could.

Some trick with Lucy dressed up like a big paisley mailbox.

"Somethin' I been meanin' t'check on anyway," she told me. "Wanna see a genuine prehistorical critter 'fore we take off again?" We floated at the intersection of a dozen tubular tunnels in the rock, each one color-coded to avoid confusion. Theoretically.

"What are you talking about?" I looked nervously over my shoulder, imagining Hamiltonians, CIA agents, and Communists at every bend in the tunnel. There were a *lot* of bends. This wasn't any time for sightseeing, though I confess I'd grabbed the opportunity to replenish my *own* life-support: a box of native-grown cigars securely tucked beneath my arm.

"Don't wanna hurry anybody loadin' Single-H, Winnie. That stuff's downright tempermental. You remember how I said I wanted livestock out on Bulfinch? Well, there's more calories on th' hoof in this place than you ever saw in yer life! Gonna stand there gawkin' or come with me?"

I shrugged and seized one of the cables snaking through a convoluted purple tunnel. Due to a modest spin and the varying composition of the asteroid, there were more gravitic anomalies here than on a roller coaster—something like being inside a loop of Salvador Dali's intestines. At another complex intersection we took a sickeningly greenish fork, which dropped us at the entrance to one of the enormous bubbles that filled most of the volume of the asteroid.

"Lucy, I think someone's following us! Two of them, taking the same branches we did. Somebody in a red smartsuit, and a big, solid-looking guy."

"Aww, yer just nervous, Winnie. It's th' stimulatin' environment. Now come on, an' mind where y'step—they got meadow-muffins in here'd swallow up th' *Bonaventura!*"

PLEISTOCENE PLAZA. At least that's what the sign said. It was chilly inside, and took a little while for my suit to adjust. An artificial sun was shining brightly, though, and beyond the transparent plastic tunnel we found ourselves in, it looked just like a prairie day in Colorado.

Except for the glaciers.

There they are, Winnie! Gimme ten years, I'll have a herd of my own!" She pointed out over the rolling plains.

"Elephants? Lucy, you should be ashamed! Who ever heard of eating elephants?"

"What you think that burger was you had for lunch? They give milk, too, gallons an' gallons of it—though y'have t'use a mighty long-legged stool! Better look again, Winnie, those ain't elephants at all."

I held my hood in front of my face and stepped up the magnification. Great curving lengths of ivory, massive, heavy heads and bodies.

Hairy heads and bodies. "Lucy, those are *mastodons!* Huge, woolly mastodons!" I couldn't believe it. Had the Confederacy's time-line diverged before I thought it had? *Thousands* of years before I thought it had?

"Them's mammoths, Winnie. Imperial mammoths, cloned from a little bitty test tube fulla tissue frozen in Siberia. Keepin' 'em here t'build up their immunities—there's a lotta diseases developed on Earth since they went extinct."

I watched a group of half a dozen animals wandering slowly across the plain. "That's why the plastic tunnel, then, although I wouldn't want to be out there with them, under any circum—"

"Wouldn't be no problem, Winnie. Look close here, by th' ground. See that plastic mesh about eighteen inches up in th' tall grass? Plenty of footroom, but it keeps 'em from runnin'. Otherwise, they'd be practically flyin' around in *this* weak a pull."

"Like Dumbo, huh? Mammoths—that's really neat."

"Yeah, an' let that be a lesson to ya. Here's a critter th' world woulda never seen agin, resurrected by the very science your United Statesians think is *sooo* nasty. Same science gonna give me back m'body in another few months."

"Your body? You mean you don't have to go on like—"

"Like Dorothy's Tin Woodman? Not as long as there's nice thick juicy elephant steaks t'gobble, an' whiskey t'be drunk. *Never*, if we can find Eddie in one piece! I'm plannin' on bein' a *person* agin, steada comic relief!"

I knew that tone of voice. Someday there'd be tears to go with it again. If only Clarissa—

"*Hey you!*" Down the tunnel a figure was running toward us, waving a long, deadly looking artifact. He shook it at us, hollering his lungs out. "Stop, I say! Stop!"

"I *told* you we were being followed! See, there's the other one, right behind him! I'm getting tired of this!" I went for my gun. Suddenly a metal arm clamped my wrist.

"Not in here, Winnie. If you break th' glass, it could kill all th'critters!"

I hesitated a moment, then ran the other way, Lucy following. At the end of the plastic tunnel another well-sealed door awaited us. Lucy started pushing buttons while I drew my Rezin, standing guard. The assassins pounded down the tunnel a hundred yards away.

"Got it!" Lucy whisked me through the door and pushed it closed, punching in more numbers. Somewhere a siren started wailing, accompanied by slamming sounds on the other side of the door. "That's th' fire alarm. Tunnel's sealed. I imagine they're takin' quite a bath in there by now. Let's get back to th' flivver."

⋏

Thus we were off again in a streak of light and a cloud of dust and a hearty "Hiyo, Sowbellies"—silver presently being on the skids, speculation-wise. Every now and again I gave Ed's Broach-detector a look, and Lucy adjusted our course minutely to center the disturbance in our navigation sights.

I took a shower and tried to nap and fixed some sandwiches and watched Lucy watching me eat them. We played tic-tac-toe and nim and Botticelli and watched Mike Morrison and Dirty Harry and Diana Rigg kill all the baddies. I thought about our own baddies and how close they'd come to getting us back at the mastodons, then cleaned my Rezin (the bugranch had dulled its finish noticeably—some bugs!) and played with the Makarov and bit my fingernails and argued with the pilot.

Space travel could stand some improving.

Finally, the Nomad Cluster swelled before our instruments. At an average of a thousand miles apart and a mile in diameter, there wasn't much to eyeball through the windows. Lucy started trying to match one of the rocks with the paratronic screeching of the Broach.

"That's th' one, Winnie. Gotta be." She held up a 'com pad in my face.

"You mean that little one down in the corner?"

"Naw, that's just a crumb from that last sandwich of yers. This one here, Bester 9656, accordin' to th' registry. Biggest rock in th' Cluster, if y'call a dozen miles big. I'm gonna do a little sneakin', now—don't wanna announce our arrival. Can y'stand buttonin' up yer suit?"

"Sure. How come?"

"I'm gonna git us pointed right, then turn everything off, includin' life-support. We'll take a slow roll that'll make us look like a natural hunka rock, an—"

"Yeah? And what happens when whoever's out there gives us a blast of his meteor-defense lasers?"

"We're gonna pass close, but clearly a miss. Be more trouble'n we're worth t'pulverize us. I'm plannin' t'walk th' rest of th' way—an' lookie here: while you were snoozin', I was knittin'." She held up a clothlike copper wire mesh, with long dangling fringes.

"Swell. Get yourself some steel wool and knit me a gun. What the hell is it?"

"Sort of a Franklin cage. Ill drape this over me an' let it trail to th' ground. Oughta perteck me against them medallions."

"And make you one hell of a radar target. I'm zipping up, now; you can roll the windows down." With the lights out and control panels dead, I began to get an entirely different view of space travel, not at all the empty black loneliness I'd expected. The sky was awash with color, enough damn starlight to read by—although Lucy wouldn't let me use the Gigacom—and the erratic wobble she encouraged in the car only served to make it a 360-degree panorama.

Problems and all, I discovered I was *liking* it out here, and even if everything (by some miracle) came out all right, Laporte and the Confederacy—hell, even *Earth*—were going to seem mighty small from now on. Maybe if Clarissa was all right...

"Okay now, Winnie, git ready t'jump! Don't worry which direction, I'll jet around and get us headed straight. I got th' plumbin' fer it, an' you don't—good thing we ain't got power doors on this crate."

At her signal, I knelt on the upholstered seat and *pushed* myself through the open door into the starry void. We'd picked a spot a few moments after passing near the asteroid when the meteor watch (if any) would be letting out their breath in relief and going back to their chessboards and foldouts-of-the-month.

I tumbled stupidly, hoping Lucy hadn't lost control of herself again or something, then felt a firm manipulator on the rubbery nape of my neck. The universe swam around upright and I was looking down on the rugged darkened surface of an undeveloped asteroid.

Except for the titanic machinery, labeled APHRODITE, LTD.

Scattered over the surface were structures that made the Great Wall of China look like kindergarten blocks. If there was any order or purpose to the assemblage of enormous beams and girders, frameworks and metallic grids and coils, it defied me. For a moment I seriously wondered whether we were being invaded by extrasolar aliens after all, and this was their idea of House Beautiful.

Then, as we drifted closer and I got the scale and angles straightened out, a pattern began to emerge, a familiarity my mind had rejected at first because it seemed so ridiculous.

I'd once held a laboratory model of this thing in my hands.

Suppose, for example, that you'd stumbled across an ordinary light bulb, made of ordinary glass with a little stem inside supporting a hair-fine tungsten filament and a pood old familiar brass screwbase at the bottom with the usual little button of solder on the end. Would you recognize it right away? Sure you would.

Unless it was five miles in diameter...

The last time I'd seen machinery like this, it had been at the cosmic other-end of a closet on the corner of Colfax and York. A Broach. A perfectly ordinary Broach, big enough to pour both sections of Niagara Falls through, with room to spare for the Amazon River, piranhas, crocodiles, headhunters, and all.

We drifted closer, each wrapped up in stunned amazement. No *wonder* this thing was making noises detectable half a System away! And there, a tiny, insignificant speck resting on the rock beside some sort of dwelling complex, was a sight I found even more astounding, somehow. A flivver.

Well, more of a spacegoing bus, really. Lots of room inside for plenty of passengers. And Telecom equipment.

Even room for the Voice of the Stars himself, Voltaire Malaise.

At least that's the way it looked.

16: FIRING-SQUAD MORNING

Saturday, March 20, 223 A.L.

Malaise's network velocipede was locked up tighter than a virgin's pantyhose. I hung there from its door-handles while Lucy sniffed around for signs of electronic activity on the asteroid. The noises we'd been homing on had gotten intermittent during the last leg of the journey. Now the titanic machinery lay silent and deserted. And so was the conventional ether. I didn't like that, it implied we were *expected*. But then I wasn't liking much of anything these days.

Unlimbering the Webley, I stickied up my feet and practiced looking like a crater or something equally unobtrusive. The surface dwellings had the hasty appearance of quonset huts, and there weren't any windows—a minor break, anyway. Overhead, the Broach construction reached up like a cast-iron highway overpass, and underneath it, my imagination populated every shadow with boogie men. Hamiltonian boogie men.

I signaled Lucy and sticky-footed over to the entrance, wondering how silently it could be cycled. Most of them make noises like a garbage truck in labor, but this, thank Vaselina, goddess of doing things the easy way, was a lot simpler, a single, relatively uncomplicated but well-sealed door, unlocked—for travelers needing emergency shelter—like they used to do in Alaska before the Teamsters and the Feds improved the crime rate. Not an airlock at all, which meant hard-vacuum inside, and that struck me as passing peculiar.

Inside the corrugated hemicylinder, an eerie bluish twilight lay upon long rows of steel benches and hermetic lockers. Plenty of standing room, and at the other end, another door. The whole damned *building* was an airlock, capable of handling a construction gang in one big hundred-person gulp.

We ghosted through as silently as possible—floors and walls conduct sound, too—until Lucy caught her antielectronic frock on a tool rack. Her muffled curses crackled through my suit receiver, but she managed to get disentangled without too much noise, leaving the snarled copper mess behind her. About that time, I tripped over someone's abandoned lunchbox, and wound up bumping my head on the ceiling. It's damned hard to tippy-toe around and keep your feet firmly glued to the ground. In a hundredth-gee, anyway.

The inner door turned out to be a double one, I supposed for times when groups in less than platoon strength wanted to come in and visit the plumbing. Experiencing a few moments of worried claustrophobia, we soon found ourselves in an air- and light-filled corridor. The whole place had the unmistakably portable, temporary aspect of a pipeline construction camp.

But where the hell were the constructors?

I unzipped my face and followed my gun, Lucy treading on my heels. Why this joint should be so deserted—

"*Urrk!*" I spun around, half-afraid I knew what was bothering Lucy. She was whirling in place like a top, while I cast wildly about for something or somebody to shoot—somebody with a bronze medallion.

Crunch! For the first time in my detectiveship, I'd gotten blackjacked from behind. Dumb thing to think of. *Crunch!* It hurt. I turned groggily, waving my gun, and *crunch!* I took it on the forehead just above the eye, and *crunch!* I didn't know where that one landed, but I seemed to be a lot shorter all of a sudden, realized I was on my knees, and *crunch!* I found myself wishing dimly that they'd do a more professional job, and *crunch!* I vaguely remember three or four hundred more like that, then throwing up.

And endless blackness.

⋏

They were making me watch TV, the bastards. This act with seals, and it must have been 3D like the Telecom, only a whole lot better; the seals kept slapping me in the face with their cold, wet flippers. Or maybe a dead fish.

Or was I?

The channel changed, I was watching the news. Pretty boring, except they seemed to be mentioning my name: *"Bear,* can you hear me now? *You idiots, how many times did you hit him?* Bear, pay attention! We've got the old lady, Bear. Who else did you bring with you? Where's your ship?"

So many questions at once.

I blinked up through the blood dripping down my face. What, oh, what had I ever done to get Voltaire Malaise so angry? Wasn't I rescuing him? Wasn't I making nice, interesting news? Wasn't that the smell of vomit rising from the seat they'd strapped me to?

Well, they *were* making me watch TV, after all—probably Lawrence Welk.

"For Alex' sake, pour another bag of water over him. And watch it this time—this is a new sweater! Bear! Who *else* did you bring with you?"

"George Strong-arm Custer," I mumbled, marveling how it all seemed to make sense, "and the U.S. Seventh Cavalry, out there hiding in a crater. They'll be here any minute, just in the nick of time—no, that was at the bugranch. Anyway, you'd better let me and Voltaire go. Give yourself up."

This rhetorical extravaganza generated little violet-colored sparks before my eyes, so I decided to relax and enjoy the shower I seemed to be taking. Abruptly things swam into focus and I was looking up at good old Voltaire again. Only he didn't seem to be in quite as much trouble as I was.

"Bear, I'm running out of patience with you. I want some answers and I want them now!"

I spat out what I hoped wasn't a tooth and waited until I could think a little more clearly. At some far corner of my vision, I could sense a seedy-looking type leaning on a big gray filing cabinet, swinging something small and black and heavy by a thong around one finger. It'd be a little leather bag, I knew, filled with several ounces of lead shot, its contours matching the dents in my personality. I was going to groan, but I was tuckered out from calling General Custer.

Malaise broadcast another exasperated expression and addressed the sap-swinger. "Look at the blood on this carpet! Blasted *amateurs!*"

I remembered not to shake my head; it wouldn't do any good, and it would hurt a lot. A second guy, the one who'd been slapping me with a wet towel, stammered back at his boss, but I put a hand up as far as the straps would let me. " 'Sokay—it's my blood, I'll pay for the drycleaning. Can I have a drink?" I peered at the System's premier newscaster. "So you're the one behind all this. No wonder you could never find J.V. Tormount! Mind telling me what 'all this' amounts to? You interrupted me in mid-detect."

"Get him a drink, Harry. I hate to revert to clichés, Bear, but *I'm* the one asking questions now. Tell me where your ship is, how you got down here, and how many others there are."

I took a deep breath. Somebody'd kicked me in the ribs when I was down, the rat; I couldn't have fallen *that* hard in this gravity. I don't know who loosened the straps, but I took a squeeze of something that warmed nicely, and looked around. An office, stark enough, but not as sparsely furnished as the rest of the place. Judging from the plastiboard boxes scattered here and there, Malaise was either moving in or moving out. I took another sip, not really caring which.

"Malaise, you're gonna kill me, anyway. Do a tired old cop a favor and tie up some loose ends."

He plastered a concerned look on his face. "I assure you, I don't intend to have you killed, not at all."

"Oh, yeah?"

"We're simply going to let you die a clean, natural-appearing death."

"Oh. Yeah."

He sat back behind his desk and steepled his fingers. "Still, I don't suppose it'll hurt to tell you just a bit. Mind you, don't breathe a word of it, now. But first, who came with you besides the crippled old woman?"

"What crippled old— Oh, you mean Lucy. Two flivvers," I improvised, "our Stanley and a Tucker. If I'm not out of here in two hours, they're coming in—and calling the Rangers."

He shook his head. "Try again—you expect the truth from me, don't you? Anyway, you've been here far longer than two hours already."

"How time flies when you're having fun. All right, just the one car. Our friend, a Dr. Scott from Ceres, is hiding out there somewhere, wondering about us by now. We're the 'asteroid' that tumbled by—whenever it was. Check with your skywatch."

"I'll do that." He signaled to the towel-flapping flunky. "And have them man the lasers again." To me: "Your doctor, if he exists, is going to *need* a doctor."

Well, at least they'd waste a little of their time and manpower. A small victory, but a meaningless one. "Now how about telling me what *you're* up to?"

Malaise tried getting up and pacing, but it doesn't work too well in nearly zero gee. He returned to the desk, squirted himself a drink, even squirted another for me. I discovered a split lip I hadn't noticed before.

"It was the War, of course, Antarctica, Hawaii, watching thousands die on both sides every day. Realizing how deeply, fundamentally, inherently *evil* human nature truly is. And stupid, criminally, wastefully stupid: you know, the Confederacy could have turned its victory into a world-wide hegemony, imposed a rational, orderly rule, But would they do that? *No!*

They'd rather go back to their Telecoms and liquor, their suburban split-levels and hoverbuggies, instead of finishing the job they'd started."

"Before my time—in the Confederacy, I mean. But it seems to me, the Czar's the one who started it—he had ideas about a world-wide hegemony, too."

"He *lost*, which proves he wasn't qualified to rule. I moved out here in 211 A.L., just after the United States were discovered. Things were getting tough for Hamiltonians about then, and I required a little more freedom to act. And *allies*—are you following this?" He glanced at his watch.

"Sure. I even have some of it figured out. After you got set up in Ceres, you came out here and built yourself a Broach, determined somehow to contact various unsavory characters in my world."

His eyebrows shot straight upward. "You really are a halfway decent detective, you know that? We carried the machinery aboard that network newsbus, and yes, I piloted back to Earth—your Earth—myself. Let me tell you, dodging all those radar defenses was quite a trick. But I settled neatly into the middle of enough primitive orbital trash to hide myself, and gradually got in touch with your Federal Security Police."

"SecPol—and they're not mine, friend. Why didn't you just use an Interworld Terminal? Wait—let me guess. You didn't want anybody seeing the famous Voltaire Malaise trafficking with—"

"Correct, but there was an even better reason: your planet-bound governments took my message *from orbit* very seriously, particularly when it was translated into one of their own childish codes. My onboard computer cracked it in a day and a half."

"Very clever. So for once you really *were* the Voice from the Stars."

"A man who appreciates a joke. In any case, it appears that times are getting difficult for duly constituted authority in your world as well. I realized, as soon as open trade was initiated, your people would choose the selfish, undisciplined, hedonistic path the Confederacy has, so I offered your government—and others—a deal."

"Which was?" I laid the whiskey bag against my forehead. I don't know how he got the ice cubes into it, but they felt good.

"The obvious: Confederate technology and wealth for their personnel and power. They graciously lowered their radar curtain, and I brought back the first load of SecPol and KGB agents that very trip. Later, we acquired a small fleet of heavy-duty vehicles and began transferring people by the thousands. Can you guess the purpose?"

I mulled that one, but came up temporarily empty. To keep from looking stupid, I said, "I'm going to get out a cigar and light it—if your thugs didn't break them again." The smoke stung, rising past the abrasions on my face. "Tell me how the brain-bores and the missing women fit. Surely you're not...Oh, no—it's just too silly!"

He looked genuinely pained. *"What's* too silly?"

"Building yourself a hidden Hamiltonian colony out here. Good God, man, the frontier is expanding so quickly, your secret wouldn't last a year! Especially using *kidnapped* women—for what, breeding stock? Pretty cold-blooded." Which is what I was trying to be, keeping my mind off Clarissa.

"Bear, you're amazing—and so *close!* But still you're *parsecs* away. We're building *starships!* Genuine starships! Two hundred thirty of them, on *your* side of the Broach, where *neither* culture can detect them, using asteroid materials easily located from the correlating strikes made over here. You're right about the women, though, *nearly a quarter of a million of them*, a hundred for every man. We're going to *grow* out there, Bear, find hospitable planets, built up as quickly as we can, and then, in a hundred years, sweep back in our billions to bring both Systems under proper leadership! Imagine: an interdimensional, interstellar Empire!"

I had to hand it to the guy, not the faintest glimmer of fanaticism in either eye. "Neat. Although not very gentlemanly. Did you know, Malaise, that the women you've had brain-bored are *aware* of ft, hating you every tortured second they live?"

"Irrelevant. They'll serve their purpose, and their children—girl children exclusively, at least for the first several generations—won't hate us. We'll be their *gods!*"

"I get it: short life spans for them, immortality for you." I had one last, wild idea: "I don't suppose you'd be accepting any new recruits this late, would you?" Maybe I could live long enough to—

"Hmm." He frowned. "No, I doubt that would be wise. Another nice try, Bear. You certainly don't give up."

"That's my *next* move. When are you and your merry little band of sex fiends taking off—and why can't you let Lucy and me live through it?" If I'd had more guts, I would have mentioned Clarissa.

"Well, first of all, because I don't like you. You've cost me personnel and wasted a great deal of my valuable time. Most of all, because I don't want either Earth expecting us a century from now. I'll tell you what, though: if you can survive until we leave, and providing someone rescues you, it's up to you."

"That *is* sporting, Voltaire. What're you going to do, bury me up to my head and let the ants eat me? Not too many ants out here, I'd guess."

"You'll see, Mr. Bear. Our interview is at an end. Take him down and dispose of him in the usual way. I won't be seeing you again."

"That's the way it looks, *Malaise!"* I snarled but I had to admire their technique. They left my legs fastened together (I must have weighed all of a pound and a half on this rock), tied my hands, and carried me downstairs like a victim of safaricide. My Webley was long gone, of course, as was my Rezin—not that they'd have done me much good. Maybe I was imagining

it, but the corners of my little .25 seemed to be gouging my sternum inside the front of my suit. Either they were careless, or what they were about to do was pretty final. With nothing much to lose, I squirmed and fought the best way I could. Even connected once—fatally, I hoped—with my heels, right to the jaw of the sap-wielder trying to carry my feet. He floated away, a basketball-size blood gobbet oozing from his mouth and ear.

That's when I found out what I had to lose.

My consciousness.

I came to, lying on the floor in a room even more bleak and depressing than before, a bare metal cube maybe twelve feet on a side. There was me, the walls, floor, and ceiling, a slowly-dripping utility sink.

And a door.

Carefully being welded shut from the outside.

17: DURANCE VILE

Tuesday, March 23, 223 A.L.

In the movies, the hero would've jumped right up, rushed over to the door, and pounded it indignantly, shouting at the villains, maybe burning his hands a little on the steel where they were welding it.

Movie heroes don't get sapped down twice in one day, not for real, and not as inexpertly as I'd been. What I did was lie there on the floor, sort of fading in and out of reality for what my suit said later was a day and a night. At some point I must have zipped up my hood on the theory it might help hold my broken head together. Sometimes, when I was more or less conscious, I'd count the rivets in the ceiling, wondering when I was going to die.

Soon, I hoped.

The suit must have done its job, though, because to my annoyance I eventually found myself wondering about a couple of other things. Like where the light was coming from, and ditto for my next meal.

I sat up sort of gradually and checked the clock display in a lower corner of my vision field, just as if I planned on going somewhere. The light seemed to be oozing from the thickly laid-on paint covering the steel walls, floor, and ceiling. Dark, irregular patches all around the door showed where the welding had scorched it. And "oozing" was just the word—a sickly shade of glow-in-the-dark toy-plastic blue. It might have been better to do my dying in the dark. My stomach growled. I growled right back. Another thing about movie heroes: first thing they want when they come out of a bad guy-induced coma is a drink, whiskey for PG through X, water for the Disneys. I watched the faucet in the galvanized corner sink, drops hanging from it big as golfballs, falling like feathers in a broad, funnel-shaped drain. Hungry as I was, the thought of drinking *anything* from that basin turned my stomach.

Which growled again like a qualifying-lap at Indy. After maybe an hour and a half of this, I cranked myself to my feet, excruciatingly particular not to lose adhesion with the floor. I needed another bump on my head like—well, like I needed another bump on my head. I didn't quite have the guts to touch it, not wanting to find out what *brains* feel like.

This room was originally intended as an outsize janitorium of some kind, about the height of two tall men in every direction, stark, fluorescent-coated metal, utterly featureless save for the sink and four thousand seven hundred and sixty-two rivets. Don't bother checking; I *know*.

Every running inch of the imitation submarine-type door frame had been carefully beaded shut, a job old Karyl Hetzer would've been proud to call his own. It was a mystery how I'd survived this long without suffocating. Maybe air was coming up the sink trap. There certainly wasn't any surplus of it; every few hours, especially if I was fairly active, I had to zip my hood again and let the suit do my breathing. After some indeterminate while, the telltales on my arm would go green again and I could take my hat off. It was a break in the routine. Like a good Boy Scout, one of the first things I did was inventory my meager possessions. My captors hadn't been very thorough, but then again, they didn't really need to be. There was the suit, of course, with its considerable talents, and, sure enough, tucked down inside my *uncolletage*, the little stainless steel Bauer, capable of hurling a massive fifty-grain slug at 810 feet per second, generating a full 73 foot/pounds at the muzzle. Just about enough to chip the paint off the walls, perhaps a little too lively for playing handball.

Besides the artillery, I had four cigars, each and every one of them unbroken, thanks to Murphy's Law (I'd save them until I didn't *care* how much oxygen I had left), a pocketful of smallish gold and silver pieces, the keys to my luggage, which was undoubtedly vaporized by now on its return trip through the meteor defenses, and a Bic lighter.

Finally, in my right thigh-pocket, I encountered a minor miracle and knew at least I wouldn't pass from this vale of tears *unentertained*: Clarissa's thoughtful present, my goddamn noisy wonderful Gigacom. I once heard a Denver disc jockey maintain that the world would be measurably improved if all clock radios played jugband music. Hard staying depressed to Kweskin's "Sadie Green, the Vamp of New Orleans," which opus I put on and immediately felt better, possibly even ready for that drink.

This I obtained fastidiously through a pseudocellophane cigar peeling held against one of the outsize drops collecting on the tap. Flat and metallic-tasting, but it shut my stomach up for a while. Kweskin's final kazoo chorus came crashing to a halt, I punched up a rare Mike Morrison flick where there aren't any horses (didn't want to be reminded of food just now), the detective thriller, *O'R.*

Now what the hell would Mike do in a pickle like this? Bash through the walls with his bare fists? Try finding out how bad he was hurt so he could stoically ignore it? Well now, if this suit could broadcast my image to another suit's receptors, why couldn't I kid it into transmitting *me* to *myself*? It took half an hour, and I missed the usual Morrison-movie barfight, but I finally turned the inside of my hood into a nanoelectronic mirror.

And promptly turned it off.

Funny, I hadn't *recalled* being thrown down seventeen miles of industrial-grade staircase at three or four gees, nor even realized my left eye was swollen shut.

And I was really going to miss those three teeth. Shit, nearly sixty years so far, I'd avoided needing dentures. For that matter, I was probably *still* going to avoid them.

I slept as much as I could, then found my smartsuit's medical overrides and helped myself to sleep some more. It filled the time, as did experimentally determining that I could burn precisely three-eighths of an inch of cigar before I had to put it out, more from pollution than anoxia (although there was that, too). I also found that even smartsuit waste-containers have to be emptied after a while, and felt grateful for the sink drain—and the water to wash up afterward.

Another interesting discovery was that the waistline of my suit contracted all by itself, about a quarter of an inch per day slower than I did. Some technology—couldn't even tighten my *belt* by myself.

On the third day it occurred dimly that perhaps I wasn't alone in this predicament; I felt stupid for not thinking of it sooner. Maybe it was all the sapping. Or maybe it was just the sap, himself. There'd been a lot of missing persons recently; though I couldn't figure out why Malaise was preserving my remains for posterity this way, maybe there were others in the same condition.

And of course, Lucy. One of these cubicles would effectively protect her against even the most persuasive control impulses. Hell, she'd probably been herself again longer than me. I resisted the urge to rephrase that and concentrated my minimal intelligence on the problem at hand: this wasn't any Chateau D'if, I'd never fingernail myself into the next cell, but maybe I could generate some companionship one steel wall removed. I shut off the Gigacom and shuffled over to a wall, my .25 in hand.

Better unload it first—could be a slug in the guts was exactly what I needed most right now, but I've always been a sissy where gratuitous pain's concerned, and it wouldn't do my posthumous rep any good to be discovered accidentally finished off by my own pocket popgun. Like Lucy'd said: humiliatin'.

On the other hand, maybe I never *would* be found. Then it wouldn't matter. I realized this thought had cheered me, glanced at my oxygen warning lights, and sealed up again. I thumbed back the magazine release, pulled out the little clip, slid the safety off and jacked the chamber-round into my hand. Then I turned up my audioreceptors as loud as they'd go, draped myself artistically along the baseboard, and rapped the pistol sharply against the wall.

My ears stopped ringing an hour and a half later.

This time, I kept the sound off while I did the tapping, *then* boosted it. Nothing. I tried again, with the same results. Next, the opposite wall, with similar reward. Either I was here alone, or the walls were awfully thick. Or they'd kidnapped a bunch of deaf people. This left a third wall which I tried, and the one with the door, which seemed silly—ought to be a corridor out there—but I gave it a shot anyway. Also the floor at several locations: one thing I had plenty of was time.

Finally, stretching my intestines to the limit of their fortitude, I stickied every suit-surface capable of it, reoriented what was left of my thinking, and crawled up the wall to the ceiling. It would have been a great way to escape—wait until the jailer brought my dinner and spring down on his back like the Scarlet Pumpernickel. Only my hosts weren't cooperating in the cuisine department; just as likely they'd forgotten by now that I existed at all. And anyway, the upstairs neighbors weren't at home, either.

All this exercise must've gone to my head; in the odd moment now and then, I found myself imitating a detective again out of sheer perverse habit. I don't know why Malaise had lied to me. Pure meanness, maybe. But a lot of what he'd told me—and a few items he'd left out—didn't add up.

Take that bit about the Broach, for instance, the one installed in his network trolleycar? If he'd had *that* at his disposal, then why the conspicuously monumental architecture mounted on the outside of this rock? Sure, he had a fleet now, but there was enough capacity here to transfer every ship that ever sailed any sea, and you could throw in a hundred years' production from Detroit for good measure. Seemed uncharacteristically wasteful.

And another thing: aside from the impostor who'd greased Ranger Trayle, there'd been exactly zero (count 'em) other male—well, field-workers executing Voltaire's dirty work. And, more significantly, an equal number of simians and cetaceans. This was entirely consistent; Hamiltonians have little use for our hairier or soggier citizens—they feel they're being generous acknowledging the existence of folks with low albedos and foreign accents.

But this left me with a couple of problems: just who the hell broke into my stateroom? There were friends of mine apparently involved somehow with Aphrodite, Ltd. No matter how I stretched things, I just couldn't see Ooloorie or Deejay, or even Freeman Bertram cooperating with the Federalists.

Nor the one who hurt the most, Koko Featherstone-Turncoat.

Here I'd *had* the goddamned cliché interview with the villain-in-chief already, and I was *still* a long way from unraveling the truth.

And I was likely to *die* in that condition.

⅄

Saturday, March 27, 223 A.L.

"Listen t'me, kid, n'listen good. Ya won't do yerself no good goin' ta pieces every time y'fill some train robber fulla...holes. Ya didn't decide he was gonna be no train robber. Y'didn't make 'im try fer this payroll. He decided all that fer hisself. Ya mighta shot 'im, sure. But th' way I lookit it, it was his finger on th' trigger, all along. Look, kid, we're th' best guns Wells-Mulligan's got—-anybody'd break inta our boxcar's just plain committin'...suicide. An' everybody's got th' right to commit suicide, ain't they...kid?"

Four days and twenty-seven Lone Star Republic Pictures later (I'd been doing as much sleeping as I could), I woke up barely able to move and guessed I'd finally reached the end of the trail. Hell, I'd thought you could go longer than a week without eating, provided you had air and plenty of water. So I lay there feeling sorry for myself. It didn't seem fair: I'd been looking forward to those three or four extra centuries Confederate medicine kept promising me.

Contrariwise, if my Clarissa was one of Malaise's brain-bored breeding slaves by now, an extra three or four *minutes* would be too much burden for a single lifetime to bear. Odd, how someone else becomes your soul. Mustering every molecule of willpower, I keyed the Gigacom. If I was going to cash in, I'd do it with her image in my eyes—God, if I'd only thought to record her Telecom calls aboard the—

"Have a good trip, darling, and hurry home." There she was in that gorgeous outfit, lying sexily across our bed. *"While you're gone, I hope this gadget keeps you entertained almost as well as I could!"* I played it over and over trying not to cry, wondering why I bothered trying. The inside of my hood was plenty damp anyway, and I couldn't even open up to wipe it out. Not enough air. In fact there hadn't been enough for quite a while, and now I thought of it, wasn't it rather hot? Look at the way the water drops were boiling on the tap.

Boiling?

Without my suit I'd probably be *poached* by now! Lying on my back, I placed a suited hand against the door—and jerked it back again! Why, after all this time, were they torturing me this way? Couldn't they just let me die in peace? Or were they leaving in their starships, their interstellar exhaust consuming both the outpost and the prisoners they'd left behind?

A sudden, reflex motion had launched me on a gentle, low-gravity trajectory across the floor. I didn't have the gumption to fend off the impact with the opposite wall, but simply lay there confused, awaiting death.

Karumph! The door exploded inward in a cascade of brilliant sparks and molten metal droplets, swirling me upward through the room like a leaf, my telltales flashing green again, a sudden flood of energy rushing through me like a can of Popeye's spinach. I whipped out a hand and glued myself to the ceiling. In the shattered, twisted doorway below swayed a blocky figure, some kind of lethal burner hissing in his upthrust hand.

I breached my smartsuit long enough to snag the « little .25. Let them do what they want, I was going to take a few of the bastards with me, starting with this one. He staggered in reaction to the implosion, shook his hooded head and passed with hesitation into the room. I flipped the tiny safety down and lined up the sights, rudimentary bumps of metal on the upper surface of the slide, slowly increasing pressure on the trigger.

Abruptly, another scarlet-suited figure followed, weapon at the ready, and reached up to unzip her hood.

"Clarissa!"

18: SEMPER FIDELIO

"**P**ut away that toy, son—gonna poke somebody's eye out!" Lucy trundled in behind Clarissa, looking like she'd gone fifteen rounds with a jackhammer.

And lost.

I fastened my eyes on my wife and let go of the ceiling, remembering in midair to scoot the tiny pistol's safety lever up into its notch under the slide. I lighted fairly gracefully (okay, call it a seven-point landing), and wrapped myself around Clarissa while she was doing the same to me. After a while we Kleenexed each other's eyes and I turned to the guy with the torch, Karyl Hetzer.

"One hell of a firestick you've got there! You should've seen the blast from *this* side!" I described the door exploding into the room. Now it hung from its frame like the lid on a half-opened can of sardines. "If that thing'd come loose, it would've cut me right in half! Not that I'm complaining—it would have been preferable to—"

"Win *Bear!*" Clarissa interrupted, "how could you say such a thing?"

"Very easily, sweetheart, I'll *tell* you about it sometime." I sat on the floor, hoping dizzily that someone had brought me a roll of Life Savers— or a couple of mastodons.

Karyl scratched his beard where a puzzled expression lay buried somewhere. "Kind of hard to figure. Anything explosive in this place?"

"Hafta be out in th' hall," Lucy answered, saving me the trouble. "Lookit th' way th' door's bent inward." She rolled her bedraggled way back to the entrance, peering closer. I didn't really give a damn; I held Clarissa, admiring her smile, and wondering, just a little, what seemed different about her. Maybe it was the dashing scarlet smartsuit she was wearing, or—

"Hey!" Lucy and I shouted simultaneously.

"You're not—" I added, but got cut off at the pass.

"That makes sense," said Karyl, I think to Lucy, even if it didn't.

"One at a time," Clarissa finished for the three of us, "but first, let me take care of my slightly under-nourished husband." She untangled herself, stepped out into the hall to retrieve her medikit and an armful of other junk. She extracted something that resembled a blood-pressure cuff, wrapped it around my arm, and plugged its cable into my suit controls. "Just as I suspected," my personal Healer observed, "pretty close to empty—though not nearly enough to explain some of these symptoms." She pushed a button on the wraparound. "We'll pump nutrients directly into your system, and you'd better take these tablets—watch it, dear, they swell in the stomach."

She was right. They *were* swell in my stomach. I burped, washing them down with something from a flask that Karyl provided. Now I knew what was different about Clarissa, but wasn't sure I wanted to ask about it.

Not here, anyway.

"That's what I was tryin' t'say," insisted Lucy, running an expert manipulator around the ragged doorframe. "Sounds more like anoxia, an' I think I've figgered out why."

"Why?" in three-part harmony, yours truly off the pitch a little.

Our semi-cybernetic sidekick pointed to the formerly molten seam along the door. It had been *yanked* inward, producing little horizontal steel icicles. "Y'used up all th' air in here, dummy, that's why! Musta been pret'near hard vacuum by th' time we cut our way in."

Pretty impressive testimony to the smartsuit, creating that kind of vacuum, then protecting its wearer so it went unnoticed. "You're right, I *did* use up all the air, several times, in fact. I just zipped up my suit and—"

"An' waited while it manufactured more? Lemme see yer status lights, boy—'swhat I thought, empty as a bureaucrat's braincase. Winnie, even *microtanks* have bottoms, an' it looks like you started scrapin' 'em two, mebbe three days ago." She turned very slowly, surveying the cell, then pointed toward the sink. "*That's* where yer oxy was comin' from, that little drip of water, an' yer own recycled sweat. But it never came in fast enough, so—"

I interrupted with a brilliant thought: "So the leftover *hydrogen* is what explo— No, that blast was *inward*, damn it!"

Karyl nodded vigorously. "These walls never were hydrogen-proof— sloppiest metalwork I've seen in years. But it was tight enough to vacuum-boil water, and the door came crashing in as soon as it was soft around the edges."

I shook my head, only half hearing him. I was still confused about Clarissa. She caught me staring at her middle.

Her lovely, slim, *unpregnant* middle.

"Don't worry, darling," she told me, patting my hand, "I'm fine, and our daughter's safely tucked away in stasis at Mulligan's Bank and Grill. I'll finish her as soon as we get home—which reminds me, you'd better take this—" She handed me my gunbelt, Webley, Rezin, spare ammunition, and all. "We found it in a sort of office, with Lucy's and a lot of others. Then I knew for certain you were here."

Dead or alive.

I checked the charge level and gave the rotor knob a twist, flipping a projectile into place behind the starter-coil. "And what was Voltaire Malaise doing while you were rummaging through his ill-gotten armory?" And hadn't we better be moving along, I thought, before he found out he'd had visitors?

"Voltaire Malaise the newsman? What's *he* got to do with—"

"Everything. I think he's J.V. Tormount." I strapped my weapons on and tucked the .25 away, explaining what I'd gone through in Malaise's office.

Lucy sputtered and fumed. "But Winnie, don'tcha remember? I was standin' right behind ya while they worked y'over—paralyzed by a tenth-bit electronic thingummy!" Okay, so it *hadn't* been a filing cabinet that thug was leaning against. I didn't remember being beaten up in the office—hadn't it all happened out in the hallway?—which goes to show you something. I'm not sure what.

By the time I finished my story, Clarissa was having trouble controlling her lower lip. I think half of it was sheer outrage. "Well," she finally managed after a couple of false starts, "the place seems deserted now, what we've seen of it. We heard Lucy from the office and came running."

"You *heard* her?" I looked my cone-shaped fellow prisoner over. It was like she'd been scaled to the summit by a thousand tiny alpinists with ice axes. "What the hell *happened* to you, anyway?"

Her answer should have seeped out through a sheepish grin. "Got plumb tired of waitin', an' finally decided t'rescue m'self! I was in a room like this'n, only I had a bunk I didn't need, an' acourse, a toilet. Anyway, day before yesterday, I figgered I was gonna check out pretty soon no matter *what* I did, so I opened up m'Darling gun—*datdatdatdatdat!* You shoulda seen it, Winnie, ricochets buzzin' around like hornets! But all I managed was this little bitty hole, an'—"

"And," Karyl finished impatiently, "we found a cell along this hallway with a telescoping antenna sticking through the door, broadcasting an S.O.S.!"

She slid the aerial out through a slightly opened gunport, punched him gently in the nose, and retracted it again. "Who's tellin' this, sonny, you or me?"

Karyl placed one hand on his middle, gestured broadly with the other, and bowed deeply from the waist. "Madame, I humbly beg your—"

"An' don't call me no *madame*, neither, whippersnapper! Anyway, they cut me loose, an' here we are!"

"Not for long, if I have anything to say about it!" I shuddered. "How did you find me?" Lucy pointed to the twice-scorched door; scrawled across it was a faint chalky inscription: BEAR II.

"Orderly bastards, weren't they? But that must mean—"

Clarissa nodded. "We can't seem to find him though. Do you—?"

"Except for these four homely walls, my love, and your Gigacom—where the hell's my Gigacom?" I found it lodged beneath the sink, seemingly undamaged. "Let's see if we can find him now—time we were getting the hell out of here, anyway. Everybody ready?"

"Right." Clarissa closed her bag with a snap and hitched the strap up on her shoulder where it wouldn't cramp her cross-draw. I squeezed her hand once more, nodded to Karyl and Lucy, and stepped out into the hallway for the first time in a week. It seemed more like a lifetime—and very nearly had been.

I drew my gun and slid an Owen tube over the barrel. If I saw so much as an earwig, I was going to blast a hole in it you could navigate a flivver through.

Thinking about bugs gave me an interesting tactical idea—just in case Clarissa's informal census was wrong. I motioned to my companions and stickied up my shoe soles. It was easier for Lucy on the floor of the corridor, so I walked along the ceiling. My wife and the welder took a wall apiece. Whoever we ran into was gonna be one confused Hamiltonian, and that might buy us an extra few seconds.

Karyl tucked his torch into his belt and pulled out the biggest goddamned laser I'd ever seen. We started slow; there was nothing to be seen down the dimly lit hallway for a hundred yards in either direction.

"Seems to be unfinished crew-quarters," I whispered. "How the devil did you find this rock in the first place?"

Clarissa kept her voice low. "When I got back from Mulligan's, somebody had wrecked the house—I didn't stay around to investigate." She lifted her feet carefully to avoid sliding down the wall. Her bag hung toward the floor, standing out "sideways" from her body.

"Smart lady." And pretty, too—I'd almost forgotten how pretty.

"No, just chicken-hearted. There was an outbound medical courier willing to buck the solar flare. Freshly cloned tissues that had to be delivered."

"And anyway, there *wasn't* any solar flare," said Karyl from the other wall. "I told you—"

"So y'did," acknowledged Lucy. "Mind where yer pointin' that overpowered flashlight, willya?" She waved her Gabbet Fairfax for emphasis, if not example.

"On Ceres," my wife continued, "I put out a general call for you and Koko—where is she, by the way?"

I told her in words of one syllable, most of them with four letters.

"Oh dear, that doesn't sound like our Koko, does it? Anyway, you'd already left Ceres, but I got answered by two different Healers and Karyl here, who decided to come with me."

"Needed a vacation," grinned the welder-restaurateur, "and I'd always planned on seeing more of the Belt. We traced you to Navigation Rock, and through the Patrol from Bulfinch to the bugranch. But then you didn't go where you were supposed to."

I laughed. "Trying to lose the bad guys. I didn't realize we'd be confusing anybody else—careful now!" We'd reached an intersection. I peered around the corner, as did Lucy below me, and kept an eye on Clarissa, for whom the same reconnaissance amounted to peeking cautiously over a metal cliff edge. The corridor beyond us was deserted. With Karyl and my wife jumping the gap, we moved on. "So what happened then?"

Karyl spoke up: "We knew you were hunting missing persons, so the good doctor here thought of contacting Ceres Central to see if there was any pattern to the disappearances."

"Which brought you to the Cluster." I nodded, understanding.

"Which brought us straight to *Bester*," said Clarissa. She reached across to punch me softly on the arm in gentle reproach. "We nearly caught up with you, too—at the refueling station—*remember Pleistocene Plaza?*"

"Oh hell!" I paused, thinking about the guilty fleeing where no Federalist pursueth. "But then we'd *all* have wound up in these cells, wouldn't we? How was it you came straight to Bester? I didn't get that part."

She looked stunned. "Why, it's the statistical center of all the disappearances!"

I stopped, nearly losing my purchase on the ceiling. "I'll be damned. Lucy, we lugged along all that Broach equipment for nothing!"

"So *that's* what all that junk was," said my wife. "We saw it in Lucy's flivver. You might have picked a more sensible orbit to park it in. We almost didn't catch it."

Lucy hadn't answered, but stood there on the floor, slapping her pistol in the palm of a manipulator. "Take a look at this here bulkhead, Winnie. We've found another missing person."

The streaky chalkmarks on the tightly welded door said SCHRO-EDER, P. The bugrancher's other daughter. I looked at my wife and our friends grimly. The girl had been a prisoner here far longer than Lucy and me. I tapped on the wall with my Rezin handle and waited.

No answer.

Karyl limbered up his burner again, torching a cautious half-inch hole in the door. He turned the welder off, but a roaring sound continued as a miniature torrent of air was sucked into the wall. When it quieted, and the edges were cool, I pushed some buttons on my forearm, raised the hood of my suit, and stuck a periscopic finger into the room. It wasn't a pretty sight. Huddled pitiably in one bleak corner lay a little pile of bones and teeth and hair and smartsuit scraps. She could have been dead for a week, or any time since they let the pyramids out for bid. Karyl and Clarissa had a look, too, Lucy tuning in on our suit frequencies.

I don't think any of us said a word.

We continued down the hall until we reached the end of the line; a painted arrow on the wall pointed to an airlock on our left. I weighed various factors in my mind, then said: "Clarissa, you and Lucy get off this rock and run like hell for help. Karyl—if you're willing—we'll stay and look for Ed."

My wife opened her mouth to protest; Lucy exclaimed, "Nothin' doin', youngster! I can set up a distress call from th' flivver, then we'll *all* tear this joint apart until—"

CLANG-CLANG-CLANG-CLANG-CLANG! Noise exploded through the steel-corridored complex. I stood frozen, the front sight of my pistol questing for a target. Clarissa grabbed my arm and towed me to the lock. We buttoned up in clumsy haste. "You sure you're still airtight, Lucy?" I dropped my weapon fooling with hoodseams and stooped to retrieve it.

"If I wasn't, we wouldn't be talkin' 'bout it!" She pointed to the rapidly widening outer door—she'd cycled us through, heedless of the risk.

We stumbled out onto the rocky surface. Behind, some radio equivalent of the alarm still blared: *"Alert! Alert! All personnel take cover! Alert! Alert!"* Above our heads a swarm of heavily armed flivvers circled like vultures, Darling guns on either fender and rocket tubes protruding from their armor-plated bellies. The muzzles of their weapons flashed and sparkled; a midwestern dust-devil churned before us on the not-so-distant horizon, a miniature tornado of swiftly marching high-velocity death.

I threw an arm up and *fired*! The Webley smashed my hand, its Owen tube wide of the mark. I racked up a second, aligned the sights and fired again. This time an aggressor skewed and wobbled in its orbit, throwing sparks and rapidly diffusing smoke. There was a flare, the buffet of a shockwave, and they were gone in a million fragments.

One down, several dozen yet to go.

"*You on the surface!*" demanded an amplified, authoritative voice. "*Stand where you are! Drop your weapons!*"

Win Bear wasn't going back to any cell! "Scatter!" I hollered, ignoring my own orders by gathering Clarissa to me. We threw ourselves into a crater, bouncing up to toss a little mayhem at the enemy. I scored on a second and a third flivver. Is it three kills or five to make an ace?

Four cars dropped out of the orbiting armada, settled in a broad-flung square around us. Men emerged, various other critters with toes in their suitfeet, running low, swinging deadly looking fléchette-guns. Overhead a smartsuited cetacean squadron jetted from the vehicles, chin-mounted lasers twinkling in the starlight as they tossed and twisted, trying to draw a bead. The rock beside me fused and smoked.

I *fired*. A shotgunner crumpled, hanging three feet off the ground, squirting blood until his suit sealed. I fired again and sensed the thrum of Clarissa's smaller weapon on my shoulder. There was a flash as Lucy's .50 joined the chorus, chewing impressive hunks out of the enemy's grounded flivvers. The different-colored flash of Karyl's laser accounted for two more bad guys.

As I groped for another magazine, the world exploded around me. When it settled down again, my left arm wouldn't work—sensible, given the fist-size chunk of tissue missing from my shoulder. A dozen steel needles sprouted from the wound like Lilliputian arrows. Oddly, it didn't hurt a bit.

Clarissa ripped the nutrient cuff off my right arm and slapped it over the wound. Now *that* hurt; I sort of faded for a moment, and when I joined the universe again, there were a lot of extra shadows on the crater floor. Our ersatz foxhole was ringed solidly with angry-looking gunmen pointing their fléchette-guns at the bridge of my nose.

A bore that size, you can actually see the shell up in the breech.

I holstered the Webley, suddenly too tired to think, and unbuckled the belt one-handed. Across the rock, more movement. "Here we go again," muttered Lucy, being frogmarched from behind her shelter. "Take yer poxy mitts off me, you...*Cossacks!*"

"Shuddup!" A burly black-and-silver-clad figure signaled to his only slightly less-impressive minions, who gathered up our guns and Clarissa's bag. Gesturing us toward the lock we'd come through, he waited for us to obey, then followed. My last glimpse of the surface was of a hundred cars disgorging soldiers; my only satisfaction the number of stretcher cases they were dragging. Come to think of it, I could have used a free ride, myself. Karyl seemed to be okay, Clarissa and Lucy were unharmed.

Okay, I'd settle for that.

They hup-hoop-heeped us through the corridor. "Where are you taking us?" my wife demanded, pointing at the wounded all around us. "These people are hurt—they need attention!"

The guard leader chuckled. "Don't worry, honey, the boss'll give *you* plenty of attention! Now *move!*" We reached an all-too-familiar-looking door. He straightened his shoulders, prodded a couple of his sagging troops erect. "Look smart, you monkeys!" It was Malaise's office, of course. The head goon rapped. Out of the corner of my eye, I caught Karyl loosening the welding torch in his belt. The seams of Lucy's hidden gun compartment were slowly growing wider. I slipped a hand up to the neck of my suit, ready to dive for the Bauer. If we were doomed, we might as well go out in style.

The door slid aside, the room beyond was dark.

"Come in, Captain! Confound it, where's the lightswitch!" The glare sprang up around us. There, leaning over the desk looking angry as hell, was Mr. Big himself, J. V. Tormount.

Known to his constituents as Olongo Featherstone-Haugh.

19: THE SHEEP FROM THE GOATS

"Fifty-seven dead, eight seriously disabled, half a dozen walking wounded. Win, how could you *do* it?" Olongo wiped a paw across his tired expression and sighed. "The policeman in you, I suppose. Once an authoritarian, always a—"

"What the hell did you expect, long-stemmed roses? Your thugs lock me up and starve me for a week, I'll be *goddamned* if I don't burn a few, first chance I get!" I elbowed away the goon in charge of me and peeked beneath Clarissa's slapdash bandaging. It still looked like strawberry shortcake, the dozen or so fléchettes embedded in the muscle beginning to throb discordantly.

Olongo recoiled. "You were a *prisoner* here?" He paused for a long time in astonished reassessment. "I'd give anything to believe that, Win. But why did you open fire on the very people coming to rescue you?"

"Mr. President, I don't know who's kidding who—whom—but we'd damn well better get it sorted out. Hell, I thought you'd thrown in with the Hamiltonians. Didn't these screws of yours call you 'Tormount'?"

The security chief peeled off his hood and took a belligerent step toward me. I met him halfway and we tried to see who could grind his teeth the loudest. He won, but I had a three-tooth handicap.

"*Gunny!*" Olongo ordered. Now I knew why the son of a bitch looked so familiar—it was Gunnison Griswold, himself. *Brrr.* "Get these people some chairs—and see to your wounded. Clarissa, apparently I've no right to ask it, but would you mind helping, dear?" She nodded and repossessed her kit, taking the local militia with her into the hall. I sat down and began exploring for a cigar.

Olongo closed his eyes, resting his broad black face in his broad black hands. "'Tormount' I am, too. A lodge name, Win: Altruistic Protective Enclave of Simians..." He spread his enormous arms, practically filling the room. "My late lodge-master's idea of humor."

Lucy, trundling out to help Clarissa, paused in the doorway. "Better answer his question, old anthropoid. How'd y'get hooked up with Federalists? Them vermin never had a kind intention toward nonhumans that *I* knowed about."

The President slapped his paws on the desk and rose, discovering, just like Malaise, that you can't pace in a hundredth-gee. He wound up leaning his massive bulk on a filing cabinet—a real one this time. It groaned and a drawer popped open. "I scarcely know where to begin, my friends. Aphrodite, Ltd., is as far from a Hamiltonian conspiracy as you could imagine: a relatively simple engineering scheme—though I suppose the scale of the thing might surprise you. I only learned recently that we had unwittingly become a *front* for something much more sinister. Which, of course, is why I came out here to investigate."

"You, too?" I shook my head in disbelief.

"*Me, too!*" replied a walking stack of print-outs which emerged from an adjoining room. "Where y'want these, Unc?"

"*Koko!*" Lucy beat me to it, but not by much. The furry little twerp set the hardcopies on the desk, flipped one of its bungees over to hold them, and ran to embrace Lucy and my wife in turn. She came back with the great granddaddy of all embarrassed, guilty looks. "Boss..."

"Don't call *me* 'boss'! You were fired the day you left Navigation Rock—in Lucy's car!" Was that a tear rolling down her leathery cheek? Maybe it was just my cigar smoke.

She sniffed, "Aw, Win, I..."

"*Ahem!*" Olongo conjured up a stogie of his own, lit it with a flourish, and, having gotten our attention thus, abused it with a long and thoughtful pause. Finally: "My boy, she acted at my request—reluctantly, for what it's worth—to help me ferret out what was going sour with our operations here..."

⅄

"Sour" wasn't quite the word. Aphrodite had been conceived nearly ten years earlier when the then-Vice President and his baby niece were traveling in the asteroids on casual vacation. He'd stayed a while, then left the fledgling enterprise in what he'd believed were trustworthy hands, returning only for rare inspections, taking care of the business end back home on Earth.

Early in the venture, Voltaire Malaise had caught wind of it. Instead of exposing it to the viewing public, he'd insisted on buying in. Olongo's partners had assented in the interests of secrecy, and out of admiration for the newsman's enthusiasm for space exploration. With the passing of time, the Voice of the Stars assumed an increasingly central role, becoming virtual overseer of operations in the Belt. Until recently, when lagging production, scheduling and cost overruns, and a rash of mysterious disappearances in the Nomad Cluster and elsewhere had prompted Olongo to initiate his first inquiries.

Whereupon the conspirators had tried to knock him off via remote control.

⅄

"Thus, my decision to pursue the matter further in person. And it served a second purpose, as well," admitted Olongo, "keeping me out of sight—and *alive*." Somehow, with that cigar in his hand, he made me think of Ernie Kovacs. All he needed was a xylophone and a derby.

I grunted. "Koko was a backup—or maybe another clay pigeon—*like me?*" I turned to glance out the door where Clarissa was administering electronarcosis. She looked up, smiled, and went right back to work.

Koko giggled. "A little of both, I guess. Uncle President needed elbow room; I proposed to muddy the water—be a noisy, visible diversion—while he simply disappeared. No one would ever suspect—"

"I *thought* I recognized that last-minute invalid they wheeled aboard the *Bonaventura*, a reddish-pelted, elderly—"

"*Elderly?*" Olongo looked insulted, then philosophical. "Well, perhaps not *all* of that medical apparatus was window dressing." He blew a smoke ring. "It was a bloody rough ride! I spent several days convalescing while Koko had to hop, keeping you—"

"Fat, dumb, and happy?" I essayed.

"*Company*," insisted the gorilla, "also running errands trying to find out what was happening here on Bester. The Federalists' 'solar flare' didn't make that an easy task."

I looked my erstwhile assistant over. "You forgot to mention committing burglaries, *Uncle Fagin!*"

They both shriveled. First time I'd ever had that effect on a gorilla. I kind of liked it. "Er, uh..." offered Koko.

"Umm, ah*um!*" Olongo added for clarification.

"Forget it, you two ratfinks. I finally figured it out, too: the Russian assassin dropped the wrong medallion for bait in the cargo hold. I wasn't supposed to get a brain-bore controller. In fact I wasn't supposed to get anything but dead. But it screwed up the Hamiltonians' plans; their hit-lady had to proceed thereafter, however inefficiently, on preprogrammed skulduggery. That's why my luggage got swiped—and it's why Koko turned my stateroom upside-down. You wanted that medal for your own investigation!"

Olongo spread his hands. "We'd heard about the brain-bore, and—"

"I said forget it. I might've done the same, in your place—*though I'd probably have confided in my friends*. Did I hurt you much, incompetent apprentice?"

She grinned. Apparently her smartsuit had repaired her knife wound well enough. I dabbed the blood leaking from beneath my own makeshift bandage. "Why'd you take so long getting out here yourselves? And why the Marine Corps assault?"

Koko snorted. "We sent three teams—borrowed from various registry patrols—and they vanished. We figured whatever we did next should either be very cautious or highly dramatic."

The President chuckled. "Koko argued for dramatic, naturally. There's very little else to tell: I used a lot of precious time and money importing a small army, and here we are. I'm sorry they wound up attacking an empty base—and innocent parties—believe me I am."

Clarissa finished the last of the casualties, came in, and started on me. "I'd believe you a lot more readily—"

"Ouch, honey! That hurts!"

"Didn't mean to take it out on you, dear—a lot more readily if you'd mentioned, any time in the last half hour, what Aphrodite's *real* purpose is out here."

Lucy pivoted, fixing her optical surfaces on the big simian. He glanced at Koko, who shrugged, then back at us: "Clarissa, Win—and you, especially, Lucy. You know I've fought the Hamiltonians in Congress, in Uganda, Antarctica, Hawaii. Have a little faith in me on that account, if no other. When I can speak freely...But there are partners, shareholders, parties sworn to mutual secrecy. Fortunes could be lost with a single careless word."

I stomped my cigar out. "Which means you're not going to tell us."

"That's what he means," observed Lucy disgustedly. "My Eddie missin', folks gettin' murdered all over th' place—Olongo, we deserve better'n this."

The gorilla smiled and shook his head. "Indeed you do. I'll make it up to all of you, rely on it. In the meantime, I have personnel combing every cubic inch of this rock. They'll find Ed if anybody can. He's my friend, too, my dears, a brother-in-arms on more than one occasion."

The door slid open and Gunnison Griswold ran in. "Chief! Check the Telecom—channel 47-D!" He tried to stop, but slid around the desk and nearly crashed against the wall. Olongo reached out an easy hand, righted him as if he were a plastic chessman, and projected the suggested channel on a wall screen.

"*Sector Nine*," said a disembodied voice, "*we have a bandit breaking off, reference B for Bakunin...*"

"Meteor watch?" I asked. Olongo nodded, shushing me. The viewpoint of the 'com surged outward, centering on a shiny dot, which puffed up into the outline of a flivver—a big one, more of a bus, really. "*Malaise!* The bastard's getting away!"

Olongo stabbed buttons. "Try and disable that—"

Flash! The spacebus vanished, leaving emptiness behind and little purple dots dancing on our retinas. "That was a Broach!" I said, unnecessarily. "He's on the other side now, probably heading for his fleet." *Which meant they hadn't taken off yet.*

"Olongo!" As quickly as I could, I summarized my conversation with the System's Most Trusted Criminal. "You people have Broach equipment here, I saw it. Is there any way we can—" The gorilla pushed more buttons as we watched; a familiar cheerful voice answered. Olongo repeated what I'd told him, and, thirty seconds later, the office door slid aside again to admit an old friend.

Deejay Thorens.

"Hello, Win, Clarissa, and is that—*Lucy!* Olongo, I'm going to need another hour to calibrate before we can follow that flivver. Converting a stationary rig for mobile use..."

A small word about Deejay, who looks more out of place in a physics lab than I would in Haight-Ashbury. I'm told she's one of the great theoretical minds of the age, with an added and unusual flair for the sort of applied tinkering American "pure" scientists frequently scorn. One look into those orchid-colored eyes and even Heisenberg would've known for sure.

I love my wife, but I'm not blind.

Deejay bent over Olongo's desk, zipping facts and figures past a 'com screen. Occasionally she'd stop to answer questions or issue orders to her crew, wherever they were hiding. I sat still, thinking furiously—or trying to—while Clarissa pulled little steel shotgun darts out of me. Reverse acupuncture.

"Ouch!" *Plink!* Good thing for me Olongo had brought his army from Earth; Gunny Griswold and his gang were sharp—"Ouch!" but *here* they were out of their element. Fléchettes need an atmosphere for their little stabilizing fins; in a hard vacuum, they'd tumbled randomly, which is why—"Ouch!"—I was still alive. *Plink! Plink! Plink!*

More or less.

One of the nasty little things had gone in fins-first backward!

"Ow!" A 230-ship fleet was parked out there invisibly, on the other side of reality. Were they piping Malaise aboard even now, for the long jump to the stars? "Ow!" That didn't make much sense, for how could he be sure he wouldn't materialize—"Ow!"— right inside one of his ships? Now *that* would be some explosion. "Ow!" Let's see: the asteroid Bester probably existed on the other side as well, and—!

"Ouch! Goddammit, stop a minute, honey! Deejay, could you get a Broach cooking *right here*, and fast?" With the regiment of gunsels Olongo'd brought along, we might be able to cancel this Federalist excursion.

She turned to look at me, bewildered for a moment, then: "Of course! We have a battery of research machines. Come on down to the lab!" She was gone with a twinkle of smartsuit-covered ankles and a swirl of labcoat-tails. Clarissa smoothed a flap of suit material over my wound. Once again I gathered up my weapons and friends, following the physicist. Griswold glanced around at the bandaged, sleeping portion of his crew, then took up a disgruntled rear-guard.

Minutes later, with hardly a chance to admire Deejay's shiny new laboratory, I stepped carefully between the pole-pieces of a freshly opened Broach, back into my home universe. Bester was here, too, all right, but the Hamiltonians' ideas on architecture were markedly—and typically—different. I was in the middle of a wide, corrugated, barnlike structure, cruelly illuminated, divided, like a National Guard armory on 4-H day, into countless pens and cages, uninhabited, and unspeakably filthy. One whiff and I suddenly knew exactly what an eighteenth-century slaveship must have smelled like. The captives in their thousands were gone, but they'd left behind an almost tangible aura of the misery the Federalists and their allies had imposed on them.

And would continue to, unless we stopped it, now.

Somebody needed killing. I hoped I'd get the chance to do it.

I turned and watched my friends step through a ghostly circle floating in midair. Deejay came last, pressing a hand-held control. The Broach shrank to an almost invisible dot, but didn't quite vanish. Important, if we were going to get back home again.

We spread out through this harshly lit gallery of horror, grateful that our suits carried their own supply of fresh air. Everywhere I turned, a maze of excrement- and blood-encrusted bars confronted me, moldering remnants of food that was probably poor to begin with, skittering furry little things, and here and there the graying bones of a few potential breeding slaves who hadn't survived.

Maybe they were the lucky ones.

Atop one skull, like a giant plastic leech, the casing of a brain-bore glittered obscenely. I finally reached the end of the enclosure where a door led to a series of corridors. I stepped inside and—

—found myself looking straight and stupid into the muzzle of the biggest little pocket pistol I've ever seen. Sixty caliber, and behind it stood a highly familiar-looking figure.

"*Ed!*"

He grinned—my grin—and let his gun arm drop wearily. "Brother, it's good to see your homely face again. Thought I was stranded out here forever. Where's Lucy?"

"I,er..."

"Eddie!" Lucy wheeled through the door, nearly bowling me over. Clarissa joined us and I put my arm around her, turning so that Ed and Lucy could have some privacy. They were going to need it.

Olongo puffed into our ken, and if gorillas can look pale, that's what I was seeing now. "I can't believe it! There must have been *thousands*—"

"*Tens* of thousands," Ed said grimly. Koko stumbled toward us, sobbing openly.

I felt my stomach turn over. "A quarter of a million was the figure Malaise mentioned. Ed, what are you doing running around loose?" I was beginning to experience an odd, calm, detached feeling about all this; I knew I'd pay for it later, in dreams that would haunt my nights for months.

"I've been free for days, hiding in broom closets, pantries, latrines—in a place this size, and with a smartsuit—besides, the prisoners were *controlled*, they thought. No need for guards." He paused. "Where they went, well, come with me. You won't believe it if I just tell you."

A long, complicated tour found us in a smaller room, circular, with an enormous, generatorlike contraption in the center. Deejay inspected it carefully; the rest of us hardly noticed: outside, through wall-size windows, was the second-most impressive sight I'd ever seen. (The first? Clarissa coming through the ruined door of my cell.) A few miles away hung the Hamiltonian fleet, 230 metallic globes, each perhaps a quarter of a mile across. In countless minuscule rows, their portholes were alight. A hundred thousand flivvers stood away in silent, empty profusion, the last and nearest in line, Malaise's network bus.

They were buttoning up for a giant leap.

"*Reference!*" At Deejay's sudden shout, I gave a giant leap myself, and peeled Koko off the low ceiling. "*They've cracked the navigation problem!*"

"What?" I turned to watch her running hands over the infernal machine. Ablaze with twinkling lamps amidst a myriad knobs and buttons, it was shaped a bit like Lucy in her present incarnation, only four or five times bigger. It rested on the floor below us and protruded up into the room through a railed, circular opening.

"Look," lectured our friendly neighborhood physicist, "the problem with traversing the Little Bang universe is that all its spatiotemporal points are geometrically common, so there's no way to tell them apart, right?"

"That's what they told me on Ceres," I answered, "Which is why they gave up on the—"

"Well, this machine is the Hamiltonians' navigational reference point. It generates a beacon of Broach noise so raw and loud that it can be used as a sort of compass, even in an alternate universe. This is how they'll—"

"*There they* go!" Ed exclaimed. I could see it too, a faint bluish aura enveloping each starship as it warmed up, answered by a sort of coruscating, crawling surface-discharge from the machine in the center of the—

Kabo! Blam! DitDitDitDitDit! I guess everybody got the same idea at once. When the smoke cleared and I'd reholstered my Webley, I noticed Clarissa tucking away her little .11 caliber. Ed blinked and gave up jerking the trigger of his freshly emptied derringer. Even Deejay was standing with a slowly cooling laser in her hand. Olongo and Koko saluted each other with the muzzles of their guns over the wreckage of the Hamiltonian device, and Lucy's Darling quick-shooter was folding back out of sight like the bellows on an old-timey Polaroid.

Griswold blew smoke through the barrel of his .476, let the slide down on a fresh magazine, and slammed the weapon back into its scabbard. Even he had been too slow; outside, like a flock of flashbulbs going off, the Federalist fleet winked out of existence.

Koko looked confused. "Did they blow up, too?"

"No," answered Deejay, "they've gone to the stars, just as they planned. Only—well, none of them will wind up where they intended. Each ship will have to jump blindly, again and again, until it finds a habitable planet to settle. They're scattered randomly across dozens of parsecs—and thousands of years—with no way to come home, ever again."

"Good heavens!" shuddered Olongo.

"Good riddance!" snorted Lucy.

20: WILL YE ALL BE KINGS AND CAPTAINS?

Doomsday, 224 A.L.

D. Nolan Fraser got elected President last week. In the Confederacy, it's "None of the Above" for the second time this century. Information specialists at the Emperor Norton University have finally deciphered those mysterious signals from the stars—with a little help from Deejay and her paratronics crew. It didn't come as much of a surprise to hear Voltaire Malaise, deBroached and unscrambled at last, whimpering across the light-years for *help!* Any kind of *help!* The Confederacy—or anyone else, *please?*

Unfortunately, it's stale news. He's centuries dead by now. Radio's notoriously slow at interstellar distances. There are scientist-entrepreneurs in the System groping toward a more reliable star drive, based on some entirely different principles, but old Voltaire'll be centuries dead *again* by the time anybody gets to him and his makeshift, randomly established colony of would-be sultans.

At least he'd really had a chance to be the Voice of the Stars; you can still hear him on a quiet winter night. He hadn't much chance at being anything else, especially an immortal god to helpless slaves and worshippers. Ed had seen to that; busiest little monkey-wrencher since FDR conned the Nipponese into ending a Depression the hard way.

Must've gotten pretty crowded out on Bester toward the end—that *other* Bester in the section of the cosmos where I used to hang my hat. Where the Federalists had built their ill-starred fleet. So full of brain-bored harem-candidates they'd had to put the overflow—like Lucy and me—in Aphrodite country, this side of the Broach.

In all that moving-day confusion, Ed had sprung himself, thanks to a trick he'd learned from me: a second, hidden gun. One night when they were feeding the First Class jailbirds, he blew away a pair of attendants and lit out for the nooks and crannies. They were suffering a manpower shortage at the time—one of his keepers was a former French-Canadian Prime Minister—and the electronic zombies weren't doing any talking, so it was relatively easy for Ed to hit and run and hit again from hiding. Good thing he'd moved when he did: his final meal killed the four-legged rats who'd gotten to it. Swell bunch of guys, the Hamiltonians.

Ed didn't waste the time he'd bought himself. Scraps of goonish conversation were enough to piece together what was just about to happen. I'm proud I taught the boy to hit below the belt: one by one he searched out every cache of geriatric goodies waiting to be loaded; one by one he substituted sugar, corn syrup, inert electronics—anything that looked right—for the real thing, which he smashed and flushed down the plumb-ing. At the time it must have seemed a small revenge, but it was something.

Ditto for another item of adroit sabotage: brain-bores operate on guccione cells, just like Confederate flashlights and flivvers. Ordinarily, they last a long, long time. But all good things come to an end (or at least require recharging), and when the original power units begin to fail, the Hamiltonians will discover (*have* discovered—it's a crazy universe) that what they'd thought were crates of new cells are actually my former partner's last-minute rock collection. *Plus* emptyings from his smartsuit.

I like Ed, he reminds me of me.

Give 'em two years at the outside. The tiny minority of male "gods" are going to wind up with an extremely large, angry female lynch mob on their hands. Ed couldn't keep a quarter-million innocents from being shanghaied, not all by himself—but he'd given them the chance to seize control of their own lives again. And on an even basis with their kidnappers. That's better than nothing—and a hell of a lot better than what Malaise and his gang had planned.

Which makes me wonder what's transpired in the centuries since Voltaire discovered the mess he and his accomplices were in. What kinds of civilizations are growing up among the two hundred thirty random stars where the lost fleet has come to its scattered rest? Deejay tells me some of them may have flickered back in time as much as five or six thousand years. Others, having accidentally blinked into the future, won't be arriving yet for an equal length of time.

Weird.

If they'd all been Confederates, there wouldn't be much doubt about the kind of prosperous, aggressively progressive anarchistic societies they'll have created by now. But the women are mostly from the United States and other countries in my homeworld, as are the bulk of bureaucrats and dictators who dreamed of owning worlds.

The few individuals from this side of reality—the Hamiltonians—are philosophical throwbacks.

Five thousand years. That's a lot of time for the successive rise and fall of one perverted, totalitarian culture after another. Most of them will lose their grip—gradually, or all at once—on the very technology that took them to the stars. Maybe more than one world is a radioactive ruin already, while others struggle through a new Stone Age.

We'll go out someday and take a look.

But we need a better way of getting there, and in the meantime, we have other fish to fry. Deejay's been filling our heads with lots of other weird and wonderful notions since Olongo finally invited us out to see for ourselves what Aphrodite, Ltd. was really all about. This necessitated another spaceship ride, aboard the less-luxurious (but roomier, owing to the highly select passenger list) *Indomitable Spirit*.

"Now you're sure you have everything, dearest?" Last time we'd visited her folks in Antarctica, she'd forgotten diapers. It had been a long, long plane ride, subjectively, until we found a drugstore in Marie Byrd Land.

"You're never going to let me live that down, are you?" She smiled sickly sweet, shut the suitcase, and turned to watch Lucille, who was doing her damnedest to eat the bedspread, little chenille balls and all.

"Forget it, honey. Vacations always seem like *work* to me, especially with our little friend here." I took my lovely wife in my arms and squeezed her, suddenly regretting that we were leaving so soon. "This is certainly going to be a hell of a trip for her—something to tell her grandchildren." I released Clarissa, lit a cigar, then turned up the bedroom ventilators to protect Lucille's tiny, brand-new lungs—hardly out of warranty yet, seemed like a shame to spoil them.

Lucille kicked her naked little legs and giggled, drooling idiotically. The doorbell asked if we were expecting visitors, so I went downstairs to answer it. There was Ed, a rented Studebaker piled with baggage thrumming in the driveway behind him. And waiting in it—

"*Lucy!* Does this mean we don't have to visit you in the hospital any more? I was getting pretty tired of the smell of disinfectant."

"*Now* he tells me!" A slender, not quite pretty, dark-haired girl dismounted from the driver's seat, smoothed her skirt down over boot-tops, and ran up the rubber-covered drive. She grabbed me crushingly around the neck and kissed me on both cheeks. "So much fer th' formalities, Winnie—don't stand there with yer choppers hangin' out, I wanna see m'namesake!" She bolted through the door and upstairs to the bedroom.

I ran my tongue self-consciously over the cloned incisors Clarissa had implanted several months ago, imagining with a shudder what life would be like for "aged cripples" like Lucy and me or a billion others in the kind of paradise Malaise had wanted. Like the man said, nasty, brutish, and short.

Ed grinned, combed a hand through his hair and massaged the side of his nose, a gesture I recognized eerily as my own. "You realize how pleased she was you named your only-begotten after her?"

"How could it be otherwise? Lucy is Honorary Grandma, after all."

"Which makes me Lucille's accidental uncle and honorary grandfather at the same time. Sounds like incest. Well, Lucy may not look it any more, but at least she's got enough seniority for the job. I'm only sixty—I sure don't *feel* like a grandpa."

"Let's see...she's now about twice your age. By the time you're 160, she'll only be 250—you're gaining on her, slow but steady."

He laughed. "First thing she does with her brand-new body is take me surfing in the Davis Strait Mitigation Zone—she broke seventeen bones. Good thing she isn't any younger, I can't keep up with her now!" We followed at a more sedate velocity to the second floor, where Clarissa had apparently finished packing.

"Well, sweetheart, about ready for another interplanetary voyage?"

"As long as we go together this time." She looked down at our daughter and frowned. "*And* as soon as you've changed her—again. It *was* you who insisted that we pack *all* the diapers, wasn't it?"

ᴧ

Let me warn you here and now that freefall sex is highly overrated. And extremely messy. If you time things wrong, you can even wind up on opposite sides of the room, just at the supreme moment.

Luckily, we spent most of the next thirty days at constant boost, where things like wives—and dirty diapers—stay more or less where you put them. Our voyage ended at a set of plastic handstraps hanging in the polarized windows of an orbiting junkyard where *Indomitable Spirit* had dropped us off—before fleeing prudently Outward once again.

I couldn't decide whether it was harder getting used to Lucy as a healthy young woman again, or seeing my baby daughter wearing her very first smartsuit. At least it solved the changing problem, as I said, no small consideration in zero gravity. Until she was old enough to handle them intelligently for herself, her suit controls would be located in the middle of her back. In the meantime, I was trying to figure whether there was a market for computerized rubber didies back on Earth.

And wondering if anybody's thought of making smartsuits for cats.

It was almost as difficult accommodating to the scenery outside those windows. If anyone had ever told a certain overworked and tired Denver cop, a decade and a half ago, that someday he was going to see a sight like this, I'd have laughed myself straight into a coronary.

Now, here it was, a fuzzy ball of cotton, far too brilliant to bear looking at without dampering the windows. Through the deeply darkened plastic, the world below us seemed to occupy a starless void. The sun was on the other side of the station, and there'd never been a moon here. Until recently. I heard a door whoosh open behind me and swiveled on my handstrap just in time to catch Ooloorie entering the observation deck, followed closely by her partner.

"Well, my finely furred landlings," said the porpoise, bobbing four feet off the grating, fluttering a suit-covered tail now and again to maintain that position, "how do you like my planet out there?" Her ventral impellers whispered briefly; she drifted to the windows, reaching out a suit-mounted manipulator to stop herself on a handstrap.

Deejay grinned. "Twenty-nine months in orbit, now she thinks she *owns* it!"

"Indeed, insubordinate calf, a full $5\frac{1}{4}$ percent, blue-chip, iron-bound, and potentially quite lucrative. The same as your share, my dear."

The human physicist grinned again, at me this time. "I understand Olongo passed a little profit your way, too."

"A tenth percent for each of us, provided this ridiculous scheme comes off on schedule." I still didn't know what we were being rewarded for. My own blunderings hadn't accomplished that much. Evil has a habit, generally, of destroying itself—though it never hurts to help it along a little. "Personally, I'm not sure this neighborhood's healthy, are you?" Even half a million miles away, the planet looked too big and deadly. Like a time bomb.

"*Cowardice,* from my Supreme Guru in Chief?" Koko ricocheted into the room behind her uncle, a jaunty yachting cap perched on her head.

"Simple caution, O Formerly Fired Flunky, that's a dangerous toy down there."

"Not near as dangerous," Lucy observed, "as th' toy that's on its way. Sure wish you'd filled us in sooner, O Prime Pongid—(Shucks, now they got *me* doin' it!)—I'd like to've checked yer 'rithmetic."

The ex-President thrust a stubby finger toward the physicists. "*Their* arithmetic, er...O Former Funnel. That's why Ooloorie was stationed here so long, to make sure we had every motion, force, and vector nailed down. Consequently, in approximately...twenty-three minutes, we'll each be several billion ounces richer—a cheerful prospect, and one, I trow, that merits a libation. Koko?"

"Not my department, Uncle Has-been, I'm a spitsole, now!"

"That's *'gumshoe'*" Koko, and *I'll* get the champagne, okay?"

"You're the boss, Boss." Puzzled, she inspected the bottoms of her feet.

"Also the waiter, it appears. Drinks for everyone?" Enthusiastic nods, even from the cetacean delegate. *That* should be interesting to watch. Lucille burbled and started nodding, too.

"Gets her alcoholic tendencies from her daddy," Clarissa contributed. I stuck my tongue out, and started nursing gigglewater from a wall-tap. Other crewfolk joined us and the observation lounge began to fill as champagne baggies were quickly emptied and replenished.

Five minutes to Zero.

Acceleration warnings sounded as the station began backing gently away from the planet. Windows became floors, tickling my acrophobia a little, but I couldn't help staring down between my feet anyway.

Suddenly, the solitary globe below was joined by an intruder, rocketing from nowhere—though all of us knew where it had started, months ago. Now, at a carefully calculated fraction of lightspeed, the asteroid Bester, driven by ravening, matter-annihilating giant Broaches on its "stern," was rapidly closing on Venus.

Venus: a world satisfactorily as close to hell as places ever get. The most inhospitable, desolate, useless, impossible planet in the System.

Venus: mass approximating Earth's, probably quite close to that of whatever primordial body became the Asteroid Belt (or never quite became a planet), the same potential goldmine, a hundred times as rich.

Bester swelled with proximity, uninhabited now except for mechanisms maintaining its course, the glaring, pulsing drives still consuming mass as they had nearly half-devoured the asteroid already. With majestic, inexorable grace, it plunged into the planet. Even through the clouds, we watched the crust bulge upward, spewing magma, erupting outward at velocity sufficient to spread the worthless planet's fragments out along its orbit, slowly cooling, hardening. A second Asteroid Belt, one that wouldn't spend its wealth profligately gouging-raters from the moons and surfaces of other planets, or fling it wastefully toward the stars.

Out there, somewhere, a thousand souped-up, toughened little fighting flivvers—Olongo's "debris patrol," an accidental parting gift from the Hamiltonians—were making sure nobody else's territory got splashed. Otherwise, the lawsuits would eat up any profit this venture might show for the next couple of millennia. Koko had wanted to fly with the squadron—until Lucy pointed out that "ace" can be spelled and pronounced a couple of different ways.

"Listen, you guys," I broke the utter silence aboard the outbound station. "I didn't want to ask before, but—well, won't this slop the whole gravitic balance of the Solar System out of kilter or something?"

"Oh, that," muttered Lucy. "You want us to file EPA forms in triplicate? Only folks who're interested in that kinda ritual are gone now with Malaise!"

"But you've got to admit," I persisted, "it was one hell of an environmental impact!" Outside, Venus swelled into a cloud of glowing debris, a trillion tons of popcorn going off inside a nuclear explosion. Or, I remembered suddenly, like those high-speed photos Remington used to publish, of a high-velocity bullet hitting an orange. *Splat.*

And three-tenths of one percent of it (Olongo had insisted on a belated birthday present for Lucille) belonged to my family. Well, *let* the authoritarians have the stars a little while. Both systems were well rid of them; the progress of liberty back home would accelerate a thousandfold—a millionfold—without them in the way, breathing down everybody's necks. Meantime, we'd have the Belts, half a million little worlds, to Malaise's two hundred and thirty.

Lucy contemplated the Wagnerian scene below—or maybe "Kryptonian" is a better adjective. "Tell y' what, Winnie. Haul th' family out to th' Old Belt agin while things're coolin' off down here. Planets're obsolete. Shucks, we might's well leave the Earth— it's a water world, after all—to th' porpoises!"

"Oh, no you don't." Ooloorie chuckled. "You seem to forget this whole thing began with cetaceans reaching for the stars. We're *built* to live in freefall; you're not going to stick us with a worn-out second-hand planet!"

I squished a little champagne out of my baggie, swirled it around in my mouth, and swallowed. "You still haven't answered my question: aren't we screwing up the Solar System?"

She turned to look at me. "Well, if it'll make y'feel better, sonny, Mr. Tormount over there's finally taken me on as an engineer. Next year, just t' balance things out, *we're gonna blow up Neptune!*"

Neptune? Well, raise the ante, then: a *million* little worlds, give or take, one for each and every man, woman, child—of whatever species—who wants one. I wondered how I'd like it, being sovereign of my own tiny planet.

The preservationists back home—what few hadn't gone with Malaise—wouldn't like it much. Once they found out: funny to think that stepping through a Broach out here would "bring" a solid, useless planet back into existence. But hell, *all* life has environmental impact, just by virtue of its *being*. Intelligence *manipulates* its environment, purposefully, instead of the other way around. The Ehrlichs, Commoners, Naders, and Gores to the contrary, to do less is to resign from being sentient. To denounce it is to renounce intelligence.

Which, I suspect, was their point all along. To hell with them; let the bastards freeze in the dark.

My daughter wanted down to see the pretty fireworks. Clarissa set her gently on the transparent floor. She reached out, trying to hold the glittering fragments in her hand.

She wouldn't know it for a few years yet, but they were hers already.

⅄ ⅄ ⅄

A novel about freedom
and what could be... $9.99

www.PhoenixPick.com

Read it the way the author meant it
to be read... $7.99

Coming Soon: L. Neil Smith's,
The Crysal Empire

www.ingramcontent.com/pod-product-compliance
Lightning Source LLC
Chambersburg PA
CBHW022128170626
46808CB00002B/894